Murder Most Howl

Margaret H. Bonham

WolfSinger Publications   Security, Colorado

Chapter One

The wind at 10,000 feet is mind numbing, especially in February in Colorado. Unprotected from the ravaging wind as it scoured the fourteen-thousand foot peaks and the great mountain, Silverheels, I wanted my parka and my gloves. My hat lay in the truck far away, leaving my head exposed and unprotected. The snowmobile was dead—empty gas tank. I was stuck in the wilderness—the nearest help was miles away. But of all the things I wished I had, I wanted my .44 magnum even more.

I leaned against the snowmobile, barely able to stand. My leg ached from the .22 caliber bullet Matt Rayburn's murderer had fired as I tried to escape. Alone, cold, and desperate—the murderer was coming for me.

It wouldn't take long. The murderer had good sled dogs. Harness them up and go—they don't know a killer from a cop. That's one of the reasons why so many people own dogs—dogs don't care if you're rich or poor, sophisticated or uncouth—they're the ultimate in positive regard. Dogs don't suffer from the foibles of the human condition—they don't cheat, lie, or betray one's trust. If they steal, there's a straightforward reason—they're hungry or they like the scent on the item. And they don't suffer from greed.

My name is Stephanie Keyes and I'm a musher. That's the term sled dog drivers call ourselves. It comes from the slaughter of the French word *marche*, which means to go forward. The English settlers who heard the French order their dogs must have thought the French said, "Mush!" But, I was not thinking of mushing or marching at this moment—I could barely walk. I was wondering how I was going to get out of here.

I was maybe a mile into National Forest when the snowmobile coughed and sputtered. I sat down again and tried giving it more throttle, but to no avail and it coughed twice before expiring. I hit the electric start, but the machine stayed defiantly dead. For some reason, the image of an old miner's burro popped into my mind. I wondered if this was how the old gold prospectors felt when their mules wouldn't budge. Only, they could shoot the mule to end it. I didn't even have a gun.

I stood up and looked frantically around. I had stopped at the crossroads between the main forest service road and a narrow jeep/snowmobile road that went across Beaver Creek. The creek was more or less frozen now to a slushy consistency. Aspen, fire willows and other scrub grew in the creek's bed making a ten-foot tall maze throughout the gulch. Giant ruts, a foot or two deep and several feet long crisscrossed the area as though somebody had taken their Labrador Retriever up for a romp in the snow. I hadn't seen any dog tracks off the main road, so I didn't know what they were.

I swore and tried to start the snowmobile again. Nothing. I sat there for a moment or two to consider my options. I couldn't wait here for the murderer to come and find me and I couldn't walk to Fairplay.

I stood up and my thigh cramped again. Gripping my leg, I dragged myself towards the dense thicket that grew around the creek. I walked with a weird jerky motion, almost as though my leg had fallen asleep. I stumbled to the creek and put a foot on the ice. It crackled and I pulled my leg back. The cold water rushed deeply here. I couldn't walk across.

I turned left and walked onto the frozen marshy grass between the fire willows. The uneven ground made it tricky to move and I stumbled a few times. Once or twice sharp pains shot through my leg and I nearly screamed. Instead, I collapsed into a whimpering ball of jelly until the pain subsided enough for me to go on.

That's when I found the moose. I was so focused on the pain that I wasn't looking where I was going and I nearly stumbled into her. By Alaskan standards, she wasn't a very big moose—maybe about the size of a horse—but by Colorado standards, she was plenty big enough. She was dark brown with the goofy Bullwinkle head and huge knobby knees. She looked up from browsing and eyed me suspiciously. I froze. Now I realized the giant ruts were moose tracks. They were made when the moose's legs cut through the snow.

Moose have three modes: charge, stand, or flight. I was probably too close for flight, so I hoped the moose would settle for stand. Never mind the killer, the cow moose would finish me off. Since she hadn't attacked yet, I prayed for stand. I said nothing and slowly backed off, hoping my jerky movements wouldn't upset her further. The cow moose lowered her head and took another bite of roots, still watching me. I retraced my steps and got out of sight. I took another direction through the brush.

I didn't realize how much I'd been shaking until I stopped when I thought I was safe. The cold wind chilled my sweat-drenched skin and I shivered violently. My fingers were numb. I crouched and wondered what had possessed me to get involved in Matt Rayburn's murder. It wasn't as if I liked him. In fact, Matt would laugh if he saw me now. *Stupid girl,* he would say. *You stuck your nose in something you had no business in.*

He would be right, of course, but I wouldn't admit that to his face. He was a Grade-A jerk. He treated everyone like trash—everyone, except his dogs, perhaps. But even they were commodities to be used to his advantage. We can pick our dogs, but unfortunately, they don't get much of a choice. He took good care of them and maybe they should have said that in his eulogy. Not that I cared right now. Not that anyone really cared.

It all started a week ago in Frisco, Colorado at the Gold Dust race...

Chapter Two

Five, four, three, two, one!

Time seems to stand still in the brief moment when the sled dog team leaves the starting chute in a race. Everything slows down as your body pumps adrenaline into your veins. The wild frenzy, the barking, the mad and joyous confusion takes on a surrealistic quality. There is nothing but you, the dogs, and the snow-covered trail now...

I don't have to scream "Hike!" The dogs hear the snaps from the snubline that holds them back and feel the tension release. We launch. The noise suddenly abates. We are silent. We fly.

I am part of the team. I think as they do. We must run as a pack. Here, we are equals. Yes, I am the Leader, the Alpha, but only because the Team wills it. I crouch, gripping the driving bow a little too tightly as the sled careens around a corner. Like a frightened yearling too afraid to stretch it out, I chide myself. I try to relax.

The snow is soft and mushy. The temperatures are already a little too warm. I can hear the dogs' panting keeping time with the pounding in my ears. The dogs slow their lope—Jasmine has already dropped to a fast trot. "Hike it up, Jazzy Girl," I urge. She glances behind at me, hearing her name. Blue eyes peer from a grizzled face. "Hurry up!" She soars back into a lope.

The first mile is flat frozen lake. Then, we go uphill onto a little island. The dogs pause; there is slush at the bottom of the hill from unfrozen lake water. Mocha and Sam don't hesitate; they take us uphill. We wind through the woods until we break out into the open again. I relax my grip a little.

I am hot. The relative temperature is probably somewhere around zero because of the wind, but I am sweating. We take a turn and I lean hard to warp the sled for the turn. Drag a foot into the corner, set up the line, warp tight at the apex of the turn, and use my foot to pedal against the snow to bring the sled around. Do it all over again. Pedal. Pedal. Pedal. Up a hill. Drag feet. Down a hill. There is no real need for commands here—this is sprint racing. Mocha and Sam only need to know to go. Go and stop and nothing else. Maybe "easy."

Another team is ahead. I catch a glimpse of the cobalt parka as his team breaks for the woods. Lee Johnson maybe. He vanishes into the forest like an ethereal specter, but the dogs are quick to give chase.

We enter the timber again. I see another team on the outward bound trail that runs close to the inward bound trail. It's Liz and her team of eight perfectly matched, white Samoyeds. I don't recognize Liz per se, beneath the parka, hat, and goggles, but I know her team. We wave as we pass.

Then, the ground disappears from under me.

"Whoa! Whoa!" I scream.

The team shoots down the treacherously deceptive hill. Mocha and Sam, my two lead dogs, don't look back despite my yelling. They aren't going to let a little thing like a twenty-foot vertical drop slow them down.

My foot instinctively hits the brake as the sled goes airborne. The dogs lope down the hill—I nearly flip the sled in mid-air. Hanging on desperately, I land smack on a log that stuck out halfway down the hill and my foot slams on the brake. I hear a loud crack. We're speeding up, not slowing down. A shattered piece of kindling is all that's left of the strong oak board and iron brake claw.

We hit bottom and run through the slushy lake water. Occasionally there's overflow where the lake meets the shore. The dogs pull out; the flat energizes us as we charge towards the free zone.

Lightning, my wheel dog, glances behind. I hear the panting of another team behind. Matt Rayburn? "Come on, Mocha! Come on, Sam! Hike it up!"

My leads redouble their efforts. The free-zone marker is just ahead. "Let's go home!" I shout. "Go home! Go home!" Those magic words are music. Tongues lolling, sinews straining, the team knows the finish line is near.

"Trail!" Matt shouts, but we're across the free zone line.

"Free Zone!" I shout.

"Damn it, Steph! I called 'Trail!'" Matt hollers.

"Too late!"

"Bitch!" He shouts. "Goddamn bitch! Your team is too slow!"

"Still ahead of you!"

We lope across the flat and pass yet another team. It's a musher with an 8-dog team of Siberians. I look beyond a mile away towards the parking area and see several trucks besides mine. How many mushers entered the eight-dog race?

Matt's lead dogs, Shep and Blue, run next to my leg. I can't pedal.

"Hold your dogs back!" I shout. I try to kick to see if I can pedal without kicking his dogs. Snow from my boot sprays in his dogs' faces.

Matt is really mad now.

I don't care.

"Go home! Mocha! Sam! Go home!"

"Matt, she's in free zone!" I hear Alan Freeman's voice. "Get back!"

I glance behind. Alan's perfectly matched team of Siberian Huskies follow close behind.

"Don't let him pass, Steph!" Alan shouts. "He wouldn't let me pass earlier!"

"Free zone!" Matt sneers.

"Not before."

The crowd along the finish line grows as we race to the end. Mocha and Sam pull me across the finish line as the crowd cheers.

~ * ~

I pulled the snowhook from its holster on the sled and slammed it into the packed snow. Its talons dug in and my dogs stopped with a jerk. I exhaled in relief—I didn't even realize I was holding my breath.

Matt Rayburn drove his dogs beside me. Six-foot tall and over two hundred pounds he slammed the snowhook into the snow beside me. "I called trail!" he shouted, stomping over to my sled. He curled his fist and loomed over me. His face was blotched and purple from rage. I was sure he was going to take a swing at me—and it wouldn't be pretty. I'm only five-six and he had seventy pounds on me. At that moment, Alan's team pushed past both of ours. Out of the corner of my eye, I saw Alan deftly pop Matt's snowhook out of the snow with a toe as he skidded by. Matt's team lunged forward and took off.

"Loose team!" Alan shouted. He winked at me as his team slid by. "Matt, you've got to watch your team."

Matt shot me a dirty look and ran after his team. The dogs nearly mowed down a group of spectators before Sam Horton, another musher, ran out and caught the lead dogs. The team's force was so intense, they knock Sam over. They dragged him until Matt could catch the sled and step on the brake.

I didn't watch anymore because Amy, my handler, appeared. She glanced quizzically towards Matt's team and then grasped Sam and Mocha's neckline.

"Let's go, I'll explain later," I said. I pulled up slightly on my own snowhook allowing it to drag, but still slow us down. She brought the team back to my dog truck. It's a blue mid-seventies ¾ ton Dodge with a dog box conspicuously devoid of sponsors' logos. Amy had already strung out the picket line where we attached the leaders' neckline. Then, we slowly attached each of the dogs' collar rings to a snap on the picket line.

"Did you win?" Amy asked from the tailgate. She's a little new at the racing thing, but she's great with the dogs. I could hear her pouring water into the dogs' bowls.

"No—that's not how it works," I said absently as I rubbed Mocha's shoulder. Mocha, a chocolate and black colored Alaskan Husky with blue eyes—in case you were wondering—leaned into my hand for a good rub. Mocha doesn't look like what most people would consider a husky. He's houndy, going back to the old time Wright Hounds or Aurora Huskies. "Can you toss me the bottle of Algyval—it's in the med-kit. Mocha's a little sore." I heard her rummaging in the medical box and tossed the white liniment bottle to me. "Thanks," I said. I pulled off my gloves and poured the aromatic stuff in my hands. Mocha melted under my touch as I rubbed the liniment into his shoulder.

"Well, who won then?" Amy asked as she put the water down for Sam the husky. Sam lapped water, splashing it and saliva all over me and Mocha. Mocha pulled away, shoved Sam's muzzle aside, and greedily lapped the cold water.

"Nobody—yet. This is just the first heat. Tomorrow is the second heat. Those two times make the race time. We leave the starting chute one at a time, so our time matches up against everyone else's."

"So, you can still be in first even with someone finishing ahead of you?" she asked dubiously.

"Yes."

"That's silly."

"Not really. Otherwise, we'd have to have a mass start and that would be really scary. Can you imagine thirty teams leaving at once?"

"It'd be exciting."

"We don't have the room."

"Well, did you do good, then?" She put the last bowl down for Lightning and Jasmine, my two wheel dogs.

"Not bad, except I lost my brake," I said, looking back at the shattered piece of wood. "Matt and Lee are probably ahead of me. I don't know where Alan ended up." I swept the box of dog biscuits off the tailgate. Sam and Mocha began hopping up and down. "Go home!" I said, tossing them each a biscuit.

Amy frowned as she saw the sled. It's a heavy oak sled that has been through a lot. Most people run Risdon and Moody sleds, which weigh less than 20 pounds—my sled weighed in at a whopping 35 pounds—more than twice the normal sprint sled. I had bought my sled used years ago, back when I didn't know whether I wanted to run sprint or distance. Sprint races are one mile per dog in the team. Distance races are much longer and may take several days. In Colorado, there is very little distance racing above 20 miles a day, so I had decided to stick with sprint. Amy set down the water bowls before the dogs and examined the sled closely. "Gee, you really did a number on it. What happened?"

"Hit the log on the last hill," I said. "Caught the brake on the darn thing. Where am I going to get a brake around here?" I paused and rubbed Sam, who was getting very jealous. He looks like a Husky: wolf gray with a dark mask. "You are such gooooood dogs!" I crooned at them. They beamed back, still panting heavily. Dog slobber covered me, my hands reeked of Algyval and dog fur covered them, but I didn't care. I went from the leaders to the point dogs—the dogs behind the leaders—and gave them the same treatment. All the way back to the wheel dogs who are right in front of the sled. They all got treats and hugs.

"I saw Mary selling harnesses earlier," Amy said. "She'll probably have a booth set up tonight. Maybe she'll have a brake."

I brightened slightly, but I wasn't so sure. Outfitters bring harnesses, lines and backpacks to races, but seldom bring something as hardware intensive as a brake. I unhooked Rowdy, a red Alaskan Husky, and began removing his harness.

"Hi ya, Steph!" Alan Freeman peered around the dog box. He no longer wore the heavy military parka. The sun was out and felt warm. He raked back his sandy brown hair with his left hand as he held up something in his right hand. "Nice run."

I did a double take. "My brake!"

"What's left of it," he said. "You're lucky it didn't fly right into your leg."

I tossed Rowdy's harness to Amy and lifted the husky into the dog box. My truck has eight compartments which can carry up to sixteen dogs. You get pretty strong hauling 50-70 pounds of husky in eight repetitions. I turned and took the brake from Alan. It was a foot long piece of wood with an iron claw at the end. The wood was jagged at the break—it wasn't clean. "Well, I guess that's it for that."

"Why? You could splint it. Got duct tape?"

I chuckled. "Yes, but I don't have anything to splint it with."

"Let me look around," he said. "Somebody might have a board or something." He paused. "By the way, the results are in."

"And?"

"Lee Johnson's first, but we knew that. You're in fourth just behind Rayburn."

"Matt's pissed."

"Yeah well, Matt's complaining again that Johnson's using steroids."

"Not likely."

"He's filed a complaint about you, too."

"Great—about the free zone thing?"

"Yeah."

I sighed. Of course, he would file a complaint. Moron.

"Don't worry. Cindy won't put up with it—especially since someone else mentioned his unsportsmanlike conduct." He grinned.

"You?"

He chuckled. "I'll look around and see if I can find a board. Going to the dinner tonight?"

I turned to unharness Yukon. Amy had begun unharnessing the other dogs and I was beginning to feel guilty. "Yeah, it's at *Megan's* isn't it?"

"Yeah, downtown Frisco," he said and turned away. I watched him walk to his own truck: a new red Ford F250 crew cab.

Amy slipped behind me. "I think he likes you," she whispered so no one else could hear.

I lifted Yukon and put him in the dog box. "He's got Siberians. It's a bad mix."

Amy raised an eyebrow. "I don't think so."

Chapter Three

I was only half joking when I told Amy Siberian Huskies and Alaskan Huskies are a bad mix. Don't misunderstand me, I love Siberian Huskies and think they're gorgeous dogs. I mean, who wouldn't fall in love with those startling blue eyes, those wolfish looks, and that devil-may-care attitude? They're not for everyone, as any Siberian Husky rescue may attest, and they are very different than the Alaskan Husky.

The Siberian Husky—called Siberians—and the Alaskan Husky—called Alaskans—have been at odds since the first Siberian Huskies appeared at the *All Alaskan Sweepstakes* in Nome in 1909. Back then, Alaskan Huskies were just known as mutts. Gold prospectors bought—and stole—dogs from the Lower 48 to hitch into a sled team along with the native Malamutes. The Malamutes were big dogs weighing anywhere from 75 pounds to well over 100 pounds. The resulting dogs were more freighting dogs than racing dogs.

When the Siberians made their debut, they nearly blew the competition away. They were tiny, compared to the Malamutes, weighing in at 35 to 60 pounds, and speedy like a racecar. After the three-day race, the Siberians took third place—admirable, since they almost beat the legendary dog driver, Scotty Allen. He was able to out-drive the competition, as any good musher should. But, the Siberians had made their mark and the next year won the race. Always the innovators, the Alaskan mushers began adding Siberians to their breeding stock, mixing a little of this and a little of that.

The Alaskan Huskies became smaller and faster. The Siberian Huskies became registered as purebred by the American Kennel Club (AKC), but the Alaskan Huskies remained the "outlaws." Mushers bred the Alaskan Husky strictly for speed and ability—the Siberians were being bred for both show and working. Ironically, in the compromise, the Siberian was not able to keep up with the Alaskan's unlimited gene pool.

If your breed is AKC registered, you can't breed your dog to a non-registered dog to have registered puppies. Alaskan mushers, being the independent sorts, never bothered to register their dogs and certainly didn't want to limit their dogs' breeding, so the Alaskan Husky remains a mutt. A mutt with a substantial pedigree. Most mushers can recite their dogs' lineage eight or more generations. I know I can.

The rivalry between Alaskan mushers and Siberian mushers exists to this day. Siberian mushers have an increasingly harder time finding good racing stock within their limited gene pool without inbreeding too much. Alaskan mushers will sometimes breed their dogs to German Shorthaired Pointers, Borzois, Greyhounds, and other breeds to add variety and speed to their dogs. For example, it's very popular to run German Shorthaired Pointer crossed with Alaskan Husky in the top sprint race in the world: the North American. Whatever is fast.

Because Alaskan Huskies have a varied background, you can imagine they can look quite different from each other. Some look almost like Siberian Huskies; others look like big hairy flop-eared hounds. Many aren't pretty and won't win beauty contests. I call the ugly ones "screaming weasels from hell." You get the idea.

What the Alaskans aren't in terms of looks, they make up for in speed. The winners of every major sprint and distance race nowadays are Alaskan Huskies. Sure, you'll find an occasional Siberian team that competes with the big Alaskan teams, but they're a rarity. When I got into sled dogs, I wanted to win. I chose Alaskans.

In recent years, many Siberian mushers have demanded a purebred class or purebred-only races. The term "purebred" applies to those dogs that are AKC registered. Those dogs include Siberians, Samoyeds, and Alaskan Malamutes. The Samoyeds and the Malamutes aren't fast enough to compete with the Siberians, so in essence, the winners are Siberian mushers. I've looked on this with a certain amount of skepticism.

~ * ~

Dinner was at 6:00 p.m. at *Megan's*, a small Italian restaurant located near the highway on the edge of Frisco. It's at the base of Mount Royal, the tall mountain just north of the town. The most distinguishing feature of Mount Royal is the large avalanche scar that runs from its peak to halfway down the mountain where the ill-fated town of Masonville sat. Masonville was a mining camp in the late 1800's. On New Year's Eve, the miners had gone into Frisco to party when the avalanche hit. Luckily, no one was back at camp, but so ended the illustrious career of Masonville. You can still hike up Mount Royal and find the ghost town.

Frisco has just one main street with an eclectic mix of late 1800's and modern buildings. If you take the secondary highway, Highway 9, it will take you to the Breckenridge ski area and eventually over Hoosier Pass, which will drop you into the real Southpark. Some of the mushers who live that way use Hoosier Pass to avoid the ski traffic on I-70 to get home. It's longer by at least an hour and a half, but it is less stressful.

Megan's is primarily a pizzeria—which suits most mushers just fine. Mushers live on pizza. Pizza and Sunny Delight—and beer— but that's another story. Amy and I walked in. The wonderful aroma of baking pizza greeted us. I was immediately hungry—the only food I had was a hot dog the Siberian Husky Club sold as a fundraiser. We walked down the red and black carpet towards the sign pointing us toward one of the private banquet rooms. The hall turned and we saw a few booths and a large line near one open doorway.

As we approached, we saw Mary Palmer at one of the booths arguing with Matt Rayburn about something. She's only five feet tall, but she drew up to her full five feet to glower at Matt. "Where's my money, Rayburn?" Her voice sounded menacing. "You still owe me five hundred dollars for that used Risdon." Risdon—a top of the line racing sled.

I decided to check in for dinner first. I motioned in the direction of the ticket booth and Amy nodded. We stood in line, hoping to avoid hearing any more of Matt's whining. We weren't that lucky.

"I paid you a month ago."

"No, you didn't," Mary stated flatly. "The check bounced. I want cash."

"Look, I only want to buy the hook from you now. My old hook didn't hold—there's got to be something wrong with it. I nearly lost my team."

"I don't care. I want the five hundred dollars."

Matt shifted his gaze from her to the line and fidgeted as several people glanced over in their direction. He lowered his voice. "Look, I don't have the five hundred with me—how about I bring it to Granby? You'll be at Granby, won't you?"

"Yeah, I'll be at Granby—you know that," Mary sighed.

"I'm desperate, Mary, I need that hook."

"Will your check bounce?"

Matt grimaced. "No."

Mary laid the snowhook on the table. It was a heavy-duty grabber type hook—same as the one I had, except it had fins welded to the front of the hook, giving it a wider profile. It looked about 6 pounds or more and ended in two sharp talons. Matt reached for it but Mary gripped his wrist. "Watch it—Ken sharpened the talons for ice."

Matt carefully picked up the hook and studied the two talons. "Yeah, they're sharp."

We were next in line. Cindy Travis, the president of the Western States Sled Dog Club, was taking money and handing out little red numbered tickets. Cindy was somewhere in her mid-fifties with salt and pepper hair and bright blue eyes. She laid a firm hand on my own as I put ten dollars down for Amy's and my meal.

"What's that about?" she whispered conspiratorially. Those inquisitive blue eyes peered from a round, weather-beaten face.

"It's Rayburn," I whispered back, though I couldn't think of a reason why I was doing so. "Stiffed Mary again."

Cindy wrinkled her nose in disgust. "What now?"

"A Risdon."

Cindy shook her head. "He is such a pain in the butt. He's been nosing around in club politics too." That was the first time I heard of it. She continued. "How much?"

"Five hundred."

"Oh my! I wouldn't have given him it for less than seven."

I nodded. Risdon sleds aren't cheap. The best ones have composite runners and are works of art. They also cost over $700. Add something like aluminum or titanium snowhooks and other exotic items and the cost really adds up. Little wonder mushers are poor. I was about to move on, when Cindy gripped my wrist. "You know, Matt filed a complaint you wouldn't let him pass."

"I heard."

"Freeman says you were in the free zone."

"Yeah, I was." I extracted my wrist from her vice-like grip.

She met my gaze curiously. "We had our spotters go out to the place where they said they saw you two together. It looks awfully close."

"I was in the free zone." I stated.

"Whatever." She paused. "Oh, hang onto those ticket stubs—there'll be door prizes afterwards."

I pocketed the stubs. Amy slid next to me. "Great—is she going to disqualify you?"

"Hope not," I said. And I meant it. It wasn't my fault Rayburn was a pain in the ass. In retrospect, I supposed I could have been nicer—if it had been Lee Johnson or Alan Freeman, I probably would've yielded the lead. Probably. Racing is, after all, racing. But Matt was an asshole, pure and simple, and the rules said once in the Free Zone, you don't have to yield the trail. So, I didn't have to yield, and Matt was full of shit.

The room was dimly lit so it took a moment or two for my eyes to adjust.

"Hey, what's the hold up?" A strong hand pushed me from behind and I nearly tripped. I whirled around and glared. Matt pushed by me. "You're as slow off the trail as on. Too bad you have to cheat to get where you are." Before I could come up with a good retort, he made his way to the far corner where I could see the tall, thin form of Lee Johnson sitting with his wife, Sherri. Lee smiled and waved. I waved back and continued forward. Their table was full. Matt, always the suck-up, sat down beside Lee. He glanced up once in my direction and smirked and then continued talking with Lee. Gina, Matt's wife, sat beside him. She flicked her straight blonde hair back over her shoulders as though making a point.

"Lee's bored," Amy whispered.

I chuckled. "Yeah, he's probably hoping we'll rescue him." Normally I would, but there just weren't any seats.

"Hey Stephanie!"

I turned and saw Alan Freeman sitting at an all purebred mushers' table. There were two seats left right beside him. "Come on, let's join him," Amy said.

"I don't need a matchmaker!" I hissed but Amy was already moving forward.

"Come on, Steph, don't be a spoil sport," Amy grinned, sitting in the seat next to Liz Smith, a Samoyed driver. That left the seat next to Alan. Chagrined, I sat beside him.

Alan smiled. His dark eyes considered me thoughtfully. "Steph, Amy, do you know everyone here?"

I looked around at the faces and shook my head. "I know Liz. I know your dogs, not your names," I admitted.

That elicited a chuckle from everyone. "I'm Vicki Thompson," said the woman by Liz. "I run Sepp and Sepp-Alta Siberians."

"Paul Jorgenson—Malamutes," said a large blonde man with blue eyes.

A thin dark-haired man extended his hand. "Ray Bryce. Siberians."

"I'm Stephanie Keyes. Amy's my handler." That raised a few eyebrows. Handlers are hard to come by. "I run Alaskans."

"A mixed breed driver," Vicki said with a sniff. She was a thin blonde woman with green eyes. Her sweatshirt sported a black and white Siberian Husky with a full mask and blue eyes with the logo I 'Heart' Siberian Huskies.

"Uh yeah," I said cautiously. I didn't like her tone—she made it sound like I did something gauche like mix a salad fork with a dinner fork at a ritzy restaurant. Amy looked sidelong at me. "But they're the most pedigreed mutts around," I added.

Vicki smiled condescendingly. "I'm sure they are. What do you do to get these dogs? Breed Malamutes and Siberians together?"

Bitch. A common misconception. It was my turn to sound arrogant. "Uh, no," I said. "These dogs come from racing lines that produced proven Open North American winners. Most Alaskan drivers start with proven stock. We've got pedigrees as long as your AKC registered dogs." I paused. "Maybe longer."

"But you mix purebreds in."

"Occasionally mushers outcross to a purebred dog. Most don't bother because it takes a lot to breed back in enough husky to make the outcross worthwhile. It usually takes three or four good generations before you can produce something worthwhile. The latest thing is to outcross to German Shorthaired Pointers."

"Those dogs aren't cheap either," Alan remarked. "What does an Alaskan go for?"

I could kiss him. Maybe purebred racers weren't so bad. "Three hundred to a thousand around here. A North American dog, like the ones from Heikki Seppanen—you're talking thousands."

"Speed costs money," Alan quipped.

"Sure does. Got to buy young ones if you're going to stay on top," I said. "A dog starts to slow down at five. So, I place the dogs in a slower kennel or use them to train pups. And buy more dogs. Or breed them, but that's expensive."

I knew I'd lost her. I could have gone on about the carefully planned breedings, the training, everything, and all Vicki would have seen was a bunch of mutts beating her purebreds.

Amy smiled sweetly and took a sip of water. "The record speaks for itself," she said. "Alaskans dominate the winners."

"Not entirely," Liz chimed in. "Alan's in second."

I looked at Alan in wonder. "Second?"

"Right behind Lee Johnson," Vicki added.

"Those pups are something," Alan admitted. "They're awesome. They're a repeat Quest and Lila breeding."

"Are you going to breed them again?" Ray asked.

"This spring, Lila's due to come in season. I'll be breeding her then."

"What's their lines?"

"Oh, Quest is out of Champion Silverheels' Blue Thunder and Icy-Paw's Silver Sunset," Vicki interrupted. Her own kennel name is Icy-Paw, which means the bitch came from her breeding. Silverheels is the name of Alan's kennel. Alan probably bought the bitch from Vicki a few years back and used his own dog to breed to her. Vicki began to recite the entire five-generation bloodline of Icy-Paw's Silver Sunset.

About that time, the pizza was ready and I was very grateful. If you've ever endured the litany of pedigrees from someone else's breed, you'll know what I'm talking about. The pizza gave us an excuse to focus on something else—anything else—besides Vicki's recitation on purebred lineage. I've discovered that what may seem fascinating to those within the breed, the rest of the universe—including Alaskan drivers—could care less. *Megan's* pizza is remarkably good, so it was easy to ignore Vicki's droning.

Alan and Liz looked almost as bored. Liz, a Samoyed driver, and Paul, the Malamute driver, cared even less about Siberian pedigrees.

"So, what's your ISDRA point standing?" I asked Alan. ISDRA is the International Sled Dog Racing Association. They sanction sled dog races.

"I don't have one," he said, somewhat chagrinned. "I let my ISDRA membership lapse when I tried distance racing in the fall."

"You tried distance?" I asked intrigued.

"Yeah, I did—I heard Siberians dominate the shorter distance races."

"Do they?" I asked.

"Not really," Alan shrugged. "You get a good Alaskan team and they'll wax you."

"Did you hear, Alan saw a moose out in Southpark?" Liz asked, changing the subject.

"No way!" I exclaimed. "A moose in Southpark?"

"Not just a moose," Alan said. "Lots of moose. There's moose tracks all over the place."

"Wow! I knew they were in Northpark and Middlepark," I said. "But Southpark? How in the heck did they travel all the way to Fairplay?"

Alan shrugged. "They must have come over Georgia Pass or something."

"But where did they come from? Breckenridge?" Amy asked, somewhat seriously.

We all laughed. The idea of a moose travelling through the re-sort town was ludicrous. "So, when did you see one?" I asked.

"The darn thing burst out of the woods in front of my team," he said. "I hit the brakes hard and dug my snowhook in. I was lucky it didn't turn and charge my team."

Everyone nodded. Moose are notoriously ill tempered especially during mating season and late winter. In 1994, Susan Butcher lost her chance at winning the Iditarod for the first time when a moose attacked and killed two dogs in her team and seriously injured others. Every musher takes moose seriously, in spite of their goofy looks. You don't enrage a ton of animal that can stomp you and your whole team flat. Each year, tourists accidentally provoke bison, moose, and elk in Yellowstone because they think the animals are tame. They only learn when it is too late—after a moose or bison charges for encroaching too close.

"So, did you hear Alan and I bred Shadow and Tasha?" Vicki asked. The moose conversation had not deterred her from going back to the pedigrees. "We've got six beautiful puppies we're co-owning."

"How old are they now?" Ray asked. Ray had Siberians—he'd be interested.

"Nearly four weeks." She pulled out photos and passed them

around. "Shadow is Icy-Paw's Shadow Stalker and Tasha, I believe is Silverheels' Grey Morning...?" She glanced at Alan for confirmation. Alan nodded. "Oh, they're simply gorgeous pups. I can't wait to run mine."

I sighed and glanced at Amy. Amy shrugged back.

"So, what are the chances at you winning an ISDRA medal this year?" Liz asked.

Vicki must have finished because the table grew very quiet. I felt self-conscious. "Johnson's got the gold sewn up in eight dog," I remarked. "I'm nowhere near O'Neill for the silver."

"What about you and Matt?"

"Matt's an uneasy third," Alan said before I could reply. "He must be less than twenty points before Steph."

"He came in before me."

"You could still beat him."

"Not this race. Not unless he disqualifies or something," I said. "He's got third right now. I'm hoping to make it up by travelling to a few extra races."

"Assuming Matt doesn't do likewise."

"Well, there aren't many races left and he would have to travel. I don't think he would necessarily go to Utah or Wyoming."

"They may be canceling Utah," Alan said.

"Why?" I asked.

"No snow."

"Shit." There went my hopes. "There's still Granby and the Snowy Range." I knew Matt wouldn't go to Utah, but he'd definitely go to Granby and if we were close, he'd go to the Snowy Range.

"Wyoming's dry too," said Liz. "You'd have a better chance in Jackson Hole."

I frowned. It would be a long drive and some tough passes.

"So, what did Cindy say?" Alan asked. I must have grimaced at the question because then he said: "She didn't disqualify you?"

The others looked at me querulously. "I don't know. Cindy didn't say I was out."

"What happened?" Vicki's eyes held a glimmer of delight that I could possibly contribute to some sort of juicy gossip.

"Steph's the musher who held up Matt in the free zone."

Liz laughed and clapped her hands in delight. "It was you!" She reached over and patted my arm. "Good job!"

"Good for you!" said Paul. "It's about time he got a taste of his own medicine! Free zone indeed! He treats it more like a free-for-all zone! He kicked my lead Malamute once because we were going slow."

"No doubt you were 'holding him up,'" Vicki said. "'Hey, get your Sloberians out of the way! They shouldn't even be allowed on the course,'" she added, imitating Matt's tone.

I stared at them in bewilderment. I knew Matt was obnoxious, but evidently didn't know how much. I was about to reply when I heard voices raised at the next table. I looked over to see Lee Johnson glaring at Matt Rayburn.

"My success comes from my training and my breeding program—something you are incapable of understanding." Lee and his wife stood up. "I'm tired of you and your shit! Leave us alone!" Lee grasped his wife by the arm and they both left.

Matt stood up and followed Lee out. "Wait! Lee!" Gina, Matt's wife, tried not to look embarrassed and continued talking to another woman beside her.

Amy nudged me. She was bored. Served her right, I thought, making us sit with a bunch of purebred drivers. Still, I'm no masochist. "We ought to get going. I've still got to drop dogs and feed." The dogs make a wonderful excuse in any situation.

We said out good-byes and walked out. *Megan's*, like all touristy spots, was kept too warm for mushers. Mushers tend to prefer the colder temperatures. My cabin, for example, is a constant fifty degrees.

Amy, who isn't used to the cold like I am, shivered a little. We hurried to the ¾-ton monster. I paused and poked my finger in the first dog box behind the extended cab's window. A wet nose and a tentative lick greeted me. Even in the dim light, Mocha's blue eyes stared back. I couldn't see Sam, but I stroked the dark fur pressed against the grate. Sam was probably asleep.

I hopped into the truck. Immediately, Winnie, my pet Malamute, greeted me with slurpy kisses. Dark gray and wolfy-looking, with a white face and light brown eyes, she's eighty-five pounds of wriggling joy. She had been lying on the seat in the truck dozing and now turned excitedly between Amy and me. "Over, Winnie!" I ordered and she obediently hopped into the back area of the extended cab. She prefers the seat because it isn't as lumpy as our suitcases.

"God, they were awful!" Amy exclaimed. "Are all purebred folk like that?"

I chuckled as I turned the ignition. I flipped the lever in reverse and we both cranked our heads around to see beyond the massive dog box. I got a good view of Winnie's head, but not much else. Oh well, sometimes you just have to have faith…

We made it out of the parking lot and found the motel readily. The Alpine Motel sits along Highway 9 a mile out of town. If you follow Highway 9, you will end up at Breckenridge and the Breckenridge Ski Area. Most major hotel chains won't take mushers because they don't want a load of huskies showing up on their doorsteps. I can't really blame them, but usually the dogs are quiet—with perhaps the exception of feeding time and the occasional howl. But you can bet if one team starts howling it will set them all off—hence the reason most places aren't willing to take mushers.

I drove around to the back of the Alpine Motel and followed the line of parked dog trucks in the parking lot. There wasn't much light behind the motel, just a security light near the back entrance. The only other light came from Matt's red Ford F350. Brand new, I noticed with some chagrin. Crew cab. Double-tiered dog box. Expensive. The floodlights from on top of the dog box beamed down on the dogs on the stakeout. I briefly saw Matt moving around. He was alone. Evidently, dog chores were too mundane for Gina. I drove down to the end of the line and found my own place. It was the last parking spot, farthest away from the hotel and nearest to the forest. I could still see the light from Matt's dog truck, but at least I was far enough away so I didn't have to see him.

"I need my parka," Amy said. "I left it in the motel room."

"Why'd you do that?" I asked. She was wearing a stylish down coat instead of the heavy parka.

She shrugged. "I left it when we brought up the luggage. Anyway, I'm not going to ruin a good coat feeding dogs."

I couldn't blame her. I sat in the cab, petting Winnie as the big Malamute pawed me.

Obscured by the other trucks, Matt's dogs were barking. Matt was probably getting out dog food.

Amy came back, warm in her arctic parka. I hopped out of the truck, carefully closing the door, so as not to catch a Malamute as she came flying over the seat. Winnie pawed the window fervently with both front paws, hoping to dig out of the truck. I hoped the safety glass held.

I had fixed dog food before I driving to Frisco that morning. It's a mixture of raw meat, bone meal, chicken fat, wheat germ oil, Canine Red Cell (a vitamin and mineral supplement) and dog food. The temperatures had stayed cold enough to keep the mixture semi-frozen. I broke the mixture by flexing the Tupperware container and tossing the blocks of mix into the dogs' bowls. Amy came around with hot water and poured it over the dog food.

The barking over at Matt's truck continued. "Hey Matt!" I shouted, somewhat irritated. "Feed your dogs and shut them up!"

No reply. The dogs still barked. He probably didn't hear me over the dogs.

I turned to Amy. "What a shithead," I said. "He's going to get us all thrown out with that barking."

We then dropped the dogs—that is, we took the dogs out of the dog box and put them on the picket or stakeout lines. We unloaded Mocha and Sam first. They spun on their pickets as I placed the full bowls before them. I went down the line and fed Lightning, Jasmine, Dancer, Spice, Yukon, Java (Mocha's sister), Shadow, Max, Rowdy, Skye and Thunder.

Most Alaskan Huskies will gorge themselves to death, so they always act as if you've never fed them. This is preferable because you will always know if something is wrong if your dog refuses food. A few Alaskan Huskies will be the exact opposite and would prefer to starve than eat. Fortunately, I have no such dogs.

Matt's dogs were still barking and I was going to check on them to see if Matt had simply left them unattended when I heard scratching coming from the cab. Winnie had fogged up the windows and I could see a dark nose press against the glass. Nostrils twitched and she inhaled the aroma of hot food deeply. I laughed. "We forgot Winnie!" I opened the door and she came bounding out. Usually, Winnie waits for me to tether her on a line while I put down her food. Tonight she bounded away before I could grasp her collar and she ran between the parked trucks.

I cursed and ran after her. Malamutes are perfectly camouflaged for the darkness and snow. Winnie looked like a shadow moving between the trucks. "Winnie! Winnie!" I called, trying to sound upbeat. My voice was nearly drowned out by Matt's dogs barking. "Matt, damn it! Shut up your dogs!" I shouted.

Amy ran around our truck along the opposite side, hoping to catch Winnie as she came around the corner. She didn't. Instead, Winnie turned and ran through the rows towards the main parking spaces. Amy ran after her, "Winnie! Winnie!" she called.

I stopped for a moment and peered under the vehicles. I saw movement. "Amy! She's heading towards Matt's truck!"

The barking turned to snarling. The hair prickled at the back of my neck. Winnie was fighting with one of Matt's dogs. Where the hell was Matt?

I sprinted towards Matt's truck and turned the corner to find Winnie snarling at Poco—one of Matt's nasty wheel dogs. I grasped Winnie's collar and hauled her off.

Then, I looked around. Seven of Matt's twenty-two Huskies had food bowls out. The ones that weren't fed were milling around, some pawing at the others' now empty stainless steel bowls. One dog had swiped another dog's bowl and was chewing on the rim—the bowl held tightly between his forelegs. I stared at the scene in puzzlement. Matt wouldn't have fed only a few of his dogs and certainly wouldn't have left them out.

I noticed a couple of dogs at the back of the truck pawing at something in the snow. Matt must have spilt some food back there. I held Winnie tightly as I walked around the truck to see what the dogs were so curious about.

Then, Amy screamed. She had rounded the corner of the truck the same time I had on the other side.

I looked. Not five feet away lay the body of Matt Rayburn.

Chapter Four

Winnie lunged towards one of the Huskies who had been pawing at what now proved to be an ever-widening pool of blood seeping into the snow and ice. I barely pulled the Malamute back. My throat clenched and I stared at the body for what seemed a surreal amount of time. Christ. I'd only seen this much blood when I helped my brother gut a deer during hunting season and during a dog fight, but never this much human blood. The smell of death was unmistakable though. It's a putrid smell you can't wash out of your memory—the smell of blood, bile, urine, and feces. I've seen and smelled death, trying to save an old or sick dog from it, and its one you can't easy forget.

I felt like retching.

"Here," I said to Amy, shoving Winnie's collar with Winnie still struggling against it into her hands. "Put Winnie up and dial nine-one-one."

Amy did not move, even though she took Winnie. Her face was pale and she trembled. "Is he dead?"

"I don't know," I said quietly. I lied. The smell is unmistakable. "Call the police and an ambulance."

"What should I tell them?"

I looked over the grisly sight. The man lay face down in a pool of blood. His head was twisted sideways and his eyes were half-open, staring blankly ahead. The back of the cranium was smashed and the face contorted gruesomely. For a moment, I thought I had stepped on gray matter as I had approached, but it only turned out to be his hat. "Oh fuck, I don't know—tell them we found someone behind the Alpine Inn's parking lot."

The dogs twirled nervously on their stakeouts. Then, one let out a long, mournful howl. Two others followed suit and the other Huskies, safely tucked away in the dog boxes, picked up the mournful cry.

"Who is he? Is he dead?" Amy trembled.

I pulled out a pocket-sized flashlight I keep in my Carhartt overalls. I slowly crouched down and shined the light into his face. It was gray and the unseeing eyes stared blankly ahead. Trembling, I removed my glove and slid my hand to the body's wrist, gingerly pulling the coat and flannel shirt back as far as I dared. I kept imagining the hand would suddenly move and grab me. I shivered but kept going. The arm was starting to cool—his parka had kept the body heat trapped in. How long had he been here? I felt for a pulse. I didn't think anyone could live with such a massive head wound. "Yeah, he's dead." I paused. The features, grotesque and misshapen, were becoming bloated and mottled with blood. "You know, Amy, I think it's Matt."

Suddenly, we both heard an engine start at the far end of the parking lot. "What the...?" Amy began.

"Stay here and take Winnie!" I ordered. I ran towards the sound. A dark mini station wagon came barreling through the parking lot. It made a quick right turn and sped down the highway. I ran to the curb, hoping to catch a glimpse of the driver or license plate. It was too dark. I walked back.

"Shit!" Amy gasped. "Who was that?"

"I don't know," I admitted. I wished my truck didn't have a dozen Alaskan Huskies tethered to it. By the time I got them packed up, the station wagon could be on I-70 heading east towards the Eisenhower Tunnel.

I stared at Matt, feeling guilty. I hadn't liked him much, but I sure didn't want him dead. He took care of his dogs—people said he had the nicest kennel and dog yard of any musher. Would it have hurt my standing if I had let him by on the trail? He would have still been ahead of me and might have gotten a shot at beating Lee Johnson. Could I have given him that?

I felt sick. I wanted to cry. This really couldn't be happening, could it?

~ * ~

Amy put Winnie back in our truck's cab and went to call the police from the motel room. My cell phone is in the truck, but I keep forgetting to charge it. As I stood alone in the dark with Matt's corpse, I felt a chill run through me and I shivered from the nervousness. The flocked conifers loomed like sinister specters just beyond the light, now dimming from Matt's truck's drained battery. My teeth chattered, but I wasn't cold. I turned and focused on the empty parking space beside the truck, staring at mashed-down snow. Tire tracks and footprints all over. How many mushers had stomped through this parking lot tonight?

I aimed my flashlight at the corners around his truck—I didn't see blood anywhere except where he lay. Then, I ran the flashlight beam up and down the snow near where he had been fixing the dog food. Blood splatter was everywhere. In our clumsiness, Amy, Winnie, and I had tromped through the bloody snow.

I heard the rumble of tires as the procession of dog trucks started to fill the parking lot. Relieved at last, that someone else would be there, I stood out in the glow of Matt's dog truck lights and waved. The first dog truck crept tentatively towards me. It was Lee's white GMC pickup.

"Lee!" I waved and shouted as he rolled down the window. "Lee! It's Matt! Jesus, Lee, it's Matt! I just found him there."

Lee's brow furrowed as he tried to understand my words. "Steph, calm down."

Sherri, who sat in the passenger seat, peered over. "What's wrong, Steph? What about Matt?"

"Matt's dead."

Lee slammed the truck in park and clambered out. "What?"

I put both hands up as though to ward him off. "Stay back. Amy's called the police. They should be here any second."

As if on cue, we heard the wail of a police siren. I heard more truck doors slam and Alan Freeman and Sam Horton approached us.

"What's the hold up?" Alan asked when he saw us.

"Steph says Matt's dead," Lee began.

"No shit?" Sam exclaimed and pushed past us. Sam is a burley man of about six-four. He easily tips the scales at 300 pounds.

"Sam, no!" I shouted. "Don't touch anything!" I ran after him.

Sam stopped dead before the body. "Shit! He's dead," he whispered. He ran one meaty hand through his dark, greasy hair. "Matt's dead." He stood there, dazed.

"Yeah," I lowered my voice. "I know."

I felt Alan's hand grip my arm. "Come on, you two, let's get back a little. The cops will want us away from the scene."

"Why?" Sam exploded. His face looked splotchy red even in the dim light. "The bitch killed him!" He lunged towards me. Matt's dogs started barking and jumping on the stakeouts.

"What?" I screamed, jumping back. I barely avoided his huge

hands.

"No! No! Sam!" Lee shouted. Both he and Alan grabbed Sam before the big musher could throttle me. "Steph found the body. She didn't kill anyone!"

"Steph! You okay?" Amy's voice came from beyond the light. "I called the police."

Blue and red lights strobed across our faces and we turned to see a Frisco cop as he pointed his flashlight in our direction. Temporarily blinded, I instinctively shielded my eyes with a hand.

"Someone called in a homicide?"

Homicide? My brain, addled with the night's events, began churning. I hadn't seen anything that even remotely suggested an accident—however bizarre.

The police officer aimed his flashlight at each of our faces. In retrospect, we must have looked strange. Lee looked like a mountain man with a fringed cowhide jacket and pants and a red fox hat—complete with ears, nose, and tail. Alan and Sam were in military parkas and camouflage pants. Amy was in a black down parka and jumped up and down because she was cold. I was in my Carhartt overalls and musher's cap—complete with earflaps that went under my chin. Lee, Sam, and Alan were blocking the light that shone on Matt's body. "I'm Sergeant Tallon of the Frisco police department. What is going on here?"

Sam visibly relaxed. The tension drained from the entire group like air from a balloon. Alan and Lee released Sam and stood back. Amy slid next to me.

"Thank God you're here," I said and I meant it. I didn't think Lee and Alan could've held Sam back much longer. "Amy and I were feeding dogs. Winnie, my Malamute, got loose and we chased her here to Matt's truck. We found Matt lying here." I pointed at Matt and Sam, Alan, and Lee moved aside.

The officer gestured away from the truck. "All of you; move over there," he said. He spoke into walkie-talkie as he examined Matt's body.

~ * ~

It wasn't long before we heard more sirens. Officer Tallon directed us to stay where we were while he got our names, addresses, and our motel rooms. We stood around for a while watching the police cars and ambulance arrive, nobody wanting to move.

Mocha's distinctive barking brought me back to my senses. He has an annoyingly loud bark you can hear for miles.

I nudged Amy. "Isn't that Mocha?"

She listened. "Yeah, I think so."

I sighed. "We forgot our dogs. They still need water." I started back to the truck and then stopped. Amy was still watching the whole scene in disbelief. "Come on, Amy."

My dogs had been quiet until now. I watched as a police cruiser parked next to my truck. The dogs swirled on their stakeouts, knocking their now empty bowls around. Sam the Husky was busy watering down the tires of Summit County's finest when I arrived. I peeked into the car to see the officer talking on the radio, oblivious to the certain actions of a rude Husky.

He looked up. "Yes, Ma'am?"

"You might want to park someplace else," I said, pointing to Sam. The officer's eyes followed my finger and his eyes widened in horror as he saw the result.

"Thanks," he said gruffly. He started the car and drove off—much to Sam's annoyance.

I walked around to the truck's tailgate and pulled it open. It sticks—a lot—so I had to tug it hard. "Get the bowls," I said to Amy. "We'll give them water."

"We still didn't feed Winnie."

"Okay, can you get her?"

I pulled an extra bowl out of the plastic storage tubs. The mixed food was almost frozen. I took the quart saucepan that I use as a food scoop and pounded and flexed the Tupperware container until a large chunk broke off. I usually don't give Winnie the same food I feed the Huskies, except on road trips. It's her extra treat for being so good.

I took two meaty blocks, tossed them into the empty water buckets. I then handed the buckets to Amy, who left to fill them with hot water from our room. The meat and water makes an enticing stew that the dogs will drink—even when they're not inclined to drink water in the cold. Mushers call it "baited water." Dehydration is a serious problem with sled dogs, so you try to coax them to drink as much as possible.

I petted Skye as I awaited Amy. The little leader crooned as I held her. She's a lightweight white Husky with a black saddle and warm, brown eyes. I removed my thin, barely insulated leather gloves and ran my cold fingers through her soft, warm wavy fur. She moved her front feet up and down in an impatient little dance as I petted her and buried my cold face deep into her fur. I felt a tentative lick in my ear as I hugged her. As hard as I tried to ignore it, the radio chatter and flashing lights continued to interrupt the numbness. I wanted to find somewhere to curl up and hide.

Homicide. The officer's words haunted me. What else could it be? I wondered. The whole incident was like some ghoulish nightmare. The Huskies weren't capable of that kind of damage and there was no obvious sign of an accident. Murder—but who? And why?

A commotion stirred me from my thoughts. Gina, wrapped in a down parka over her robe and pak boots, pushed her way through the growing number of spectators. She stopped as she stood in front of the blanket-covered body. Then she began screaming. Her words were inarticulate as two policemen gently took her arms and led her away, sobbing.

Amy came back, lugging the two buckets full of water. I stood up, wiped away the tears, and took one of the buckets from her. Together we poured the water for the dogs and gave each dog a bowl.

"Miss...Keyes?" A voice turned me from the scene. I turned and saw another officer. He was heavy-set and in his mid-fifties. "I'm Detective Jenkins of the Summit County homicide bureau. I understand you and..." He paused and looked at his notebook. "Amy Smythe discovered the body."

"I'm Amy," my handler ventured. She had set down the last of the bowls.

"Yeah, I'm Stephanie Keyes."

"I would like to talk to you alone about what you saw."

Detective Jenkins led me to a police car and opened the back door. I sat inside, feeling a like a convict behind the Plexiglas. The car even smelled like a cop car—different from the normal passenger car. When we were inside, the detective turned on the overhead light.

"Sorry about the accommodations," he said. He pulled out a notepad and a mechanical pencil. "This is easier than standing outside. Could you please tell me what happened?"

I relayed the entire story, including the mysterious dark station wagon and Sam Horton's attempt to throttle me. The detective took copious notes, flipping through several pages. When I was done, he began his questions.

"So, Amy Smythe also saw the dark station wagon?"

"Yeah, it surprised us both."

"At about what time did this happen?"

I paused and looked at my watch. It was eleven-thirteen. "We'd left Megan's at eight-thirty, so, I don't know. We had fed all the dogs except Winnie probably by nine or so."

"And Amy went to your room to grab her coat?"

"Her parka—she already had a coat on, she just forgot her parka and was cold."

"How long was she gone?" He looked up at me.

"Not long—a few minutes at best."

"But you were alone."

I paused. "Not very long," I repeated.

The detective scribbled some more notes. I sat quietly wondering where this would lead.

"Why would Sam Horton think you killed Matt Rayburn?"

"Does he think that?" I asked a little too sharply.

"I don't know, what do *you* think?"

"Sam is—was Matt's best friend. He saw me there with the body and reacted wrong. That's all."

The detective clicked the mechanical pencil and scribbled more notes. The conversation turned to the "banquet"—the pizza dinner. Who was at it and who wasn't. What was said and to whom. All this time, I kept thinking about the not-so-subtle accusation. Did the police think *I* did it?

"So Lee Johnson and Matt Rayburn had an argument?" The detective brought me back to the present.

"Yeah, but Matt was…" My voice trailed off. I would have normally said "such an asshole," but I wasn't sure that was appropriate. "Well, he liked getting into fights—he did it all the time."

"Is that why he filed a formal complaint with the Race Marshall?"

"He was pissed I wouldn't give him trail in the Free Zone. It didn't really matter much anyway, his time was better than mine."

"But it could have made a difference tomorrow."

"Sure, it could. Races are won or lost by seconds."

The detective made sure he had all my contact information and handed me his card. "If you think of anything else, don't hesitate to call me."

"I will."

"Could you send Amy Smythe over?"

"Sure."

~ * ~

I walked back to my truck. I peered in and saw Amy had fallen asleep. Winnie lay beside her, tucked in the telltale sled dog curl. Amy was using Winnie's rump as a pillow. Winnie got up and Amy started awake. "Your turn," I said. "The detective wants to talk to you." Amy slid out of the cab. She walked over to the police car.

I found myself alone again and decided to do something useful. Mocha and Sam twirled nervously on their chains, occasionally barking. Skye and Spice had curled up into shivering balls. They had barely drunk their water due to all the excitement. The bowls were already icing over. I took Mocha by the collar and unsnapped the picket line. I pulled up on his collar and Mocha got up on his hind legs, leaning his front paws against the truck's side. Alaskans are very limber critters and don't mind being on their hind legs. Mocha waited patiently while I fumbled with the dog box latch.

He peered into the box of warm straw and then glanced back at me. "Okay," I said and scooped his butt in my left arm, while still holding his collar with my right hand. He jumped up into the dog box, twirled around, and laid down. Sam was next—into the same box. He's a wild dog and will jump readily into the box. He smacked Mocha in the nose as he leapt in. Mocha snarled for a moment and then settled down as Sam jockeyed for a comfortable place to nestle in the straw.

Each dog is different when it comes to the dog boxes. Some love the boxes; others would prefer less cozy accommodations. I had to pick Lightning's feet off the ground and place them on the side of the truck so I could push him in. Lightning goes limp as you pick him up. Maneuvering sixty pounds of dead weight is not easy. I went down the line with each dog.

Alan Freeman tapped my shoulder as I was loading up the last of my dogs. "Matt's dogs are still out. Gina is still too hysterical to care for them—she asked for us to put them up."

I nodded, loathed as I was to revisit what was now considered the crime scene. Still, the dogs needed attention. "Will the police let us?"

"I think so," Alan said.

We approached the police line. Matt's body was gone; Matt's Alaskans were still twirling on their stakeouts, still too keyed up to lie down. Occasionally an officer would pass by Blue or Shep and the dogs would try to reach out. I turned to the officer as he was taking notes. "Excuse me, Officer."

"Yes?" He looked up and that's when it struck me how handsome he was. Pretty dopey, I know. I'm not a sucker for a good-looking cop or a man in uniform, but with Sergeant Tallon, I could've fallen for him right then and there. He was somewhere in his mid-thirties with blond hair. Sharply chiseled jaw and, from what I could see, exceedingly muscular. Single women probably intentionally speed in Frisco just to get stopped. I wondered if he'd be worth the $100 ticket or so just to ask him out. He looked up with piercingly blue eyes. "Yes, ma'am?"

"Uh, I'm Stephanie Keyes."

"The lady who found the body."

"Uh, yeah, actually both Amy and I found Matt dead." The words sounded strange. "Matt's dogs are still staked out. We'd like to put them up if we could."

Sergeant Tallon considered me a long moment. "You mean put them in their kennels on the truck?" I nodded. "Where's Mrs. Rayburn?"

"Gina's distraught," Alan said evenly. "She's with Mary and Cindy right now. She's asked us to put the dogs up."

"Matt always took care of the dogs anyway," I added.

"All right," the officer said. "But I'll have to watch you."

"No problem." I unhooked Blue's snap from his collar ring and picked him up. He was a beautiful gray Alaskan Husky with the typical husky mask and fur. His eyes were blue, hence the name. About 50 pounds, judging by the weight in my arms. To the untrained eye, he could have easily been mistaken for a purebred racing Siberian. But, Matt would have dropped dead before owning a Siberian—that, I was certain of. There were slight differences that would have made me suspect he was an Alaskan even if I didn't know the owner. His body was a little longer and leaner. His head was not quite Siberian. I'd seen Blue move on Matt's team—he had a nice lope. He wiggled in my arms and gave me a big slurpy kiss. "Up you go," I said as I opened an empty compartment in the dog box and put Blue in. The Husky turned around and waited patiently for his partner.

"Nice dog," I commented to Alan, who was struggling with Poco.

"Blue?" Alan asked. "Yeah, that's a nice *Alaskan*."

I held my tongue and turned to unhook Shep. Blue seemed to be content to stay in the box, so I left the door open. Shep was more of a hound, with black and tan markings that made him look almost like a German Shepherd cross. His markings were where the similarities ended, however. Shep had bi-eyes, meaning one blue eye and one brown eye—or, in his case, a yellow eye. His build was long and lean like a Greyhound and his ears flopped in interesting positions. He too, was very friendly. I hoisted him into the dog box with his pal, Blue. By his weight, I guessed him to be somewhere around 60 pounds. Each of Matt's boxes were large enough to accommodate two dogs.

Alan and I went down the line. Within less than fifteen minutes, we had put the dogs up. I was about to leave when the officer turned to me. "Will you be here tomorrow?"

My mouth was cotton. "I'll be racing," I said. "I'll be here 'til eight-dog racing class finishes. I might hang around for the awards."

"I might have some questions."

"Well, if you need to get hold of me, I live in Pine Junction," I said.

Chapter Five

Early morning, the phone rang loudly. I jerked upright, disoriented, nearly cracking my skull on the overhead bookshelf as I fumbled for the handset. I could hear Amy groan in the next bed. She probably had about the same amount of sleep I had—next to none.

"Hello?" I muttered. Instead of a voice, I heard overly cheery music. The wake-up call. I looked at the clock and then fumbled the receiver back on the hook. I groaned and closed my eyes. I kept waking up with nightmares of death. I'm not an overly sensitive person, but seeing Matt's body like that chilled me. I pulled myself up and gave Amy a shove in the shoulder. She groaned again.

Winnie whined from her crate and pawed at the door. I threw on some clothes and my pac boots, grabbed my parka, gloves, and a leash, and took Winnie for a walk.

The cold air hit my face as I opened the door. Winnie dragged me outside before I could protest. The sky was remarkably sapphire blue over a blanket of pristine white snow. You only get that color at high altitude without much humidity or pollution. Frisco, at over 9000 feet in elevation, fits the bill. The beautiful weather just didn't seem appropriate for all that happened last night.

The parking lot was remarkably quiet. I noticed a few trucks I saw last night were already gone. They probably would drop their dogs at the race site instead of here at the motel. Matt's dog truck was gone too—Gina must have left early. The snow around the parking area was scraped almost to the asphalt. The motel must have hired a snowplow to remove the evidence of the murder.

Winnie relieved herself and I took out a small bag and cleaned up after her—depositing the bag into a nearby dumpster. I idly wondered if the police went dumpster diving last night and if they had found the murder weapon yet.

~ * ~

Normally I don't shower before a race, but today I did. I closed my eyes and let the hot water pour on my body. I couldn't shake the vision of Matt lying there dead. The whole night had been one impossible nightmare. It was hard to believe that it happened at all.

Now, I kept thinking about Gina screaming. I hadn't had a boy-friend in a long time—the dogs tend to scare most would-be suitors away—but I think I would be devastated if something had happened to someone I loved. I really felt sorry for her. She didn't need to see him like that.

My thoughts wandered to Officer Tallon. I wondered what he thought about all the mushers last night. Probably thought we were all crazy—and he'd be right. Still, despite the awful night, I couldn't help but think about him a bit. Knowing my luck, he was probably married, had allergies to dogs, and was an Animal Rights Activist.

I pulled myself out of the shower, dried off, and slid into the black polar fleece long underwear, the black polar fleece pants and pullover. I then zipped the Gore-Tex pants over the fleece. I hate black—it shows dog hair—but most Gore-Tex clothing comes in black. Gore-Tex is wonderful for mushing. It's relatively waterproof and definitely windproof. The manufacturers just haven't figured out a color that blends with dog hair.

Amy had boiled hot water in the little hot pot we always bring along for road trips and was eating instant peaches and cream oat-meal from a paper cup. I poured a cup of hot water and rummaged in my duffle bag for a tea bag. I found one left and dunked the bag in the cup.

"That was terrible," Amy said, without preamble.

"Yeah," I agreed, sipping the hot tea. I glanced at my watch. It was six-thirty-five. "We don't have much time—the driver's meet-ing's at eight."

"They'll have the race?"

"There's snow, isn't there?"

"Isn't that a little callous?"

I stifled a yawn. "Yeah, well that's mushing." Perhaps they'd dedicate the race to Matt or offer a prize in his honor. But canceling the race over a murder? Unthinkable.

~ * ~

I trundled out to the dog truck and grabbed the two water buckets from the truck bed. The meat had frozen solid over the night, so I dumped a couple of scoops of Eukanuba dog food into the buckets and shuffled back. The original formula is high protein/ high fat content—perfect for sled dogs. It's highly palatable too—

the dogs will seldom turn their noses up at it.

I entered our motel room. Amy was dressed and drying her hair. Evidently, she too felt a shower was in order. I entered the bathroom and filled the buckets with hot water.

"Ready?' I asked.

"Yeah—just have to pack some things," she nodded.

"Let's drop," I said.

The morning routine is a lot like the evening routine. Dogs always come first. I string out the picket lines for the dogs while Amy unlocks the boxes. Then, we both open each box together and take—or in some instances, catch—our respective dogs. The dogs that are comfortable with the dog truck often just hang back and wait for us to take each by the collar and help them down. However, a few make a game of jumping out of the truck. Skye will leap in the air the moment you open the box, so you have to be ready for her. Sam will bowl you over if you stand in front of him. Now that I think about it, he's an obnoxious dog. If Sam weren't a leader, I wouldn't put up with all his shenanigans.

After the dogs are hooked on their own stakeouts, we get the bowls and fill them with the baited water. Most will drink; some won't. Skye won't, for example, but she's a princess. The dogs relieve themselves and we walk around with a pooper scoop and deposit the waste in an empty dog food bag.

Once we sufficiently watered the dogs, we put them back in their boxes and drove over to the race site. The City of Frisco had plowed the parking area around the marina again the night before. Snow banks over 10 feet high ringed the parking area. This was the staging area for mushers. Another parking area on the far side was designated for spectators.

Lee Johnson stood at the entrance of the staging area. Gone was the fringed buckskin—replaced by high tech Gore-Tex, blue military parka, and an orange high visibility vest. He still wore that ratty red fox hat. I rolled down the window as I approached.

"You ever going to get rid of that skanky thing?" I teased.

"Not on your life—Sherri gave it to me," he grinned. "You know where you parked yesterday?"

"Yeah, why?"

"Cindy asked me to play parking lot attendant—at least until the driver's meeting."

"Lucky you."

"Yeah, well, we've had some newbies show up and they're trying to take other people's parking spots." He shook his head. "They don't understand that's how diseases spread."

I nodded. Mushers park in the same spot each day to reduce contact with other teams. Although we clean up after ours dogs, viruses and bacteria still can spread from contaminated dirt or snow. With that many dogs, it's common for an entire kennel to pick up a bug at a race. Kennel cough or an intestinal virus has ruined the race season for more than one musher. Vaccinations are not fail-safe and not every bug can be vaccinated against.

"Didn't we have the newbies here yesterday?" I asked.

"No," said Lee. "We've got a kids race and a rookie run today."

I groaned. "Okay, so it's going to be mayhem."

"That's one word for it." He eyed me appraisingly. "Tough night, wasn't it?"

"Yeah," I said, "that's one word for it."

Another truck pulled up behind us and honked.

"Better get going," Lee said and waved us through. I drove over to my parking spot next to Lee's truck. Lee has a beautiful double-decker dog box mounted on a flat bed with a blue silhouette of an Alaskan Husky running. The dog had a red harness painted on it and the words *Sky Hi Alaskan Huskies* in big blue letters across the box. *Sky Hi Alaskan Huskies* is Lee's kennel name.

I parked and shut off the ignition and we slid out. The air filled with barking from dogs as the mushers unloaded them from their trucks and put them on stakeouts. There were about twenty dog trucks here already. The trucks ran the gamut to old rusted-out hulks that were barely running to brand new, one ton dually, crew cabs that came with every option imaginable—and some unimaginable—for a cool fifty thousand dollars.

I watched in disbelief as a sky blue '75 Volkswagen Beetle with a modified ski rack (complete with sled on top) drove into the staging area. The musher smiled and waved at me as I watched him putter to his parking space. In the back seat and the passenger seat were three huge Malamutes. The Malamute in the passenger seat was a huge black and white male with a black mask and golden eyes. He hung his head out the halfway opened window, panting as they drove by. The Malamutes in the back were a sea of writhing gray. The Beetle's windows were fogging up.

"Testing! Testing!" crackled a voice from the ancient PA system the club had set up at the chute entrance to the start line. The starting chute was no more than a gap between the giant snow banks with red and blue snow fencing lining the actual chute. Along one side of the snow piles next to the start line sat the club's old yellow school bus. It served as race headquarters.

The bus still had "Gilpin County School District RE-1" across the sides in faded black. Smoke puffed from a chimney that protruded from one of the windows. Cindy had her husband install a wood stove in the bus. It kept race workers cozy when it was freezing outside—which, of course, is all the time. Along the side of the bus, whiteboards announced the latest standings. The PA crackled again and I heard The Beach Boys "Help Me Rhonda" blaring from the PA system and the loudspeakers atop the bus. You could barely hear it over the barking.

I turned and started unlocking dog boxes and the sled locks. Mushers put their sleds on top of their trucks—it's the only place the sleds will fit. I use electric conduit and eyebolts to secure the sled to the roof of the dog box. The conduit slips through the eyebolts at the corner of the box and snakes through the sled's runners. I lock both sides to ensure the sled is safe, but the system does have its drawbacks. I've known mushers who have lost a sled in a really strong wind—the wind actually ripped the sled off the truck, eyebolts and all.

"Did you hear about Matt?" I heard Vicki's voice. She sounded conspiratorial.

"No, what?" came a woman's voice I didn't recognized.

"He was *murdered* last night," Vicki said.

"No! Really?"

"Yeah, the jerk finally ticked off someone once too often."

Laughter. "How do you know he was murdered?"

"Sherri told me. Saw everything. The blood, brains, everything!"

"Ewww!" The other woman shuddered.

Their voices faded as they walked out of earshot. I frowned and glanced over at Lee's truck. Sherri wasn't around. I wondered what she had told Vicki.

The music stopped and the speaker crackled. "Attention! Attention! Driver's meeting in ten minutes!"

Nobody seemed to notice. "Surfing USA" boomed from the speakers.

I checked my watch. It was eight-thirty five. Sprint races run multiple classes of dogs. At this race, there were classes for ten-dog teams, eight-dog teams, six-dog teams, four-dog teams, and three-dog teams. They also had a rookie race, a kid's race, and a skijoring race. (Skijoring is where mushers wears skis and have one, two, or three dogs pull them). Ten-dog was supposed to go out at eight sharp and they hadn't even had the drivers' meeting. Eight-dog, my own class, would go out after that. I motioned Amy to help me with the stakeouts. We pulled the telescoping stakeout bars out from the truck's bumpers. The rear ones always get stuck with dirt and ice, so I took a sledgehammer out of the cab and began pounding on it.

"Need help?"

I tugged hard against the bar. It released and I fell backwards unceremoniously on my backside. I looked up to see Alan Freeman snicker. I could see his Siberians were already out and drinking water. I hated looking so ungainly in front of him. But, his smile was good natured and I quickly forgive him.

Amy was right—Alan was kind of cute, despite not being my breed. That is, he was a Siberian Husky musher and I, by God, was an Alaskan Husky musher. Bad mix. Can you imagine what the puppies would look like?

"I'm doing just fine," I grumbled, picking myself up.

"A little WD-Forty helps."

"I'm sure."

Alan tested the bar along the opposite side. "Can you hand me that hammer? This side is frozen too."

"Feeling charitable this morning?" I asked suspiciously.

"Last night was a bit rough," Alan said. "You looked pretty shaken up. My dogs are all dropped and harnessed, so I thought I'd help you out if I could." He smacked the bar with the hammer several times. Dirt and ice fell from the bar. He jerked the bar loose and fastened it in its extended position with a heavy-duty pin.

"It wasn't fun," I admitted. "Thanks. I appreciate it." Amy and I strung the aircraft cable with the pickets across the length of the truck.

"Did you get breakfast?" Alan asked.

I shook my head.

"Pam, from the Sammy Club, is selling breakfast burritos."

My stomach churned at the thought. "I think I'll pass."

"She has cinnamon rolls too," he said temptingly. "Would you like me to pick some up for you?" He smiled again. That smile could almost melt a frozen heart. Almost.

"I think I might take you up on it."

He grinned. "Let's drop your dogs first."

We opened the dog box doors one at a time. Some of the dogs, such as Lightning, simply lay in their boxes, quite cozy and happy to stay. Lightning is a big white dog with a crease in his right ear and a goofy expression. He loves to run, but isn't much on human companionship. Some dogs are born with a natural shyness. Poor socialization with humans early on just increases the tendency. His overall lack of socialization made him skittery with humans, although he's much better with me and enjoys the occasional pet. On the opposite side was Skye, she nuzzled me affectionately as I caught her in mid leap and gently set her down. I snapped one of the stakeout lines to her collar.

We had just put the last of the dogs on the stakeouts when Cindy shouted "Driver's meeting!"

That was the longest ten minutes I'd ever seen. It was nine o'clock.

"The trail's still kind of rough," Cindy shouted without preamble as we stood around her. Glancing around, I noticed thirty or so people were gathered. Others were still coming in. We must have looked like some bizarre cult in our parkas, brown Carhartt overalls, and coveralls standing around the high priestess of mushing. She wore an olive drab, military issue, extreme-weather parka with Iditarod, Race to the Sky, Beargrease, and other sundry race patches sewn across it. Duct tape lined the bottom pocket where it had once ripped. A thick hunter-orange wool cap covered short, wispy, gray hair. She looked down at her clipboard through horn-rimmed glasses and then up over them at the small crowd. "We got the snowcats out last night and this morning to try to smoothen up the trail. It's still rough in spots and there's patches of ice, especially along the first and last mile. This is a hard and fast trail, people. Yesterday we had several people take the last hill at full speed..."

I could feel eyes turn on me and I heard a few snickers.

"We've put markers designating slow sections for a reason,"

Cindy's gray eyes met mine. "Slow down, people, or you're going to lose control." She paused and studied the clipboard more intently. I held my breath, guessing what the next part was about. "Yesterday, we had an altercation in the free zone and there were some questions concerning passing…"

I felt my face flush. I glanced furtively around to see if anyone was looking at me—if anyone was, I didn't see it.

"We use ISDRA passing rules. This is an ISDRA sanctioned race. When someone calls 'trail' on you, you must yield the trail to the overtaking team. The only exception to this is in the 'free zone', which is clearly marked a half mile from the finish line. There was some questions regarding a team that wouldn't yield in the free zone. They don't have to do that, but…" And now her gaze was directly on me. "It's just common courtesy to let the overtaking team pass. This is a 'free zone' not a 'free for all zone.'" She paused.

"Remember this is head-on passing, folks. If your team has not head-on passed before, or if your team has jumped into another team before, I want you to stop your team and hold it while the other team passes. Incoming teams have the right of way. Your starting order is your placement at the end of yesterday's heat. Any questions?"

I didn't and after having been publicly chastised, whether or not my name was specifically mentioned, I decided the best thing was to go buy that replacement brake.

I spotted Mary Palmer's booth near the finish line. She's a local mushing outfitter that everyone buys from. She used to race twenty years ago or so, but decided selling to mushers is better than racing. Her son, Ken, races the few Alaskans she owns. She was setting up her booth for the morning.

"Hi Mary!" I said, as I watched her pull some brightly colored harnesses out of a Roughneck container. She looped the harnesses on a stand set up like a large cooking spit where other harnesses, sled bags, and other lightweight items hung.

Mary smiled, squinting in the sunshine. It almost looked like a grimace. The small woman had graying hair tied back in two thick braids and wore a thick green kusbuk trimmed with coyote fur. Her hair and tanned skin was reminiscent of an old Inuit woman. Mary was Caucasian. "I heard you were the one who found Matt."

"Yeah," I said. "Amy and I did."

"Too bad—I hear it was ugly—mighty bloody." I must have looked surprised. Mary is the local gossip repository, but somehow I didn't think she would have that information this fast. "Don't worry, everybody's heard. Can't say as I blame whoever did it." She eyed me appraisingly.

I didn't like the insinuation, but ignored the unsaid accusation. "Do you have a spare brake I could buy?"

Mary shook her head. "Didn't bring brakes this time. Usually I bring my heavy duty one, but I was short on space yesterday. John's running three-dog." John was her thirteen-year-old son. "Come by my house before Granby and I'll set you up with a heavy-duty brake. I might have a Risdon sled for sale by that time."

I frowned. "Matt's?"

"You heard our argument?"

"Yeah."

Mary shrugged. "I suspect many people did. Anyway, I'll be talking to Gina on Monday and getting the sled back. Why don't you buy it? It's better than that boat anchor you ride."

"Money," I said.

"Don't worry about it—I know you're good for it."

I gave her a puzzled look. "Matt sure wasn't."

"Matt," Mary sighed. "He was always promising me money and never paying me. You're good for it."

"Thanks," I said, but it didn't do anything for the predicament I was in now. "I've got a real problem, though. My brake's busted and there's no way Cindy will let me run without it. I've got to replace it or splint it with something."

"Try Sam—he carries all sorts of odds and ends."

I shook my head. "Sam's in a real bad mood right now. I don't think I want to get too near him."

Mary grimaced again and squinted into the sun. My eyes followed her gaze. It rested on an old school bus parked outside the starting line. "Check the bus," she said. "Cindy might have something."

I grinned and nodded. "Thanks."

I was walking towards the school bus when I heard a commotion. All the dogs starting barking wildly and louder than ever.

"Loose dog!" someone shouted.

A little red Husky came bounding towards me. She danced away from a couple of people who tried to catch her and teased a few dogs at the truck nearest to me. It was Ray Bryce's truck. The thin Siberian musher I met the night before at the banquet rounded the corner and called to her. The Husky had an impish grin on her face as she eluded him and danced backwards towards me.

I lunged and nabbed her red collar. Startled, she nearly turned around and snapped. Half-way through the motion, she saw me and instead licked my face with a big slurp. I laughed. "Silly girl!"

The dogs around us quieted.

"Your dog?" Ray asked as he picked up a dog bowl.

"No," I said, petting her. I looked around. I expected to see her owner dash up to me with relief on his or her face. Instead, everyone went back to what he or she was doing.

"I think she's got a tag," Ray said, bending down and peering under the collar.

I slid the collar around her neck, so I could look at the tag. I stared at it for a long while.

"Who does she belong to?" he asked.

My throat went dry. I shook my head and pointed.

Ray gasped as he read the name.

MATT RAYBURN.

Chapter Six

Both Ray and I stared at the tag a long time. His skin was pale white next to his red musher's cap and dark hair.

"Mary said Matt's dead," he stammered.

I nodded, speechless.

"She must have gotten out last night," he ventured.

"And found her way here?" I asked.

"How else would she have gotten here?" he asked.

"I don't know," I said. My mind reeled. There wasn't a logical explanation for this. She had to have gotten out. I thought back to the pickets on Matt's truck. I thought there was a Husky on each stakeout, but I couldn't remember. Both Alan and I had put the dogs up. Perhaps a picket had been empty on the side Alan had put up.

The tag said her name was Tasha. I pet her and she licked my face. "You're a friendly thing, aren't you?" I said to her. "Tasha! Ta- sha!" She wriggled happily as she heard her name.

Ray looked ill.

"Sit down, Ray," I said. "This isn't your problem. I'll call Gina and let her know Tasha must have gotten loose last night and I found her."

He breathed a sigh of relief. "You'd do that?"

"Yeah."

~ * ~

I walked back to my truck, leading Tasha by the collar. The City of Frisco had unfortunately plowed the parking lot too closely. Mushers, dogs, sleds, and vehicles had pounded what little snow re- mained into ice. Even with my Sorel pac boots, it was slick.

I returned to the truck. Amy had set up the sled, securely snub- bing it to the truck's bumper, and had strung out the eight-dog line—minus the dogs. She was now fast asleep in the sled's basket, just on top of the sled bag. The basket was only four feet and isn't made for humans to lie on except in an emergency, so her toes hung off. The dogs were still staked out of the picket lines and began bark- ing and yammering when they saw me and Tasha.

There are some serious misconceptions about mushers in the

general public. For instance, some people think mushers sit in the basket or lie down while driving the dogs. Mushers actually ride the runners behind the basket, standing upright. We use our weight to shift the sled (called warping or racking) side-to-side, sort of the way a skier uses his skis. You can't control the sled while sitting in the basket—it would be the ultimate in suicide runs. In the basket, you are literally at the mercy of the dogs. There's no steering and no brake. Drawings and photos of current mushers running dogs while in the basket aren't real. There's no way you'd live going around a corner or down a steep grade without the benefit of using a brake or being able to steer it.

Amy didn't move. The dogs' barking didn't faze her: the sheer exhaustion had caught up. I thought about waking her, but instead decided to slip Tasha into one of the empty boxes and go look for my brake.

"Up you go, Girl," I grinned as she allowed me to pick her up and slide her in the open dog box compartment. She turned around in the straw, apparently satisfied, and gave me a lick on the nose. I closed the door and locked it with a padlock. "Try to get out of that," I said.

She didn't look like the escape artist type, but you never know. I've had dogs climb out of six-foot tall kennels, unsnap themselves from chains, and even bolt when I opened the kennel door. My dogs either don't go very far or if they escape, they come back when they're hungry. They know they've got it pretty good—they get love, attention, high quality food and medical care, and they get to do what they love to do: run in a sled team. Tasha, however, didn't know me and it takes a while to build trust. If she could unsnap herself from a picket line, she might do that again and she would be off for parts unknown.

I headed back to the bus, watching my footing carefully. The crowd had dispersed. A few people were standing before the large white boards, writing down names and times from yesterday's heat. I looked at my time. I was in third place, right behind Lee Johnson and Alan Freeman. Matt's time would have been third had he not died, although technically his time was third best. Someone had marked a red line through Matt's standing and added DNR—Did Not Race—in today's slot next to his name. I looked at the times again. Alan was an astonishing twenty-three and a half seconds behind Lee's time—I was nearly forty seconds behind that. If I hadn't held up Alan Freeman and Matt Rayburn in the free zone, their times would have been closer still. What an accomplishment for Alan's Siberian Husky team.

I climbed aboard the bus. Inside, Cindy Travis was arguing with Sam Horton over running order. Cindy's husband, Joe, sat next to the wood burning stove in the middle. I don't think the bus came with the wood burning stove option, although I'd imagine that on some cold winter days the kids wouldn't mind. I seem to recall Cindy having Joe weld the wood stove into the bus a few years back. It took a little creativity to construct the stovepipe and the fitting around the window. Joe had the fire stoked and it radiated enough warmth to feel cozy even at the entrance. I paused and wondered how I was going to get around Sam's hulking frame when the big man scowled at Cindy and stomped down the aisle. I quickly slid into the first seat and let Sam pass. He paused and glared at me for a moment, but said nothing as he passed.

"He makes me nervous," I admitted to Cindy as I paused for a moment to watch Sam Horton walk back to his truck.

"You should be," Cindy said. "Sam could have easily throttled you last night, you know."

"You heard about that?" I asked.

"Yeah, there aren't too many secrets among mushers," she said. "Except, perhaps, who killed Matt Rayburn." She looked at me thoughtfully. "You know, Sam thinks it's you."

I drew a quick breath inward. Tried and convicted in the court of public opinion? "What happened to innocent until proven guilty?" I asked.

"That only works in court—and sometimes not even there," Cindy remarked drolly. "So, what brings you here? Matt's complaint?"

In truth, I hadn't even thought about it since last night before the murder. "No, I was looking for a plank to splint my brake. Mary Palmer doesn't have any brakes."

She looked at me over her horn-rimmed glasses. "Joe!" she shouted, although he was not more than ten feet away. "Steph needs a plank—you got any short two-by-fours?"

Joe wore short wool gloves with the fingers cut off and leather palms and he spread his hands with fingers outstretched towards the stove. He too wore an olive-drab arctic parka and a hunter-orange wool cap. Together Cindy and Joe looked like throwbacks from the 60's. Quick blue eyes darted towards the scrap woodbin he had been using to feed the fire. The woodbin was an old case that held Fetzer Chardonnay long ago. He rummaged through the bin and pulled out a foot-long, flat plank. It looked like a wood shingle. "Would this work?" he asked, rubbing the gray, day old stumble along his chin.

I hefted the shingle in my hands and then tried to flex it. It wouldn't budge. "Should work," I said. "Thank you! Do I owe you anything?"

Joe laughed. "Of course not! It'd go into the fire."

I left the bus, gripping that wooden plank like my most prized possession and hurried back to the truck. Amy was still fast asleep in the sled basket. I walked over to the sled and stood on the runners and leaned above the driving bow. If I had expected a reaction from her, I would have been disappointed. Instead, I kicked back, propelling the sled until the snub lines grew taut. Amy started awake, practically tipping the sled forward and dumping me across the driving bow.

I laughed.

"Hey! That's not funny!" Amy groaned, when she realized what had happened.

The snickers from onlookers told me otherwise. I just grinned. "Come on, Lazy Head! I've got a race to run!"

Amy pulled herself up and sorted the harnesses out of the tack box. The dogs barked and spun on their lines, dancing on their hind feet as they reached out for us. Only Skye stood placidly. The little white dog with a black saddle was once a distance dog and knew to conserve energy—unlike my lanky sprint dogs, which resembled screaming weasels from hell more than they did huskies. Skye did a tiny dance with her front feet and a small whine escaped her muzzle to let me know the self-styled princess was getting impatient.

Meantime, I searched in the tack box for the piece of brake that had snapped off. I found it beneath a spare snowhook. The wood had splintered into a jagged triangle. I took it, my newly acquired plank, and a roll of duct tape to my sled. I carefully turned the sled over and put the two pieces together. I put the plank on top and wrapped the whole splinted brake with the duct tape. Turning the sled upright, I tested it out. The splint held. It would work if I didn't put too much stress on it.

Sprint sled dog races are run by classes. Your class depends on the number of dogs you run. In this race, ten-dog class is first, followed by eight-dog class, then six-dog, then four-dog, and so on. Each team leaves at an appointed interval—usually one to two minutes apart. So, if you have twenty-three teams in the ten-dog class (as we had), and the teams are staggered at one minute, it takes twenty-three minutes for the teams to leave the starting chute. The next class is not run until the previous class comes in. So, my class, the eight-dog class, has to wait for all the ten-dog teams to finish. Since ten-dog runs ten miles (one mile per dog in the team), the fast teams, like Lee Johnson's, finish the race in about 30 minutes. The slower teams take longer, and could be as long as an hour. So, the ten-dog class may take as long as an hour and a half.

But, it never happens that quickly. Most of the time, there's a break between classes—ten to fifteen minutes. Everything at a dog race is hurry up and wait. It's not unusual for the last classes to end late in the day, even on Sundays—when everyone is tired and ready to go home. They hurry it up a bit on Sundays, but it's still slow.

The trick to running sprint races is to watch which team is going out and which team is coming back in. Lee Johnson runs ten-dog and eight-dog and by my standards, is a lunatic for running two classes back-to-back. Lee Johnson's ten-dog team had already entered the paddock from the trail, dragging both Lee and handlers across the parking lot from the race. Lee's dogs veered towards his truck. Sherri, Lee's wife, was ready with water and treats. She clipped the leaders' neckline to one of the stakeouts at the truck. The dogs drank deep and panted with grins that pulled back to their ears. Their faces were wet with foamy froth from saliva, but they didn't care—right now, they were the happiest dogs in the world. There is nothing an Alaskan Husky loves more than to run in a team.

"How was the trail?" I shouted to Lee above my own dogs' barking. Lee's team's arrival stirred up my own dogs.

Lee gave me a thumbs up with gloved hands and a grin. "Hard packed and fast—your team should scream," he shouted back. He turned back to giving water to his dogs.

Other teams were entering the paddock. There were 23 teams in 10-dog and most were already back. There would be only five minutes between 10-dog and 8-dog and we were now third of 27 teams. "Let's hook up," I told Amy.

Others were having the same idea. Soon, the entire paddock erupted in a cacophony of barking and screaming. Huskies will scream and yammer with excitement. Sprint dogs are enthusiastic and will "harness bang," that is, slam their bodies forward against their harnesses in their desire to go. Others may "line bite" or chew the harnesses or lines, so desperate in their fever to run. Mushers must sometimes run cable-filled gangline or risk losing dogs.

I'm convinced "line-biting" and "harness banging" is hereditary. I once bred a litter of puppies out of a line biter and a harness banger and ended up with nearly uncontrollable dogs. The moment I put them in the line, they began pounding and chomping away—with absolutely no chance to see it from other dogs. Most sprint mushers don't care about this. They call it "high attitude." I tire of it easily. It's rough having to constantly replace lines and harnesses from the abuse. My dream is to have a team of well-behaved huskies someday.

We started with Mocha and Sam, my two leaders. The dogs attach to the gangline through the neckline at the collar and at the tugline to the tug loop at the back of the harness. My harnesses are red and the traditional style mushers call an X-back. There are other harness types—H-back, siwash, collared X-back—but X-back harnesses are the most popular. The X-back, when viewed from above the dog, looks like a diamond with an X in the middle. Padded straps start from behind the dog's ribcage and cross over the withers to form a neck opening—the main surface the dogs must lean into to pull. The straps go downward into a breastplate—I use what is called a split-chest design—and then the two straps split and go underneath the forelegs. The two straps become one at the end of the harness at the base of the dog's tail. With the exception of the two cross pieces that form the X, the whole harness is one solid piece of 1 inch nylon webbing.

Amy held my leaders while one by one I hooked in Spice, Skye, and Lightning into the team. Then, Dancer and Jasmine. I put Jasmine in wheel next to Lightning. (Wheel is the position next to the sled). She screamed, seeing the other bitches in front. She didn't like other females. Then Rowdy—who is true to his name and pounds the line.

People always ask me which make better sled dogs, the males or the females. It is typically a preference of the musher. For example,

I've heard from sprint mushers that females are the better athletes, but then I've heard distance mushers prefer males. Mocha and Sam were two males that made up my leads, but most of my team is female. I would say it depends on the dog.

I finished hooking up Jasmine, went back to the sled, and stood on the brake. I waited and watched as Lee hooked up his team. Dancer, my little gray husky, pounded the lines, jerking the sled with each bang. Lee hit the quick releases on his snub lines and his team shot off. The brake scraped loudly against the ice, trying to gain purchase. It sent two small plumes of ice and snow into the air as he pulled away.

My team barked, whined, and pounded the lines harder. Dancer began chewing the line in frustration. "Dancer!" I admonished. She dove guiltily underneath the line, trying to hide.

When you step on the sled, time slows and reality shifts. The barking is so loud I can't hear Amy shouting even a few feet away. I wave and give her the thumbs up. I hope she understands I'm releasing the team. I pull back on the quick release of one snub line and the snap pops open. I stand on the brake, knowing it won't bite into the icy road. I unhook and we lurch forward.

Amy runs in sort of a weird, clumsy dance. She tries to hold onto the team and hold them back, but that's my job and the brake won't bite into ice. She raises her hand as she approaches the next team in the line. I step harder on the brake. Somehow, we stop.

I look at the musher's bib number in the team right before us. Twenty-nine—Alan's number. Alan's Siberians are as skittery as mine are. I am bib number twenty-five.

I don't hear the countdown or the "go!" but instead, I see Lee's team in the chute leave at a lope. Alan's team strains forward as Alan tries to keep his own dogs from pursuing Lee's team. He thunders into the chute and the workers grasp his dogs and sled and hold it firm. It takes five people to hold his dogs and the sled.

It feels so odd to be behind a Siberian team. They're not supposed to be this fast, but somehow Alan has discovered a magic combination. I'll need to make up time today to beat his team, but I don't think I can. Yesterday, with the exception of the failed brake, was a pretty clean run. I am thankful Alan and I aren't competing against each other for ISDRA points.

"Five, four, three, two, one, go!"

Alan's dogs fall silent and take off. They're beautiful—even I admit it. A team like that would make me switch to purebred if the politics weren't so crazy. My own team chases his. I don't trust my newly repaired brake, so I unholster my snowhook and let it catch into the snow and ice. We stop right at the starting line.

"Thirty seconds," says the timer.

Who killed Matt Rayburn? The thought continues to nag me as I shift uneasily on the runners. Oh, there were many people who didn't like him, but who would be driven to actually kill him? I lean back and carefully loosen the snowhook so I can pull it from the ice. Whoever killed him had to be strong—whatever the murder weapon was it had to be heavy and sharp. Whoever it was, was strong—like a musher. Matt wouldn't have gone down easily.

"Fifteen seconds."

Mocha looks back at me. He senses my mind is elsewhere. Sam is acting like the typical idiot and is barking loudly and banging against his harness. Amy holds him by the X-back, but control is tenuous. I wonder if she is going to go deaf from his barking. Rowdy is chewing the lines again in frustration and Jasmine is screaming, cat-like. Dancer is pounding her harness. Only Skye, Spice, and Lightning seem calm.

"Good Mocha! Good Sam!" I call out, although my optimism is false. Sometimes you have to pretend enthusiasm, even when you don't have any.

"Five, four, three, two, one, go!" the timer and workers say in unison.

Chapter Seven

Amy releases Sam and quickly backs away. The other workers back off as well. I pull the hook and yell "Hike! Hike! Hike! Hike! Hike!" For the record: nobody uses the word "mush" anymore. "Mush" is too soft sounding a word to command dogs, so most mushers use "Hike!", "Let's go!", or "Get up!"

The team falls silent and we bolt out of the chute. I drag my feet to provide some sort of control as we fly across the lake. The team is moving faster today—maybe we do have a chance at catching up with Alan. Lee's team, however, is too far ahead to contemplate. Mocha and Sam have started at a faster pace than I expect and everyone's tuglines are tight. Even Jasmine is focused ahead instead of on the other females in front of her.

Lake Dillon is flat and wind-swept. The race takes us across two miles of the frozen lake until the trail meets the islands and climbs upward to land. The flat, snow-covered lake makes a perfect racecourse for the dogs. The sun is shining and the sky is a deep sapphire blue but the wind comes off the mountains that ring Dillon and Frisco. The cold wind bites into my exposed skin.

We're running maybe twenty to twenty-three miles per hour. That's fast for a sled team, especially at this altitude. A friend of mine once borrowed a radar gun from a cop and aimed it at various teams. The fastest he clocked one was at twenty-five miles per hour. But that was at a local race. The big teams—the unlimited teams that race in the Northern American in Fairbanks, Alaska—probably run closer to thirty miles an hour at times.

The snowcats made a hard and fast trail and the dogs fly across it. We're nearly two miles when we reach the hill. The hill is actually an island in the lake. We climb up the hill after a brief hesitation, hardly slowing down. Once we crest the hill, the trail winds its way through coniferous trees. We run through the trees and the island levels a bit. The trail winds along the open snowfields. I see another team pulled over to the side of the trail. It is Alan Freeman.

His team is strung out along the side of the trail. Alan is off his sled and working on a dog's tugline. I hesitate before slowing the team down. As I step on the brake, I can feel it flex dangerously under my foot. I will need to use the snowhook if I am going to stop. In a split second, I make the decision.

"On by!" I tell Mocha and Sam. "On by!"

I'm still slowing a bit, so I turn to Alan. He is snapping the tugline back to the dog's tug loop on the harness. "Need help?" I shout. I want to go by, but my conscious won't allow it.

Alan waves me on. "We're okay! Had a tangle! Go on!"

I wave back. Tough luck. Occasionally, even experienced teams can have a dog or two get tangled up in the lines. Some tangles are harmless, but many can injure a dog, especially if a line is wrapped around a leg or neck. I must have gotten there while he had finished untangling the dogs. I was in second place, assuming nothing else happened.

The team, energized by the pass, begins to lope. I idly wonder how far ahead Lee Johnson actually is. I stare ahead into the whiteness. He started two minutes ahead of me, which would mean I would have to at least see him before I had a shot at beating his cumulative time. I couldn't see how I could possibly make up that much time without another lucky break. Two breaks during a race was asking too much of the mushing gods.

The sun beats down on the team. Out on the snow, the reflection is excruciating. Without sunglasses or goggles, you can go snowblind. It's also hot. Even if the ambient is only ten to twenty degrees, it can feel like seventy. I strip off my gloves and grip the driving bow with bare hands. Still hot, I pull hat was off, too, and slip it into the glove bag on the sled and unzip my parka. The wind feels good against my face. I look ahead; see something move two hills over. Lee Johnson?

I began pedaling, standing on one runner and using one leg to push off with a swinging motion. I stay focused. Damn it, I want to win! I hope I am not imagining Lee's team—but the sun off the snow can play with your eyes. Did I see Lee or did I see that copse of trees to the right? I feel elated, hot and tired all at once. But I don't dare stop pedaling. Not now.

The trail runs up and down a few hills. "Get up, Sam! Get up, Mocha!" I shout. Sam and Mocha lower their heads in response and pull harder. Sometimes a good lead dog makes all the difference between a mediocre and a winning team. We crest the hill and look around the flats that run back towards the last hill and back onto

Lake Dillon. I see Lee's team a mile away: black dots against the snow. He is moving at a phenomenal pace.

My heart sinks. There is no way we could catch him. Still, I don't let the dogs know that. We lope down into the flats and pass the free zone marker that yesterday had caused such consternation. I remind myself to be more careful on the last hill where I had broken my brake. From the top, I see Lee already crossing the finish line.

"Drat!" I grumble. "Easy, Mocha. Easy, Sam." I applied the brake as we crest the top of the last hill and slide down it with little more control.

Our run to the finish line is uneventful. "Stephanie Keyes, number twenty-five is in second. Good run, Steph," the loudspeaker greeted me as we crossed the finish line. I give the announcer a smile and a thumbs up sign. The crowd clapped. Amy is there; ready to grab Sam and Mocha's neckline.

~ * ~

As I rode the brake, I reflected on the romance of mushing. The truth is, there isn't much romance. It's a lot of hard work. The dogs need care all the time—whether it's dropping them, feeding them or patching them up. People get involved in mushing without understanding the time and monetary commitment. That time and money pays itself back on the trail. In sprint racing, that's less than an hour. Distance racing gives you more time on the trail, but you increase your commitment substantially. From September to April, mushers train constantly. The dogs won't run at their peak performance otherwise. Everyone asks how many miles you have on your dogs. It depends on the year, but as a sprinter, I put about 500 to 600 training miles on my dogs that season before they run their first race. The distance mushers easily double or triple that number. Iditarod dogs usually have run the mileage in the Iditarod (1200 miles) two to three times over in one training season before they even get to the race.

"How'd they do?" Amy shouted as she led the team across the parking lot, bringing me back to the present. The sun had turned the ice to slush and my runners bit into blacktop.

I hopped partway off and nearly had the sled torn from my grasp as the huskies, without any real drag, pulled in earnest. The sled flipped over on its side. I held on. "Whoa! Whoa!" I tried to right myself and failed. The dirty slush splashed in my face and I closed my eyes to avoid getting the grit in them. My mouth already tasted of road salt and mud.

I opened my eyes for a brief moment and then shut them again as the sled lurched forward. Amy had stopped and the team nearly folded onto itself like an accordion. I still hung on, hoping road rash really didn't hurt as much as I've heard it does. Rule Number One in mushing is never let go of your team. A loose team is a dangerous thing. The dogs can easily tangle and drag to death. If a musher loses a team in the wilderness, it can mean death for the musher. It's a long walk to civilization and most of the survival gear is in the sled.

Suddenly, I was upright. My foot instinctively went to the brake and I stopped. I opened my eyes. Officer Jack Tallon was gripping the driving bow.

"Hi," he said. "It looked like you could use some help."

I made a wry smile as I wiped the slush from my eyes. "Ick," I groused. "Thank you."

Amy led the dogs back to the truck and hooked Mocha and Sam's neckline up to the stakeouts. I turned the sled upside down to provide enough friction. The slush was too soft to sink a hook in.

Amy had water ready to go, so she and I gave the dogs their water and then I pulled out the biscuits. Jack Tallon was standing there, studying the team and me behind those mirrored aviator sunglasses. I pretended not to notice, tossed each of the dogs a biscuit with a "go home," and then turned to him. Amy elbowed me for my rudeness.

"Thank you for helping me out Officer Tallon." I wasn't sure what to say. "Did you need to talk to me?"

He straightened up slightly. "No, I was just here on patrol." He smiled. "I'm glad I could be of help." He continued to stand there for a time.

Watching the races, no doubt. Or watching me? "Got to take care of the dogs," I said awkwardly, hoping it was a good enough excuse. I turned back around, unsnapped Skye's tugline, and began removing the harness. I had a chance to look over after Amy and I unharnessed the point dogs and put them back into the dog boxes. He was gone.

"I think he likes you," Amy said as I started to slip Lightning out of his harness. "He's been watching you, you know."

"I'm a suspect," I grumbled. "He's supposed to watch me." But, somehow the entire notion did flatter me.

~ * ~

It's common for race-giving organizations to run sprints 3-dog, 4-dog, 6-dog, 8-dog, and 10-dog on the first day and reverse order on the second. So, I had plenty of time to take care of the dogs, get something to eat, smooze what media was there (Channel 8—a new Denver local station), check my placement in the race, and do some PR work for mushing.

Channel 8's reporter, Barry Sanders, saw me at one point and came over, camera and all, to take photos of my lead dogs and me. I woke Sam and Mocha up from their naps and pulled them out of their dogs boxes so they could get their faces plastered over the evening news.

"I'm talking to musher Stephanie Keyes about the wonderful race up here in Frisco," Barry was saying. The camera panned to me. "Stephanie, what makes these dogs run?"

"They love it," I grinned. "I can imagine their minds are out on the tundra going after caribou when they run."

"Ah, that's great!" He grinned back. "Isn't it cold for them, though?"

I almost laughed. "Hardly! These dogs love to moon-bathe when it's twenty degrees below zero. They're built for minus fifty—it's the humans we've got to worry about."

"Great, that's a take," he said and the cameraman went over to take some shots of Mocha yawning. He turned to me. "So they really love to run?" he asked.

"Oh yeah—I couldn't get them to do it otherwise."

"No whips?"

I laughed. "Nobody uses whips anymore. They're outlawed from ISDRA races anyway. At one time, whips were used as signaling devices—the allowable whips were about three feet long and popped over the sled. If you look at the distance between the sled and the start of the last dogs—the wheel dogs—you couldn't physically reach the tip of a dog's tail with such a short whip. Furthermore, it was and still is illegal to abuse a dog. You've been reading too much Jack London."

He grinned back. "That's good to know. I'm glad they love doing it."

"So am I."

He left and Amy slipped around the side of the truck. "Poor Mocha!" she said as Mocha looked up at her indignantly. "The price of fame."

"Can you believe he asked the whip question?"

"Mocha looks a little thirsty—the price of fame, I guess," Amy said. "There's some baited water in the truck's bed."

I opened the truck's tailgate. I stared in utter bewilderment. "Amy, did you leave a snowhook out?"

"No," said Amy. "Why?"

"There's an extra one in the truck bed," I said. I picked it up and examined it. It was a standard heavy-duty grabber hook, like the type I saw Matt purchase from Mary Palmer the night before at the pizza dinner. The snowhook was made of welded tubular steel in the shape of a isosceles triangle with curved talons at the corners of the triangle base. The top of the triangle was where you tied the rope that anchored the sled. It had flat metal fins welded to the talons to grab snow and a handlebar for grabbing just set back from the curve of the talons. It was painted flat black with no chips in the matte finish. The talons had dried brownish splotches as if from rust, but the end tips gleamed silver as if it had been sharpened. I hefted it—it must have weighed a good six pounds or more. "Well, it's a grabber hook. A little old, but in good condition."

"Gee, someone must have thought we lost one," Amy shrugged.

I turned it over and looked at the label affixed to the crossbar. Mary Palmer's Mountain High Husky sticker gleamed white against the matte finish. A large rust-colored spot stained the label. The label was new, just stained. Stained with...

I nearly dropped the hook as I realized what I was looking at.

I put the hook back in the truck's bed, pulled out the water bucket and then, quickly shut the tailgate. Amy stared quizzically. "What's wrong, Steph? You're as white as a ghost."

I pulled her closer so no one would hear above race's din. "We got to get rid of it and fast."

"Huh?"

"There's blood on it. A lot."

Amy took a quick inward breath. Her blue eyes were wide with fear. "Blood, how?"

"That snowhook is the murder weapon," I said, as much to myself as to Amy. "It was used to kill Matt Rayburn!"

Chapter Eight

"Are you sure?" Amy gasped.

I bit my lip. My mouth had become cotton and I felt nauseated. "Very sure."

"But why is it here?" she asked. "It wasn't here earlier."

"Have you seen anyone around the truck?" I asked.

"Yes—I mean, no, I mean—there's been so many people." She sighed. "I didn't see anyone open the tailgate—but I wasn't here all the time."

I nodded. I couldn't blame her for not hanging around the truck every second.

"What should we do with it? Shouldn't we turn it into the police?"

I paused. "Let's sit in the cab."

We climbed into the truck. Winnie jumped up and pounded me with her paws for leaving her alone in the truck. "Not now, Winnie," I said, scratching the Malamute's ear. "Go over." I pointed to the back of the extended cab. She grudgingly obliged and glared at me from the back.

"Look," I said, once the doors were shut. "We've got to get rid of that thing. Whoever planted it on the truck is looking to frame me. It now has my fingerprints on it. You can bet the murderer used gloves."

"Then the police…"

"May be tipped off."

Amy chewed her lip. I'd never seen her so worried. "But you didn't do it."

"No, I didn't."

"Here," said Amy, thrusting a towel in my direction. "Get your gloves and wipe off the fingerprints."

I nodded. Just at that moment, I spied Officer Jack Tallon. He was standing next to another police officer and talking with him. Occasionally, they looked towards my truck. "Damn!" I swore. "I bet you the murderer has called it in. We're sitting ducks, if we don't do something now."

"I'll stall them—you get rid of the hook," Amy said.

I got out and as casually as I could, walked back to the tailgate with the towel. I now had my gloves on. I opened the tailgate and took out the offending hook. Using snow and the towel, I rubbed the snow on the crossbar, where I had handled it and rubbed it off. I kept looking around, expecting all eyes turning to me. My throat burned and a voice in my head kept saying, "You're guilty—you know that. You're tampering with evidence…"

I pulled out an empty bag of Eukanuba Dog food. I slipped hook into the bag and started towards the dumpster. Anyone who saw me would assume I was dumping dog droppings. I kept my eyes focused ahead even though my heart pounded loudly in my ears. Fifty feet. Forty feet. Thirty feet. Twenty feet…

"Stephanie Keyes!"

I jumped in surprise and almost dropped the bag. Barry Sanders and his cameraman were right there. Barry was grinning at me. "Hey! Did I startle you? I'm sorry."

"No, no, no," I muttered apologetically. "I was just preoccupied." I paused and forced a smiled. "What did you need?"

"I was hoping to get another shot of you for this evening's news."

"One more?" I squeaked. I glanced down at the bag.

"Yeah, you were great on camera."

"I bet," I said. "What did you want to ask?"

Barry straightened up and spoke into the microphone. "Tell how you take care of these dogs. You feed them Eukanuba?"

"Actually, I feed them a mixture of Eukanuba, meat, and fat," I said, looking into the camera. "Sled dogs need higher protein and fat to work as hard as they do. I feed them anywhere from three thousand to seven thousand calories a day, depending on their training."

"Wow! That's a lot of calories," he said. "Why are they so skinny, then?"

"Sled dogs aren't house pets. Most pets are too fat—pet owners are literally killing their dogs with kindness. Too many calories and not enough activity. So, when pet owners and even some veterinarians see sled dogs, they're likely to think they're skinny, when in fact, the dogs are in good condition. Sled dogs are trained athletes; they're like marathon runners in peak shape. They can't afford to carry excess weight. Unlike the dog who maybe gets a walk each day, if he's lucky, my dogs use the calories I give them."

"Wow! I didn't know that."

"In long distance races, such as the Iditarod, dogs use well over ten thousand calories a day. That is really incredible. If you compare a fifty-pound husky to a two hundred-pound man, calories per weight, the man would have to eat the equivalent of over forty thousand calories and be able to use it."

"Incredible."

"That is truly what makes these dogs so special."

"Thanks," Barry said and moved off to talk with two other mushers.

The trash bins were hidden behind mustard-brown barriers that gave the overall appearance of tidiness, presumably to not offend vacationers. There was a door-sized opening so people could slip in and pitch trash. I slid inside, pulled out the snowhook, and without a further thought tossed it into the bin. The bin must have been somewhat full of trash because I heard a thud, instead of a metallic clang. I peered out of the entrance and since no one seemed interested, breathed a sigh of relief. I walked back to the truck, tossing the Eukanuba bag in the open and unattended bed of Lee's truck. He feeds Eukanuba too and would no doubt think he had left an extra bag there.

Officer Jack Tallon was looking at a pair of Carhartt overalls Amy had pulled out when I came back. "What's going on?" I asked.

"We received a phone call stating that you might have some vital evidence on your truck," Tallon replied evenly. "Your handler was willing to allow me to search the pickup bed and box."

I did my best to frown. "Evidence? What kind of evidence?"

Tallon shook his head. "I'm not at liberty to say."

At that moment, I looked beyond him and realized Tasha was still in the dog box. I wished I had removed her collar. Instead, my eyes met Tallon's.

I shrugged. "Well, look all you like—I can't imagine what you would find interesting." I paused. "But, we'll be leaving soon." I turned to Amy. "Come on, let's get some lunch. The Samoyed Club is cooking hamburgers and hot dogs."

"That was close," Amy whispered when we walked out of earshot.

"Shhhh! Let's not talk about it." We stood in line and bought hot dogs. When we returned, the tailgate was shut and Officer Tallon had moved on.

"Guess he didn't find anything." I yawned in the warm sun. Of course, he wouldn't look at the dogs. "Let's drop dogs again and go home. I've really had enough for one day—Cindy will give me the ribbon and check if I ask nicely."

We started unloading dogs when Amy peered in the compartment with Tasha. "Who's this?"

"That is Tasha," I said. "Ray Bryce and I found Tasha wandering around. She belonged to Matt."

Amy did a double take. "What?'

"Yeah," I sighed. "Surprised me too. She must have gotten loose when Matt was killed." I felt extremely uncomfortable saying, *murdered* although there was no doubt someone had killed him.

Amy opened the box and helped her out. "Well, you're a pretty thing," Amy said. "She looks like a red fox."

"Not exactly," I said. "Foxes are shorter legged and have black stockings. Not to mention the white tip on the tail."

"Nit, nit, nit. I think her name should have been 'Foxy.'" She petted Tasha, who began licking her face. "Are you going to call Matt's wife about her?"

"Yeah, but I bet Gina won't want her back," I said. "I've heard she isn't fond of dogs."

"And married to a musher?" Amy shook her head in disbelief.

~ * ~

By one o'clock, we had dropped and watered dogs, and were heading back to Pine Junction. Winnie had crawled into the back on a cushion of suitcases and was already asleep. She knows the drill and rides well. Amy petted her as I drove down the highway. The sleepy Malamute groaned softly as Amy tickled her chin.

"Let her sleep," I said. "She'll be wild when we get home."

"Whoever killed Matt Rayburn is looking to pin the murder on you," Amy said without preamble. "The police are incredibly suspicious—I wouldn't be surprised if one is tailing us right now."

I laughed. "I doubt it." But she had voiced a serious worry.

"Suppose they don't believe us about seeing the station wagon?" Amy asked. "Suppose you're their only suspect?"

I chewed my lip thoughtfully. "Well, I *was* there at the time of the murder. I have a motive, I suppose, but there wasn't any evidence to link me to the murder."

"Until today."

"The snowhook," I breathed. "Damn! Who would kill Matt and then try to frame me?"

"Who hates both of you?"

I paused and thought about it. "I don't know. There are plenty of people who hated Matt."

"Like Lee Johnson?"

"Lee's a friend of mine. Lee wouldn't frame me."

"If it were him or you going to jail, would he consider it?"

"Amy, this is ludicrous!" I snapped. "Lee didn't kill Matt."

"How do you know—what about that steroid thing?"

"That happened years ago."

"Could he be kicked out of ISDRA for it?"

I fell silent. We started the climb towards the Eisenhower Tunnel. "Well, let's think about some other people. Other than Lee. How about the purebred people? Matt was always complaining they didn't deserve special privileges."

"That's a little vague," Amy said. "Did Matt ever try to block someone from running dogs because they were purebred?"

"Don't know," I shrugged. "There's Mary Palmer."

"Oh yeah, Matt bought a used Risdon sled from Mary and his check bounced. That was five hundred bucks."

"I don't know, though. I can't imagine Mary killing Matt for a measly five hundred dollars. I could see Mary suing him for it, but not killing him over it."

"People have killed for less," she reminded me.

"Sure," I said. "I think Mary would rather sue him or repossess the sled."

"Who else?"

"Well, there's Cindy, I suppose, but other than them not seeing eye-to-eye on things with the club, I really don't think there was much friction."

"Ok, so we have Lee Johnson, Mary Palmer, Cindy Travis, and some purebred folk. Anybody else?"

I shrugged. "They say the spouse is always the prime suspect."

Amy pulled out a pen and a notebook. "Gina Rayburn…"

"You're writing this down?" I glanced over at the pad she was scribbling on furiously. We had passed through the Eisenhower

Tunnel were starting our descent towards the Loveland Ski Area. If you're feeling especially adventurous, you can take the Loveland Pass road to Frisco—assuming it's not shut down due to avalanches.

"Yeah—who else?"

I shook my head. "Maybe somebody at his work?"

"Would they know Matt was there?"

"Yeah, it's far-fetched," I said.

"Anybody else he might have gotten angry enough to kill him?"

"Just half the members of the Western States Sled Dog Club," I said. "Honestly, Amy, I don't know. I wasn't with his group."

"Who were Matt's friends?"

I paused. That was a good question. "Well, there was Sam Horton. They hung around together."

"Anyone else?"

After a few moments, I shook my head. "I'm drawing a blank on that one."

Amy looked over the list. "Lee Johnson, Mary Palmer, Cindy Travis, Gina Rayburn, Sam Horton…that doesn't leave much."

"There's still the purebred people," I reminded her.

Amy snickered. "How about we say all the purebred drivers did him in?"

"Very funny," I said. "Somebody left that snowhook as a calling card. Whoever killed Matt wasn't fond of me."

She shifted uncomfortably in the seat as we passed the town of Berthoud Falls at the base of the pass road. "What are you going to do?"

"I'm going to find out who murdered Matt Rayburn before the bastard pins the murder on me!" I snorted.

We didn't talk much after that. I kept mulling over the list of suspects we had. None of them seemed to have good motives. Although Matt was infuriating, his death didn't seem justifiable. You didn't just kill someone because he annoyed you. Or did you? When we found the body yesterday, part of me was willing to accept it might have been a random act of violence—a robbery gone bad—although that made less sense. What idiot robber would kill someone surrounded by fifteen dogs? A dog person—specifically, a musher who knew sled dogs were not aggressive and not protective.

If Matt had a German Shepherd or a Rottweiler, perhaps he'd be alive today, and the potential murderer would be covered with bite marks. Hell, even a Malamute can be protective if someone attacked his owner. But, the murderer knew sled dogs wouldn't become aggressive and their barking would cover the noise. So, it was doubtful this was a random act of violence or a robbery attempt. The police must have known this too, because otherwise they wouldn't have spent so much time interrogating me.

My house is a tiny cabin just outside Pine Junction. Originally, a stagecoach roadhouse on the way from Fairplay to Denver, it's had a few additions added since the 1880's when it was built. Its logs have been painted brick red and it has tiny windows with storm shutters. The former occupants fitted a woodstove insert into the tiny fireplace. The stove works pretty well, but I added propane heat two years ago. The roof is corrugated tin—it can be deafening during a hailstorm. The interior of the cabin is modest. There's maybe a thousand square feet if you include the upstairs room that is my bedroom and my "study." Amy sleeps downstairs on a hide-a-bed sleeper sofa next to the wood stove. The kitchen is cramped with a little two-person table, a small refrigerator, and a stove. There's barely enough room for my microwave on the lime-green linoleum counters and there's no dishwasher. I managed to stick a stacking washer-dryer into a closet and have a plumber add a water line from the main. We're on well water with a marginal flow, but hey, it's home. Did I mention the ten acres?

Actually, it's quite a deal because part of the land is a cemetery. No, I'm not kidding. Before the roadhouse was built, a stagecoach crashed during the wintertime in this area and the occupants froze to death. When the next stage came through, they built the roadhouse and buried the victims nearby. When I first bought the land, one of my neighbors told me the story about the cemetery and I had to go look. Sure enough, old Zebediah and Elaine Mortz, James William Smith, and Miss Katherine Johnson were buried, complete with marble markers dated 1881. If you look through old Jefferson County records, you can see the house was built in 1882. Most people don't want land with a cemetery, but I don't mind. The neighbors are pretty quiet. I keep the grass cut down and lay flowers on their graves every Memorial Day. So, if old Zebediah wants to haunt the roadhouse, at least I've partially appeased him by cleaning up the cemetery. The dogs haven't noticed. They're pretty savvy about strange things.

I nearly lost the whole place when the Hi Meadow Fire swept through in the second week of June 2000. No one knows the exact cause, but the fire started on the north side of Crow Hill in Bailey and traveled northeast at an alarming speed. I was at work at the time—I work at a local veterinary clinic as a vet tech—when the fire broke out. The firefighters wouldn't let me through to my home so I ditched the little Dodge Colt I was driving and ran into the forest. I got to my house, loaded the dogs up, and drove out through thick smoke. Although the fire burned over 10,000 acres, it miraculously left my little cabin untouched. Fire is like that. I also have the smoke-jumpers and the local firefighters to thank for their work. The fire-fighters were able to save most of my land, though about an acre on the far side is burnt up—a grim reminder of the dangers of living in the mountains.

We pulled up to my garage-less cabin and started unloading dogs. The kennel pens are long—some over thirty feet. Each dog has a nice house with warm straw—which they seldom use. Most like to sleep on top of their houses or moon bathe in the snow. Lastly, I let out Winnie, who decided to run up and down the kennels, barking at all the huskies.

After bringing Winnie inside, I started a fire in the woodstove for warmth. Even with the propane heat, the little cabin can get drafty. I then began making dog food—an awful concoction of meat, bonemeal, wheatgerm oil, Canine Red Cell, vitamins, rice, water, and kibble. It can reek, so I leave the food to soak in the bathroom. As I let the hot water fill the buckets, I began to ponder the list of potential murderers Amy had constructed. The list seemed preposterous— no one I knew had a good reason to kill Matt Rayburn, and yet, here he was, dead. And here I was with a snowhook that was most likely the murder weapon in my truck that I managed to dump without (I hoped) any witnesses.

I sighed as I used my hands to break apart the chunks of frozen meat under the hot water. As I let the hot water run over my hands, the blood from the meat ran off in rivulets. I winced, quickly re-minded of the bloody murder scene. I shuddered and withdrew my hands for a moment and then thrust them back under the hot water.

Turning off the water, I dried my hands and then pulled the bucket out of the sink and set it on the floor to let the kibble absorb the water. Matt was killed by a musher—that much I was certain of—and for reasons that would perhaps escape the Frisco police. I wouldn't be safe while the murderer was still at large. He or she would find some way to pin the murder on me.

My thoughts turned to Lee Johnson. He seemed the most obvious person to have a grudge against Matt—especially with that argument Saturday night, but somehow I just couldn't see him killing Matt and then pinning the blame on me.

If it were him or you going to jail, would he consider it? Amy had asked. "I don't know," I whispered to the walls. "Maybe he might."

One thing was for certain: I had to find out.

Chapter Nine

I awoke the next day resolved to visit Lee after work. I'm a vet tech who works for one of the local vets here in Conifer. As a college graduate, I'm vastly underpaid. I have a Journalism degree and couldn't find work, so I went back to school and got an associate degree at a veterinary technical school. Someday, I'd like to go back to school and become a veterinarian, but it's a tough degree to get and still have a life. Pity too, because I'm only an hour and a half from one of the best veterinary schools in the nation: Colorado State University in Fort Collins.

It's not as if I don't have encouragement. My boss, Rachel Sanders, DVM, is one of my best friends and is constantly encouraging me to get the prerequisites and apply to CSU. In fact, that's how I met Amy. Amy goes to Metro State College in Denver. I met Amy in a calculus class—she's eighteen and a real whiz at math. I'm mediocre—so she was the perfect study partner. She found out I raced sled dogs and was intrigued. So, I made her an offer she couldn't refuse—free room and board for handling and dog yard chores. She gets to go to school and in fact, RTD (Denver's public bus system) has a bus that goes straight from Pine Junction into downtown Denver every day, so it's even cost efficient.

I had thought about calling Matt's wife, Gina, but every time I tried to dial her number, I got nervous and hung up. I wanted to tell her I had Matt's dog, Tasha, and Tasha was doing ok, but I just didn't know what to say to her. I mean, she just lost her husband, right? I could just imagine the conversation. *"Hi, Gina, I'm Stephanie Keyes—yeah, the person who was a total snot to your husband in the free zone and now prime suspect in his murder. I have your dog..."* So, I wimped out and went to work instead. Thankfully, work was busy and I didn't have to talk to anyone about the race.

After work, I hopped in the truck and drove to Lee's place. Lee Johnson lives four miles south of the town of Buffalo Creek in a small cabin off National Forest. Not far from his house is the Buffalo Creek wilderness where in 1996 a 10,000-acre fire blazed and burned some of the most beautiful land in Colorado. Luckily, the fire stayed northeast of Lee's house. There were some tense moments when I was sure he would have to evacuate his 30 or so dog kennel. Several other mushers and I offered to help transport the dogs to safety as the fire raged towards them. Then, the wind shifted, and the fire went north. I remember standing on my tiny deck, watching the slurry planes rumble overhead and strafing the fire in the Platte Valley not far from Foxton and Pine. The fire was at most five rugged miles away from my own house. If the wind shifted, I too, would have had to evacuate.

If you haven't guessed already, fire is an ever-present danger here in the high country. The land is rugged and for the most part, very arid. We get runoff from the snowpack in the spring and for a while, it rains nearly every day. However, when June or July comes around, the rains stop and the vegetation dries out. The whole area becomes a tinderbox. My home was threatened in 2000; Lee's home was threatened in 1996, and everyone was threatened with the Hayman Fire. In the Buffalo Creek Fire, fire fighters kept the blaze mostly to unpopulated areas. Unlike the Hi Meadow fire, which destroyed over 50 homes and structures, the Buffalo Creek fire destroyed six structures including the house of the Fire Chief. I always found that a bit ironic.

Just north of Lee's home were the remains of the burnt forest. The once stately ponderosa and conifer are now charred blackened fingers against the sky and the contrasting snow. The Forest Service called the fire the Gashouse Fire after the trail where it started, but everyone else calls it the Buffalo Creek Fire. Strangely enough, the flames left most of the Gashouse trail untouched near Bailey. In the early fall, you can park at the Gashouse trailhead and run 3-9 mile loops on cart, depending on whether or not you go all the way to the former Eos sawmill or take another loop. Unfortunately, the Eos Sawmill burned up in the Hi Meadow Fire. During this time, you share the road with a billion mountain bikers, loose cattle, and wild turkeys. Not the liquor—the real thing. They're huge, but they are shy, so other than seeing them scatter and hearing their gobbles, they don't pose much of a problem. The cattle and mountain bikers are far more entertaining to the dogs.

When I drove up to Lee's, a howling chorus greeted me. Lee owns fifteen acres and while his neighbors are still in earshot, the forest dampens most of the ruckus. Lee was outside cleaning the dogyard and playing with his dogs. He wore an old pair of Carhartt overalls and a muddied Kasco Dog Food cap. Several dogs were off their stakeouts and were running loose in the large penned perimeter that surrounded the dogyard. They ran towards the fence closest to me. Some stood on their hind legs to get a look at the new visitor.

"Hey, Lee!" I shouted over the noise. Amy swears one of the occupational hazards of being a musher is laryngitis. Actually, I've never had it, but my voice can get pretty hoarse.

Lee waved. "Come on in!" He shouted back. He waved in the gate's direction.

I unlatched the first gate and stepped through. He had a dual gate system on his perimeter fence so if one gate was left open, the other gate was secure. I closed the first gate and opened the second gate. A swarm of Alaskan Huskies greeted me. Fortunately, I had my Carhartt overalls on and didn't mind the muddy paws. The day was warm and sunny—it had to be at least 45°F—and the packed snow was turning to slush even in the shade. I petted the dogs within reach and continued walking, sometimes with a four-footed friend clinging to my arm.

"Damn thaws," Lee commented when I got close enough he didn't have to shout.

"Yeah," I said. "My kennel's mud-city too."

"On the phone, you said you wanted to talk to me?" Lee said. Lee wasn't one for small talk.

He scooped some poop and dumped into the waste bag beside him.

"How well did you know Matt?"

Lee paused. His dark eyes considered me thoughtfully. "About as well as anybody, I guess. He was obnoxious occasionally and a pest most of the time. Liked to ride other peoples' coattails for the most part. Bought some decent dogs from me a couple of years back. Why do you ask?"

"Just curious," I said, unwilling to tell him the real reason.

"I saw you talking with the Frisco cop on Sunday, did he put you up to this?"

I shook my head. "He was just asking questions about all of us." I paused. "You know, you made quite a scene at the banquet Saturday. You mind if I ask what that was all about?"

Lee frowned. "Is that what you're here for?"

"Yeah." I nodded. "Look, Lee, Matt's dead. The police are investigating us all. They don't know how close-knit the musher community is. They're going to finger the wrong person. Lots of people implicated you. I don't think you did it, but I've got to know what happened that night so when Officer Tallon asks me about you, I've got something to say in your defense."

He sighed. "All right then. Matt made some reference to the trouble I had with ISDRA some years back."

"The steroid accusations?"

"Yeah."

I shook my head. "Your dogs were tested and were clean."

"Damn straight they were." Lee knelt down and slapped his thigh. "Ginger, come here!" We were standing by a house with a small Alaskan Husky bitch on a stakeout. She came obediently to him. She had a short blonde coat and golden eyes. I admired her build—I wouldn't mind a dog like this in my kennels. "She's been favoring her right front. I think it's a carpal injury."

I watched as the little dog twirled on the stakeout. "Can you let her loose?"

He unsnapped the chain and the little dog bounded across the dog yard to play with her pals. I caught a slight hesitation as she used that foot. "Good eye," I said. "She ought to stay off of it."

"Yeah right," Lee said. He straightened up. He was not a big man, maybe shy of six feet. He was thin and wiry. He gathered the pooper-scoopers and full bags. He brought them to the double gates.

"You need me to get the gate?"

He shook his head. "Listen, Steph, Matt was just goading me Saturday night. I just got fed up, that's all. Everyone knows my dogs are clean. Matt was angry he ended up in third place—he kept saying you should have yielded—even in free zone."

"And?"

"I said it was your choice. I wouldn't have yielded, but that's just me. He was pretty upset Alan's Siberians blew him away. Heck, Alan isn't even running for ISDRA points."

"And that's when he dragged up that steroid testing debacle."

"Yeah." He nodded. "If there was anyone I should be mad at, it should have been Bruce Galley for accusing me in the first place."

I sighed. I had heard all about it. Six years ago, Lee Johnson seemingly came out of nowhere to compete for the ISDRA medals. A former club member, Bruce Galley, accused Lee of pumping steroids into his dogs. Lee had to answer to ISDRA and the club and provide positive proof his dogs were clean. He had blood analysis done on every single dog in his yard during the height of racing season. The tests showed no drugs—in fact, they proved his dogs were well cared for. Bruce got out of mushing a year later, but the stigma still followed Lee. The truth is, Lee spent a lot of money to buy top North American Open dogs.

Confused? The North American is one of the biggest sprint races. It's held for three days in Fairbanks, Alaska, and anyone who is anybody races the North American. Famous mushers such as George Attla, Gareth Wright, Roxy Wright-Champaigne, among others made their names running the Open North American. It's called open because of the number of dogs—you can run as many as you want. I've seen people run teams of well over twenty dogs. I personally find just ten dogs to be exciting.

"So, what does his accusation about you pumping steroids into your dogs have to do with me not letting him pass in the free zone? Are you upset with him for not beating Alan?"

"I sold him Blue and Shep," Lee admitted. "This was before I knew what a slime he was. He didn't really know how to train—otherwise his team would have been in a solid second place. I really shouldn't have sold him Shep—he's a Wright Hound, you know." Wright Hounds or Aurora Huskies were a special line bred by Gareth Wright—a big time musher in Alaska.

"I could've guessed—looks like my Mocha."

"Mocha? That's the pup I sold to you from the Coffee litter?"

Coffee litter: mushers will often name their dogs with themes. Mocha's siblings were Java, Espresso, Latte, Decaf, and Cappuccino. "Yeah."

"Then, Shep and Mocha are related. They both come out of Jumpstart."

I didn't want to admit Shep was a better dog than Mocha. Or Blue could lead circles around Sam, but I knew they were damn good dogs. "So, what was Matt's beef?"

"He whined I must be using steroids to get where I'm at because he thinks I sold him trash."

Shep and Blue were hardly trash. I would love to have dogs like those. "So, where were you when Matt was killed?" Like all mushers, I'm not known for tact.

Lee grinned. "You know, I told that cop friend of yours." He walked over to some hay bales that were under tarps and pulled the tarps off. "Look, Steph, I've got nothing to hide. You've known me for three years now—would I lead you wrong?" He pulled out his pocketknife and cut the baling wire off the hay. He pulled a large piece from the hay bale and stuffed it into the nearest doghouse. The owner came back—a large black male with white paws—and buried himself in the sweet-smelling hay.

"So, where were you?"

"We were still hungry, so we went to Arby's"

"Anyone see you?"

"Yeah, the kid behind the counter."

"Anyone else?"

He shook his head. "No one other than Sherri."

Sherri, his wife, could be considered his alibi or his accomplice. We both knew that. "Do you know of anyone who would want to kill Matt?"

He shrugged. "I don't know. Matt wasn't popular. He was always gunning for someone. Maybe he just tried his antics once too often."

We didn't talk much more about Matt's death. Instead, we caught the loose dogs and hooked them back on their chains. Stakeouts are the common way mushers keep their dogs. Unlike keeping a single dog out on a chain, sled dogs on stakeouts get constant socialization. Stakeouts were convenient for heavy snow areas, where digging out gates and fencing is prohibitive. Also, if you have enough snow, the dog is able to use the snow piles to climb out of a six-foot fenced in area. Sled dogs, unlike dogs just left tied out in a yard, get constant training for 6-8 months out of the year. Most are let out for daily romps with fellow team members to socialize and establish pack order. I live in a mountain lion area, so I can't have my dogs on stakeouts. Otherwise, I would.

Each dog gets a treat when it is hooked up to its chain, so we only had to play chase once with a big dog named Sandy. Sandy thought it would be fun to lead both Lee and me on a merry chase. At last, we cornered him and Lee caught his collar. I heard a car honk and looked up. Sherri drove her Bronco into the driveway.

"Hi Sherri!" I waved.

She waved back. "Lee, what kind of host are you?" she admonished. She put her hands on her hips and drew herself up to her entire five-foot-two-inch height. She was a pretty woman of about 40 years old, with straight brown hair pulled back in a single braid. Her face was brown from the sun and her green eyes met mine. Lee was about to respond, when she turned away. "Come on, help me," she ordered as she pulled her groceries out of the truck. We walked out of the dog yard to help her. Sherri handed Lee two bags and hoisted the other two.

"Let me take one," I offered.

"Nonsense!" Sherri scoffed and pulled open the screen door. She fumbled with the doorknob and carried the bags into the cabin. A red merle Australian Shepherd came bounding towards us, barking enthusiastically.

"Easy, Cisco," Lee said, giving the shepherd a pat. Cisco eyed me warily and then grumbled a bit. I held out my hand for him to sniff. He backed off and grumbled again. Lee laughed. "Big tough guy, aren't you, Cisco?" Cisco glanced at him and the back at me. "Leave him alone—he'll come to you and then you won't be able to keep him out of your lap.

Their cabin was the standard rectangular log variety. Some time ago, someone had painted the exterior logs russet brown and the trim in red. Inside, thick rope rugs covered wood floors. A square, iron "County Comfort" wood stove sat in the corner on raised red tiles. A blue couch and loveseat, worn from years of use and covered with dog fur, faced the stove and TV. Shelves filled with trophies and ribbons lined the walls. A large photo of Lee Johnson and his ten-dog team was the centerpiece. The caption read: *Granby, January 1997.* A large blue rosette lay beside it inscribed with: 1ˢᵗ Place.

Sherri led Lee into the open, U-shaped kitchen. She put down the sacks and rustled through them. "You like coffee or tea?"

"Tea, please," I replied. "These are really nice awards. The photo in Granby is excellent." I wasn't exaggerating. The dogs were perfectly synchronized. A well-matched team—one of the best compliments a musher could receive.

Lee grinned from the kitchen. "Thanks. That's Jumpstart in lead next to his daughter, Latte."

I nodded, admiring the dogs.

Sherri put a cup of water in the microwave on the counter and pulled out a tea bag. "Plain Orange Pekoe, ok?"

"Just fine."

The microwave beeped and she came out with a hot steaming mug. "So, what brings you out our way?"

I took the mug, noting Cisco sidling up beside me. "I was just asking Lee some questions about Matt."

Sherri glanced sidelong at Lee. "Have you spoken to the police? Are we considered suspects?"

"I think we all are," I said. "Officer Tallon is investigating the murder. He asked me a few questions about motivations."

"That argument at the banquet?" Sherri asked. "Matt brought up the stupid steroid accusations…"

"I know, Lee told me."

"Then, did he also tell you the police ought to be investigating Vicki?"

"Vicki Thompson? The Siberian musher? Why?"

Sherri smiled wryly. "You don't get out much, do you?" She sat down beside me with her own cup of hot coffee. I could smell the cinnamon mocha flavoring. Cisco crept towards me and I felt a tentative bump on my hand from a cold, wet nose. I slowly slid my hand down and scratched the Aussie's ear. Success.

"What do you mean?"

"Vicki handled a lot for Matt until about a year ago." There was a pause.

"That's somewhat unusual—a Siberian racer and an Alaskan driver…" My voice trailed off. "Oh."

Sherri smirked. "Thought you'd get it."

"But Matt's married…"

"So?"

"Did Gina know?"

"I don't know. You might want to ask her yourself."

Chapter Ten

I left the Johnsons' house and headed back up Crow Hill perplexed. It was already growing dark as I turned into my driveway. I didn't really think Lee had killed Matt, but I felt I had to question him. The dogs greeted me with a howling chorus. They're usually quiet, but tonight they were rambunctious. A change in the weather, perhaps? I turned the engine off and looked up at the clouds. They were thin cirrus—the herald for a cold front and the harbinger of bad weather. The wind had kicked up and was blowing from the west.

Amy stood at the door. "Dinner's ready—where have you been?"

"Sorry," I said as I slid out of the truck. "How were classes?"

"Okay, I guess," Amy said. "The prof in psych is a real pain in the butt. I've got to write a paper by Thursday so I won't be able to train with you Wednesday."

I grimaced, but nodded.

"Oh, and that cop called. Wants you to call him back." She grinned. "I think he likes you."

"I think you have an overactive imagination." Secretly, though, I was pleased. I walked into the cabin and shut the storm doors. Amy had latched the wood panels over the windows to shut out the cold. A fire blazed in the chimney that had a wood stove insert. It made the room hot and its occupants drowsy. Winnie lay panting next to the back door. On seeing me, she leapt up and greeted me in her usual Malamute fashion by nearly bowling me over. For the next few minutes she and I played a game I affectionately call "the Malamute scoot." Namely, I chase Winnie around the house while she runs around in a squat position with this devilish grin on her face. Until Amy throws us both out.

"Excuse me," Amy said, while I caught Winnie and gave her a good belly scratch. "Dinner?" She held a bowl of steaming chili.

"Uh, yeah," I said. I gave Winnie a hug and sent her outside into her kennel beyond the back door. Before I came back inside, I checked on Tasha. She was adapting to her new accommodations well. I didn't really have room in the regular kennels, so I put her in the whelping pen. I built the pen years ago when I thought it'd be fun to raise a litter of pups every spring. The first litter did me in and I spayed the rest of my bitches soon after that. I kept the pups but got out of the breeding business. It's cheaper to buy dogs than breed them.

I came back inside and found my chili on the counter. I took a handful of grated Colby from a plate on the counter and tossed it on the chili. "Thanks for making dinner. Sorry I'm late—I went to Lee's."

"Really?" Amy's eyes brightened with interest. "Did he say anything about the argument?"

"Yeah—Matt brought up the old rumors about Lee using steroids on his dogs."

"Does he?"

I shook my head. "I don't think so. There was a big stink a few years back and he had his dogs all tested. The results were negative. End of story."

"Then, why did Matt bring it up again?"

"Because Matt was a troublemaker—he enjoyed bringing that kind of stuff up and throwing it in people's faces."

"Would it be enough to kill somebody over?"

"I don't think so. The steroid rumor will haunt the Johnsons for a long time and they certainly wouldn't be able to kill everyone who brought it up."

"Maybe Matt knew something more. Something they didn't tell you about."

I shrugged. "Could, I suppose. I don't think Lee did it, though. Sherri, though, mentioned something interesting. Vicki handled for Matt until last year."

Amy's eyes widened. I had to hand it to her; she got it quicker than I did. "Did Gina know?"

"What's apparent to you or me, may not have been apparent to Gina. She isn't much into the sport—I've always thought her to be a dilettante."

"Yeah, but she's a woman—women notice these things."

She had a point. Even I would have suspected something was up. "I wonder what she's going to do with the dogs now that Matt's gone. Blue and Shep would make a great addition to my team."

Amy sighed and rolled her eyes. "More dogs?"

I shrugged. "I've got to talk to her about Tasha anyway. It's a good excuse to talk to Gina."

"Yeah, right."

After dinner, I dialed the number Jack left with Amy and got the Frisco police station. He had left for the day, but I was told to call back tomorrow during business hours. I left a message saying that I returned his call.

~ * ~

The next day I awoke to six inches of snow that covered the valley like a crystalline blanket. The sky was a brilliant blue. The temperature would hit twenty or thirty degrees and I was tempted to pile the dogs into the truck and drive to Fraser. Instead, I went to work.

Tuesdays are usually slow days at veterinary clinics. The really hopping days are Mondays, Thursdays, Fridays, and Saturdays. There are spates of busy times on Tuesdays and Wednesdays, but today wasn't one of those: just a teeth cleaning and a vaccination in the afternoon. I told Rachel about the murder as we inventoried supplies.

"That's too bad about Matt," Rachel said when I finished. He was a client of Rachel's, as were most of the other local mushers. She seemed to have a knack of understanding that working dogs are very different from pets. She pulled back her dark hair into a ponytail and tied it off as I finished counting the Clavamox. "Do you know whom the police suspect?"

I shook my head. "I'd guess anyone there in Frisco is a suspect. Matt wasn't very popular." I paused. "Rachel, did you have any trouble with Matt paying his bills?"

Rachel shrugged. "He might have bounced a check or two. Why?"

"The night before he died, Mary Palmer was arguing with him over a bounced check for a sled."

"Really?" Rachel's brows furrowed over her blue eyes. "How much would a sled cost?"

"Mmmm, five hundred bucks." I finished writing down the number of bottles of soloxine and thyroxine.

"That's a fair amount, but I wouldn't think it would be enough to kill someone over."

"Maybe he owes her more."

"Maybe he owes someone else."

I paused and considered Rachel. "Who?"

She shrugged. "I don't know. He owes me about two hundred dollars in back vet bills—perhaps he extended himself further with someone else. Anyway, if someone bought equipment—wouldn't the owner be able to repossess it?"

"Not always," I mused. "People lock up their sleds and equipment on dog trucks."

"It'd be harder to kill someone."

She had a point, I admitted as I finished counting the jars of nitrofurazone. "Maybe he bought a new dog he stiffed someone out of."

"Pull up his records," Rachel said.

I went to the files and found Rayburn. The folder was thick with name cards. I counted them and counted them again: 40 cards. Quite a few, but not necessarily unusual for a musher. A quick perusal showed he brought Shep in last week for minor diarrhea. Out of curiosity, I looked for Tasha's card and saw he had purchased her last year. She was four years old, but otherwise had nothing interesting on her card. I went over to the computer and cross-referenced Matt's name and found an outstanding balance of $182 for various routine work. Nothing flagged his file as being alarming. Most mushers carry balances with their vets because they pay so much in veterinary care. In fact, looking through Matt's expenses, it became obvious his bills had gone down from previous years. I'd seen Dogs For Sale signs on his truck this season. He'd been reducing his kennel a bit.

"How many dogs does Matt own?" I said aloud.

Rachel shrugged. "Check the vaccination records. I do his rabies."

Duh. Of course, Matt would have had Rachel vaccinate his dogs against rabies. The cards in the client's file cover every dog Rachel sees. They're not removed if the dog is sold or even euthanized. The rabies registration gives a more accurate picture of how many dogs Matt owned. Matt vaccinated his dogs last August. At that time, Rachel issued eighteen rabies certificates. That left twenty-two other cards unaccounted for. I checked each name registered against the cards in the file and they matched up. That left twenty-two dogs without rabies vaccinations or twenty-two dogs Matt had sold or euthanized.

Flipping through the cards, I found one ten year old that was euthanized because of terminal cancer. None of the other cards listed dogs older than seven years old. The records went back four years. "Twenty-one dogs in four years," I murmured. "He sure liked to stay on top."

"He was always coming in with a new dog," Rachel said. "Until recently. I think his wife told him to get rid of some."

"Really?"

"Do you know Gina?"

"Not very well, no."

"She doesn't like dogs much," Rachel said. "She was always talking about getting a Himalayan or Seal Point."

I nodded. A cat person. "Does she have one?"

Rachel chuckled. "With all those dogs?"

I snickered too. She had a point.

~ * ~

The clinic was dead so Rachel let me off early. I called up Gina and asked if I could come by. She sounded strained, but was grateful to have someone to talk to. Gina and Matt lived in a largish house up on Conifer Mountain. I had been there only twice—once to see about buying a high-priced dog from Matt—but I remembered the way. Kennedy Gulch, the road up to Conifer Mountain, goes behind the Safeway and winds its way through a little valley before turning upwards. Although it was only four o'clock, the sun had passed beyond the mountaintops and threw the entire valley into a premature twilight. Patches of packed snow and ice still clung to the road in the shadow of the mountains. I took a turn up a dirt road and started my ascent.

Gina's house is typical of the new homes built in Conifer. Blonde cedar with huge picture windows, it sits on a mountaintop and proudly proclaims itself the ruler of all it surveys. Too bad it's north facing and surrounded by trees. It never gets any sunlight, so Gina's heating bills must be enormous and her driveway is one ice slick. But compared to my little hovel, it must be grand to live in. I trust mountain driveways only so far, so I parked my truck at the bottom of her drive and walked up.

The first thing I remembered from the last time I was there was

I couldn't see any dogs. For a musher's house, that's a bit unusual. Sure, there were the ubiquitous "Sled Dog Crossing" signs and the cutesy husky-type banners I've seen at other people's homes, but no dogs. Matt had built a dog yard some distance away behind the house. As I walked up to the front door, I heard a howl emanate from somewhere behind the house.

"Quiet!" I heard Gina shout. I tentatively pressed the doorbell.

I heard a flurry of footsteps and then Gina opened the door. Her eyes were red-rimmed and her face pale as though she hadn't slept since Matt died. She probably hadn't. Usually she wore her long blonde hair loose—today she had it tied back in a bun. Gina was tall and thin—like a dancer—I could see her majoring in ballet or dance in college. She wore stirrup tights and a baggy sweatshirt with an appliqué gingham cat on the front. "Come in, Steph, please come in."

"I am so sorry," I began as I stepped onto the polished wood floors. Feeling self-conscious in my Sorel Glaciers, I unlaced the boots and stepped out onto the smooth floor in stocking feet. The wooden floors, the white carpet, the pristine furniture, all spoke of no animals allowed. She led me past a study lined with bookcases. The room was dark and cordoned off with double French doors. I could see a large teakwood desk inside.

Gina smiled sadly. "You're the first person to have come by since Matt..." She paused and chewed her lip. "Since Matt died."

"I'm sorry," I said again, feeling utterly helpless. What do you say to someone whose spouse was murdered? We stood for an awkward moment in the hall until she waved her arm and ushered me into the teakwood kitchen.

The kitchen was light and airy with two large skylights overhead in a cathedral ceiling. Decorative blonde wooden beams crossed overhead. The kitchen had real white ceramic floor tile and matching counters. All the appliances were white and matched. I made a mental note to purchase the same color appliances when I got around to it. The avocado green stove and the harvest gold refrigerator at my home kind of clashed with the log walls.

"Coffee?" she asked.

I nodded pathetically. I hate coffee, except with lots of sugar, cream and some sort of mocha flavor, but I couldn't turn her down. "No one has come by?"

She shook her head as she poured two cups. Mine was in a mug with a blue sled team running across a snowy field. "French vanilla roast." She pushed the cream and sugar towards me which I gratefully accepted. I was trying to think of something to say when the phone rang.

"Can you excuse me for a moment?" Gina said. "I'm expecting that phone call."

I nodded, leaving my untouched coffee on the counter. I slipped into the hallway.

"Oh, hi Jeff," I heard Gina say. "Did you get the last statements? You did, good…"

I turned and walked back to the study. For a second, I stared at the brass handles on the French doors' smooth, bleached wood.

"…the mortgage payment?" Gina was saying. "I don't know—Matt used to handle all of that…."

I carefully pushed down on the handle and the door swung noiselessly open. I hesitated and then walked in.

"…what will all that cost?"

The study's floor-to-ceiling bookshelves had very few books in them. They held instead assorted Alaskan knickknacks: plates with frolicking husky pups, a carved Alaskan ulu knife (used by the Inuits to cut meat and hides), a miniature basket sled—perfect in every detail, and various carved items including a sled team running along a caribou antler. Along the other walls were several framed prints by Donna Gates King, John Van Zyle, and Bev Doolittle. But I was interested in the desk. It had a blotter, a plume pen, and several pretty brass accessories. I slid over to the desk and picked up a stack of mail Gina or Matt had shoved into a brass mail holder.

"Look, I'm going to have to think about that…" Gina was saying.

I thumbed through the letters. VISA, MasterCard, VISA, mortgage envelope… It was already open. I pulled the bill out of the envelope and nearly gasped. Their mortgage payments were twenty-seven hundred dollars per month. I flipped through a few more credit card bills and found an opened one. The balance was ten thousand seven hundred dollars and thirty-two cents.

"I have to go now," Gina was saying. "I have company…"

I slipped the bill back in its envelope and rearranged the stack in the mail holder.

"We'll talk later. Yeah, thanks for all your help. Good-bye."

I practically bolted out of the office and almost banged the French doors. My feet, clad only in socks, became ice skates on the newly waxed floor and I did a passable single axel before landing on the floor next to the entryway table.

"Steph?" Gina said, coming out of the kitchen.

I was facing a picture of Matt's team. The caption said it was taken at Granby three years before. "Nice photo of Matt," I said, pretending to study it.

"Yeah, Matt always liked it," she said. "Come on in, your coffee is getting cold."

She led me back to the kitchen. "Sorry about the phone call—that was my accountant. He and I have been playing phone tag for the past several days."

"No problem." I paused and got an idea. "Is he any good?"

Gina blinked. "My accountant?"

I nodded. "I've been looking for one for a while to do my taxes. Someone who might know business deductions."

"Jeff's really good with that," Gina said. "I think I've got a card from him somewhere…" She walked over to the counter where the telephone sat. "Yes, here it is. Jeff Dreyer CPA." She handed me his card.

"Gee, thanks. This will really help me out," I said, pocketing the card.

"I really want to thank you for coming by to visit," Gina said. "I didn't think I'd have swarms of people coming by, but I didn't expect anyone. I guess Matt really wasn't all that popular."

"I don't know," I shrugged. "He could sometimes be a little abrasive."

"A LOT abrasive," Gina corrected me. "Matt was very competitive and that made for enemies. He often irked people like he did Lee Johnson that night. Nobody really understood Matt—he just wanted to be accepted."

I nodded, although I didn't agree. Matt could've picked a better way to look for people's acceptance. "That doesn't make sense. Why would people hold that against you?"

"Everyone's so, cliquish," Gina shrugged. "Certainly you've seen it, Steph. Half the Colorado mushers don't want anything to do with you unless you're winning or you're looking to buy a dog. It's what you can do for them—nobody is interested in friendship." She paused and sipped her coffee. "That's why I'm really glad to see you."

"I'm glad I could be here," I said, feeling guilty. I felt now I was just one of the clique, using her to get something. Perhaps it didn't have to be that way. "I am truly sorry we've put on such a bad show." I meant it. "Look, Gina, there's something I've got to tell you. I found one of Matt's dogs at the Frisco race yesterday."

Her breath drew in sharply. "Are you sure?"

"Yeah, she had a tag. She must have gotten out somehow Saturday night…"

Gina's lip quivered and her eyes began to fill with tears. "Oh Steph, it was awful!"

I patted her hand, not knowing what to do. She pulled a box of tissues off one of the kitchen shelves and blew her nose with it. "I'm sorry. I'm just so upset."

I nodded. "You've been through a lot."

"Is the dog all right?"

"Yeah, she's fine."

Gina took another tissue and dried her eyes. "Do me a favor—keep the dog for a while. They're a handful as it is."

I nodded. "I thought you might want me to hang onto her." I gripped the mug between my hands and took a sip of the coffee. I tried not to make a face—I hate coffee. "Gina, you mentioned Lee Johnson—were Lee and Matt not on the best of terms?"

Gina shook her head. "Actually Matt spoke highly of Lee most of the time. Occasionally he would get mad if someone else's team proved better than those dogs Lee sold him. Matt was pretty annoyed a bunch of purebreds beat him out."

"Alan's dogs? Alan Freeman?"

She shrugged. "I don't know. Some purebred guy."

I couldn't think of any other competitive purebred teams besides Alan's, but I couldn't imagine anyone taking umbrage over Alan's team. I had to admit I was a little perplexed how Alan had put together such a competitive team in a relatively short time. I would probably be seeing Alan on Wednesday at our normal training area, so I could ask him then. I took a sip of the coffee and mulled over whether or not it needed more cream and sugar.

"Gina, we both know Matt could sometimes rub people the wrong way, but that isn't a reason for killing him. Can you think of anyone who would have reason to kill Matt?" OK, so I'm not tactful.

Gina's eyes widened and for a moment. I thought she was going to cry. She shook her head. "I can't think of anyone. Sure, he was competitive, but it was just dogs."

I lay my hand over hers again to comfort her. "How about work?"

She shook her head. "He was a medical technician at University Hospital—he had no enemies there."

I must have looked at her in surprise, because she said, "He made good money as a technician. We were always able to get the loans."

I nodded stupidly. Yeah, he had them mortgaged to the hilt. I ran my finger along the mug's sled team. The next question felt awkward. "Who did Matt train with?"

Gina frowned and I knew I had hit a sore spot. "I don't remember everyone he trained with," she said. "There're just mushers."

A silence ensued. I sipped the French Vanilla Roast and hoped fervently she wouldn't throw me out. "So, what will you do with the dogs?"

"I don't know yet," Gina said. She drained her cup. "More coffee?"

I eyed the quarter cup of sweetened, muddy liquid and shook my head.

She poured herself a cup and continued talking. "I may be selling them. I don't know. Would you be interested in any?"

"I would," I said.

"Well, you're not the only one, I guess," she sighed. "I've gotten phone calls from people expressing their interest in the dogs and a few interested in the Risdon. I told them I hadn't decided what I want to do with the dogs. As for the Risdon, I returned it to Mary. You see, she loaned it to Matt to see if he liked it."

I nodded. The lie was blatant, but understandable. "Well, let me know when you decide on what you're going to do with those dogs," I said. There was an uncomfortable pause. "So, you don't know anyone who would have killed him?"

Gina paused as if considering a thought, but then seemed to dismiss it. "No, I don't. I wish I did."

"What do the police say?"

"They're *investigating*," she said in a sarcastic tone, as though she really didn't believe it. "They don't tell me anything. Imagine that! Me, his wife!"

"That's hard," I agreed, not willing to add she might be a suspect. "Tell me, did you notice if anything was missing?"

Gina shrugged. "The police took a bunch of stuff as 'evidence,' but I didn't notice if anything was missing. Why?"

I chewed my lip. "I don't know. Maybe there's something missing the police wouldn't look for."

"Like what?" she asked.

I finished the coffee and gazed out the window. The shadows were growing deeper and it would soon be dark. I looked at my watch—it was almost five. I had to be leaving soon. "I don't know."

"Maybe if you took a look at the truck?" Gina suggested brightly.

I nodded. "I could do that, if you want me to."

She nodded and led me to the garage door. "You wouldn't believe how long they held the truck," she said as she opened the door and turned on the light. We stepped down into the garage. Like the house, Gina and Matt's garage was pristine. The walls were white and the floor was painted gray. Not a drop of oil anywhere.

Matt's red F350 sat parked in the left space. His sled sat on a bench next to the truck. It was an older model—maybe a Moody or some other sprint sled. The Risdon was gone—returned to Mary. In the right-hand space was Gina's Honda Accord. This year's model. It was shiny red with black interior and still had temporary tags on it instead of license plates. "Nice car," I said.

"Yeah, Matt bought it for me..." Her voice trailed off and she burst into tears. "Oh, Steph! What am I going to do?"

I felt awkward. I put my arm around her skinny shoulders and felt her slight frame shake with each sob. "I'm so sorry."

"No," she sniffled. "I'm all right—really, I am."

"This has been terrible for you."

She nodded. "It has been, but I've been okay." She didn't look ok. I just nodded. She wiped her eyes with her fingers and straightened up. "Do you think you'll be able to find anything?"

"I don't know."

She walked around to the tack box at the back of the truck and opened it. Unlike my truck, Matt's had a two-tier dog box with a large cargo area in the back that extended down the middle. Gina walked to the cab and turned on the interior lights. I peered inside. Both the side and back walls were pegboard with hooks fastened into the side. Harnesses hung from the hooks neatly, according to size. I recognized them as being Mary's standard sizes. I prefer custommade harnesses, but then I didn't have the large number of dogs going through my kennel that he did. I found one snowhook, three or four gangline of various sizes—one made out of cable that I guessed he used to train puppies and dogs that chewed the lines. Buckets and bowls were lined neatly in the back. The stakeouts hung on a peg next to the ganglines.

There was a medical kit in front of the bowls and buckets. Opening it, I found cotton gauze, tape, antibiotics, suture material, and a number of other items.

"Do you see anything missing?" Gina asked.

"I don't know," I said truthfully. "Nothing looks obvious."

She chewed her lip. "I was afraid of that."

I closed up the back and walked around to peer in the cab. The tan interior was empty.

"I'm sorry, I removed everything," she said.

"That's okay," I said. "It's getting late and I've got to go anyway. Thanks for letting me look around. Call me if you need anything." I excused myself and left.

Chapter Eleven

Wednesdays are training days. Normally, Amy comes with me to train but since she was at the university's library, I would have to train alone. The weather was pleasantly clear. Snowplows and sun would take care of what was left of Monday night's storm, so I put the team in the dog box.

Colorado is an enigma. On one hand, its weather can be very harsh and it isn't unusual to have dumps of two to three feet of snow. On the other hand, you won't find more beautiful winter days. In Denver, the temperatures can soar to forty or fifty degrees Fahrenheit. Today, it would be easily in the mid-forties. Where I train would be in the twenties or thirties.

Mushers train wherever they can find enough snow. Lake Dillon still had the trail from last weekend's race, so I took the opportunity to train on it. It was nearly seven a.m. when I arrived in Frisco. The trail itself is at the Frisco marina on Lake Dillon—in summertime the parking lot is filled with boaters not mushers and the docks are full of ships not ice. When I drove up to the dock, I found Alan's blue Chevrolet 3/4 ton parked at the trail's entrance. The empty stakeouts told me he was somewhere along the trail. I parked beside him, but not too close to where my dogs would fight with his should we both be here at the same time.

I turned my attention to my own truck. When I opened the old pickup's bed gate, it creaked loudly in the cold air. Tossing aside my green parka, I slid into the brown, thermal-lined Carhartt overalls. The Carhartts are very warm and on days like today, they can cause you to build up quite a sweat. For this reason, I only use them over my clothes when I am feeding or handling the dogs. They're the toughest thing against dog nails, cable stakeout lines and cable ganglines. I dragged the Roughneck container that held my lines and harnesses from underneath the dog box.

I extended the stakeout bars from both sets of bumpers and stretched the cable across them. I'd brought nine dogs with me today—the eight I had planned on running and Tasha. I had brought Tasha along because after the run, I was thinking about trying her out. Gina had nearly given me the dog—I wondered how well she might fit in my team.

My dog box has eight compartments that can carry up to sixteen dogs normally, but I didn't want the hassle of trying to pull out two dogs at once. The only box I needed to double up was Mocha and Sam. They're so familiar with the routine they will wait their turn to come out. I snapped each dog on a stakeout to relieve themselves while I went over to Alan's truck and snooped a little.

I first peered into the cab. I cautiously tried the doors—Alan had locked them. I saw a worn green backpack, a coffee thermos, and a parka, but not much else. Alan locked the cargo box too, so I walked around and peered into the boxes. A few inquisitive eyes peered back.

My own dogs started barking and I turned and saw Alan's team approaching. I quickly went back to my own truck, hoping he hadn't seen me snooping around. I slipped out of the warm overalls and into my parka, but found the parka too warm as well. I threw the parka back in the cab and settled on the lightweight Gore-Tex jacket with Polartec underneath. I glanced to see Alan hooking his team to the stakeouts. If he had noticed I had been around his truck, he didn't say anything.

"How'd the run go?" I shouted above the din. The dogs were yapping wildly at the new team.

"Pretty good," he said. "Ran a sixteen-thirty-two in six miles."

I raised an eyebrow. That meant his team was running about twenty-one miles per hour. That was very close in speed to my own team. "Pretty good," I echoed.

"Not bad for a bunch of purebreds," Alan grinned. His rakish smile caught me off guard. He walked to the back of his truck and opened the cargo box. Unlike my truck, his was a flatbed with a double-tier dog box. Behind the dog box was a large cargo box where he hung harnesses and stowed water and dog bowls. He pulled the dog bowls and water jug out and set the bowls before his dogs. They lapped eagerly. I noticed they were the typically stream-lined Seppala and Sepp-Alta Siberian Huskies. A few looked longer and more streamlined than I was used to seeing. They were so well built, I couldn't help but think they would fit on my own team. Alan tossed each a large biscuit.

"Yeah, not too bad," I said. "Hey, I was wondering if you could talk for a moment?"

"Sure, Steph, what about?"

"It's about Matt. How well did you know him?"

Alan frowned. "Not very well—you'd probably know him better since he was into mixed breeds."

I almost winced, but chose to ignore the comment. "I heard he was pissed you took second on the first day of the Frisco race."

"Really? Well, that'd be no great surprise. Matt was mad at everyone that night. Hell, he was trying to get you and Lee thrown out of the race."

"So, you didn't know about him being mad at you?"

"Not 'til you told me. Why are you so interested in Matt all of a sudden?"

I shrugged. "Just curious. Sure, Matt was a pain in the butt—but did he deserve to have someone kill him?"

Alan looked at me strangely. "You sure didn't like him much when he was alive."

I shook my head. "He was a big pain and sometimes I wished he would just go away. But I never wanted him dead." I felt uncomfortable. What was Alan suggesting? That I killed Matt? I felt a burning in the back of my mouth, as though I had swallowed cotton. I could feel my eyes burn as the tears seemed to come from nowhere. "I didn't kill him, Alan. I couldn't."

Alan shrugged and went back to his dogs. I stood there for a moment and watched. Then I turned back to my own dogs and began harnessing. As I began to harness Spice, I felt the hot tears well in my eyes. It was one thing to have the police consider me a suspect; it was another matter altogether to have the rumors start about me being a murderer. I felt Spice's cold nose against my face as she licked the tears with her warm tongue. I had left my elkhide gloves on the truck's hood because it is difficult to manipulate anything with gloves on, so I dug my cold hands into Spice's fur. Her fur was slightly curly and somewhat dry from living outdoors for so long. I sat down and she crawled into my lap, licking my face. I felt Mocha's nose against the back of my head as I hugged Spice. I heard Alan's cab door close and his truck start up and drive off. I didn't bother looking up.

There is something remarkably healing about dogs. Studies show pet owners live longer on average than non-pet owners. While my dogs are not pets—no working dog is—I, like most working dog owners, benefit all the time from my canine companions. I continued harnessing each dog, letting my cold fingers knead their fur.

Only Lightning did not appreciate my attentions. The big white dog was an eighth Greyhound with funny-looking ears and a constant quizzical expression. He skittered away from my outstretched hand: he was shy from either lack of human contact or genetics. Some sled dogs dislike being touched or handled. These dogs have not been abused, but rather were bred strictly for speed and not for temperament. These sled dogs prefer canine companionship to *Homo Sapiens* and see the musher more as caretaker and trainer, but not as a friend. I'm not fond of this personality, but Lightning is an exception. When I turn my back, he will come up and gingerly bump my hand and then dash off, as though he got away with something naughty. I indulge him fully in this silly game. I then bend down and give him a big hug. He turns his head to the side with an "Aw shucks" expression. As a reward for his complacency, I harnessed him next.

Tasha stood shaking with sheer excitement. Some people, when they see a dog shake like this, think she is cold or fearful. Actually, they are so eager they shake as if shivering. Tasha coiled herself up in a spring-like movement and then launched into the air. She wanted to go. I petted her.

"Good Girl—not right now," I said as I picked her up and put her in my dog box. "You'll get a chance when I get back." I locked the box with a padlock.

The air filled with the incessant yapping of eager to go sled dogs. After I finished harnessing, I hitched the gangline to the sled with a heavy-duty, locking carabiner. Carabiners are actually mountaineer climbing equipment, but mushers use those to hook the lines together because they can take the abuse. My gangline, the "traces" that hook the dogs up to the sled, are made out of aircraft cable, covered with polyethylene rope for aesthetics. Some mushers use straight polyethylene rope, but I have line biters and chewers and I would lose my entire team even before I stepped on the runners. The gangline is a tandem design with a neckline that hooks to each dog's collar and a tugline that hooks to the tug at the base of the harness. That's it—there's no reins or steering mechanism at all. We just use commands that (we hope) our lead dogs listen to.

I lashed the sled to the truck with two quick-release snub lines and then stomped two of the snowhooks into the icy pack for good measure. I took a light leader hook out of my cargo bag and stretched the gangline out tight, hooking the end where my leaders' necklines were and pounding the hook into the snow. I slid out of my Carhartts and tossed them in the truck's bed. Then, I got the dogs.

Have you ever seen a hookup? It's joyous mayhem. Dogs howl and throw themselves against the line with wild abandon, straining to go. Each pound caused my truck to lurch forward until the drive train took up the slack and then rocked it back with each release. Some days, I think they're going to pull the truck out of park with their exuberance. When I was done hooking up, I had eight screaming weasels from hell. I shuddered to think how I was going to handle ten alone. As the old sitcom says: eight is enough.

I pulled my leader hook first, trusting Mocha and Sam to hold the line tight for a minute or two while I ran back to the sled. Hopping on the back runners, I put on my gloves and carefully pulled the two snowhooks out and tossed them in their holders. Lastly, I fumbled with the quick-release snaps and hung on.

The dogs launch and the team falls silent as we lope across the snow. We enter the starting chute and fly across the flat lake. The race markers are gone—the club pulled those up after the race on Sunday, but the trail is still here. And the dogs know where to go— they remember every trail they've run.

The cold wind is in my face, but the sun is hot and I'm quick to shed the hat and gloves. The dogs pound the hard track with their feet—the only noise is the wind, the runners, and the dogs' panting. Mocha and Sam lead, their ears flat against their skulls as they await my commands.

I don't have much to say. Most veteran mushers don't. The novice mushers chatter to their dogs, but the pros say little. The dogs hate nagging and eventually tune you out. So, I stay silent and let the wind speak. It blows the snow around us like an ethereal wraith.

My mind drifts to Matt's death. I feel as though I had all the pieces already, I just don't know how they fit together. The loose dog. The snowhook. The Frisco race. Was something stolen? Was something missing? Could Tasha have been the reason for Matt's death?

We climb the hill and I turn to look back. A few more trucks have joined mine in the parking lot. We'll have company before long. I lose sight of the parking area as the trail dips into the timber. We wind our way across the island and over hills.

I want to relax a little as I'm riding, but I know I shouldn't. I won't relax at a race. I start pedaling up hills and riding down hills. The dogs sense my urgency and pull harder. We return to the timber, down the treacherous hill, and onto the flat.

I slowed the team as we approach the parking area. I saw Vicki's, Liz's, Lee's and another truck I didn't recognize. It might have been Mary Palmer's, Sam Horton's, or another Alaskan driver's truck. Even before I approached the paddock, I sensed something was wrong. As I approached close enough to see what had happened, I slammed the heavy-duty snowhook into the ground. For a moment, I stared at my truck in dismay. Someone had shredded the aircraft cable of the stakeout line and opened the truck bed. All my equipment lay strewn about in the snow. But what was worse was the dog box. The door on the box Tasha had been in had been ripped off its hinges.

Tasha was gone.

Chapter Twelve

"Tasha! Tasha!" I screamed. My voice sounded thin and reedy in the cold air. I looked over the vast frozen lake, tears streaming down my face. A storm was coming in from the west—if Tasha were out there, I'd never find her.

Mocha and Sam were convinced I had gone mad, but waited patiently as I went from dog truck to dog truck to see if Tasha was in someone else's box. She wasn't. Whoever had taken Tasha had either set her loose, was gone, or had hidden her well. I turned back to my team.

I hugged Mocha and Sam. "Tasha's gone, Guys," I said, burying my face in their fur. Sam gave me a tentative lick. I stood up and dried my tears. "Good dogs!" I said. "I'm sorry—you think you've done something, but you haven't. You've been wonderful." I went down the line and gave each one a hug and biscuits.

I had been unable to hook the necklines to the stakeouts, so I had tried to pound the snowhooks into the ground, but there wasn't enough snow in the parking lot. Luckily, I carried an extra snubline and tied the team to the rear bumper. I found a piece of stakeout that had two lines attached and used those to snub Sam and Mocha to the front bumper. I checked their water—tasting it myself—before giving them any and then gave them more biscuits. After they drank, I put them up in their boxes before leaving to make a few phone calls.

~ * ~

"Who would have done such a thing?"

I stood inside the Frisco Visitor's Center lobby and shivered as I held onto the cell phone. "I don't know," I whined plaintively. Confused and unsure of what to do, I had called Amy at home. "Tasha's gone and my lines are cut up."

"Or someone who thinks you're getting too close," Amy mused. "Could the murderer have been looking to steal Tasha back? Who knew you had Tasha?"

My mind was numb. "Ray helped me catch her—but it could have been anyone at Frisco. I led her back in front of everyone." I closed my eyes at my own stupidity.

"I already checked the other dog trucks there—if she's there they've done a good job hiding her. Amy, I was so freaked, I barely could take care of the dogs."

"Where are your dogs now?"

"I got them put up. It was tough, but I did it. Jesus, Amy, they cut my entire stakeouts and ganglines. Why was I so stupid? I should have kept Tasha hidden. Amy, you won't believe the mess! Anything that a bolt cutter could make short work of, they did. I must have hundreds of dollars in damages. I noticed they tried the door locks, but couldn't get through the case-hardened steel. They must have used a pry bar to pull the door off Tasha's box."

"Steph, call the police. Get them out there. I'll be down there in an hour."

"What about your paper?"

"Hell with it."

"No, you've got to finish it." My voice grew stronger and more authoritative. "I'll be all right."

"Yeah, right. I'll be there."

"No, you won't," I said stubbornly. "I'll be all right. I'll call the police. Lee Johnson and Liz are out on the trail—they'll be back soon."

"Promise me you will call the police."

"I will."

I dialed 911 and calmly reported the vandalism and the missing dog. Then, I walked out of the Visitor's Center and fell apart. The clouds had rolled in from the mountains, blanketing the sky with gray cotton. A cold wind had kicked up from across the lake, causing the cold tears to sting my face. I ran back to my truck.

Liz was there. She stood staring aghast at the destruction. "Jesus, Stephanie, what happened?"

I shook my head. "It was like this when I got here."

"Did you call the police?"

"Yeah."

Lee's 10-dog team loped into the paddock. Great plumes of snow sprayed behind his brake as he tried to gain purchase on the icy ground. He hooked down and grasped his leaders' necklines, swinging them over towards his own stakeouts. "What happened?" He gestured at my truck.

"Somebody cut-up Steph's stakeouts," Liz answered for me. "And look, someone chopped open a dog box..." She stared. "Steph, there wasn't a dog in there, was there?"

I fought back the tears. "Yeah, Tasha was in there."

Liz's eyes widened and her gaze strayed to her own boxes. I could see relief on her face when she saw her boxes were intact. "Has anyone else's truck been damaged?"

"No," I said. "Just mine."

Lee had finished watering his dogs and walked over. "Who would want to steal your dog and destroy your equipment?" Lee asked. "And why didn't they go after our trucks?"

"I don't know," I said. "But they did a thorough job. All my ganglines are cut too. Maybe it had to do with..." Blaring sirens interrupted me.

"Looks like the cavalry is here," Lee remarked. He touched my shoulder. "Look, Steph, if you need ganglines for Granby, I've got some you can borrow. I don't have any stakeouts, though."

The police Blazer pulled up. In spite of myself, I smiled. It was Officer Jack Tallon. "Ms. Keyes, are you all right?" he asked as he saw the ripped open dog door and the equipment strewn everywhere.

"Yeah, I'm fine but some bastard stole my dog," I said, trying to sound braver than I felt. "I came back to my truck and found this."

For the next hour, I filled out the report with Jack. Vicki Thompson and Sam Horton soon appeared as well and gave their account along with Lee and Liz. Nobody, it seemed, had seen anything.

"Do you have any idea why someone might have done this?" Tallon asked. "Animal Rights activists?"

I shook my head. "I don't think so. I think it had to do with Tasha."

"Or maybe the murderer thought you were getting too close," Jack remarked.

"What do you mean?" I tried not to sound cagey, but it came out that way.

Jack smiled ruefully. "We got a phone call shortly after yours. Seems your roommate, Amy Smythe is concerned about you. She told us you've been doing a little investigating on your own."

I swore.

"Don't blame her. She's worried about you. Come on, you still look a little shaken up," he said. "Let me buy you some coffee and tell me about the dog and why someone would want that particular dog."

~ * ~

"Listen, Ms. Keyes," he began after the waitress served me a streaming cup of hot cocoa. We sat in a booth at the local Java the Hut. After Jack had taken his patrol hat off, he looked remarkably like any of the ski bums who frequented these resort towns. Nervous suntanned fingers ran through sun-bleached, blonde hair. I could see him easily shredding and catching air. Definitely not a two plank wank. Except something behind those piercing blue eyes told me he had seen more than he was letting on. I wondered what it was.

"Stephanie," I corrected him. "Or Steph. Nobody calls me Ms. Keyes."

"Very well, Stephanie," he said. "This is strictly confidential..."

I nodded and sipped the whipped cream off the top of the cocoa.

"I've been trying to get hold of you for the past several days. I wanted to let you know you're no longer a suspect."

I let the air leave my lungs. I hadn't realized I'd been holding my breath. "How? Why?"

"Our first clue was the dark station wagon Amy and you saw speeding away. I did a little investigation and found it belonged to a maid at the Alpine Inn. She "No hablo ingleses," if you get my drift. My Spanish isn't that good, but the Investigator's is. Come to find out the maid was watching you unload dogs and feeding them the entire time Matt Rayburn was murdered. She watched you during the fifteen minutes Amy couldn't account for you."

"Did the maid see anything?"

"About the murder, no." He took a sip of latte and continued. "She heard Amy's scream and the commotion and decided to get out of there. When I heard the general description of the vehicle, I started poking around in the Alpine Inn's parking lot, and voila, there it was."

"So, I'm no longer a prime suspect."

"Not even if you wanted to be." Jack took another gulp of coffee. "Listen, Steph, I know you were trying to vindicate yourself by snooping around and asking people questions, but something tells me you made someone a little too uncomfortable. I would like you to stop snooping and to tell me everything you've found out so far. Let us handle it."

I nodded. Perhaps he was right—the police were better at this than I was. I told him everything I learned and told him about finding Tasha the next day. I left out the part about the snowhook. He listened attentively and took notes during what I felt were salient points. I finished with the run.

"So, nobody was there when you left the paddock?"

"No one," I reiterated. "Alan Freeman had gone already."

He frowned. "Somebody knew you'd be training, then?"

I shrugged. "That's half the club. People train here all the time—it wouldn't take a detective to figure out I'd be here."

"Well, someone wants you to stop investigating," Jack mused. "And that someone thought that dog was important enough to risk getting caught. Otherwise, they wouldn't have bothered. The pry bar would have made a lot of noise."

"You think the killer?"

Jack shrugged. "It might have been. Why would someone go through the trouble of stealing this particular dog? Was there anything special about her?"

I chewed my lip. "She belonged to Matt." I mused. "I don't think she was a leader. Matt always used Blue and Shep."

"It might not have even been the murderer," Jack said. "People have a funny way of reacting when somebody starts delving into their secrets. This might have been a warning shot—the next may not be as friendly."

I sat back and nodded, sipping the cocoa. The cream was gone. "So, what should I do, lie low?"

"Skip your next race or two."

"I can't," I protested. "It's Granby and it will clinch my bronze medal."

He frowned. "Is it that important to you?"

I considered my words carefully. "Granby is the second to the last race. If I drop out now, some hot team in the Midwest will shoot right over me."

Jack smiled ruefully. "Well, then be careful." Again, I could see something flicker in those stare-right-through-you blue eyes.

"I always am," I said evenly. "So, why the interest?"

He smiled ruefully. "Let me say I've seen enough innocent lives taken."

"Pity," I replied. "I thought that perhaps there might be something else."

He grinned. "That there might."

We talked for a long while. Jack, it seemed, grew up around Helena, Montana, and was used to seeing mushers, especially near Seeley Lake. One of the toughest sled dog races starts at Camp Rimini near Helena. It's called the Race to the Sky. Aptly named, the race in past years has been as long as 500 miles and crossed the Continental Divide at least ten times. After Jack had graduated from the University of Montana, he had moved to Los Angeles.

"Los Angeles is quite a change from Montana," I remarked.

"Yeah," he agreed. "I got tired of it and decided I needed a change." Again, that strange look. Was it regret? He glanced at his watch. "It's getting late and I ought to be heading out."

"Me too," I said.

~ * ~

We parted and I returned to my truck. It was nearly ten a.m. Thick snowflakes fell from the gray sky and swirled in the increasing wind. I found the cut lines picked up and neatly stacked away from my harness bin. I found a nearly new gangline with a note from Lee saying that he, Liz, and Vicki had picked up my equipment. Lee's note added that if I needed anything, I should call them. I smiled, glad to know I had such good friends. I peeked inside the dog boxes and found my dogs asleep: warm and comfy in the straw.

I hopped into the cab and started the truck. A dusting of snow covered the windshield so I flipped on the wipers. A white piece of paper fluttered on the wipers. I turned them off and retrieved the paper. The note was wet and fragile from the melted snow, and I could barely read the blue ballpoint ink. It said, "See me at the Ski Haus—Vicki."

~ * ~

"It's like this—Matt and I were good friends at one time," Vicki said as her thin hands cradled the mug of hot buttered rum. Without the parka, boots, and extra gear, she looked small and frail. Sizing her up, I realized she barely reached five feet and I doubted seriously she weighed a hundred pounds even with her gear. Her blonde hair never looked messed up. She had braided the long strands perfectly into a single plait. If I hadn't known she was a musher, I would have thought she was too fragile to run dogs. Vicki ran four-dog only, although she had enough dogs to run in the six-dog class. I remembered her dogs were somewhat calmer than my screaming weasels from hell. "We used to train together…"

I stared into the dark rafters of the Ski Haus Bar. Vicki and I were sitting at a small table in the back. 1920's wooden skis and basket poles hung from the rafters and black and white photos of miners and old towns graced the walls. I found myself staring at an old photo of the Tenth Mountain Division and the site that became Ski Cooper—a small ski area two miles west of Leadville. Some members of the Tenth Mountain Division opened a ski area in the North after World War II, which no doubt you've heard of. It's called Vail.

"Why are you telling me this?" I asked.

"I heard you're trying to find out who killed Matt."

Jack's warning echoed in my head. I was getting dangerously close to the murderer and the cut lines and missing dog were a warning. Next time, I wouldn't be so lucky. I should have denied it. Instead, I met her gaze. "Who told you?"

"Everyone knows. I just didn't want you to think I did it or I stole your dog."

"Great," I muttered and sipped a bit of the whipped cream off the hot cocoa in my own mug.

"After you left to talk with that cop, Lee said the murderer must have done it because you've been asking questions…"

I groaned. I reminded myself to talk to Lee about his big mouth.

"I thought you might want to know my side of the story before you thought I'd done it."

I nodded and waited.

"Well, you might have heard Matt and I were kind of close," Vicki said, keeping her eyes on me to gauge my reactions.

"I heard you, uh, *trained together.*"

Vicki smirked. "Is that what they call it?"

I chuckled.

"Yeah, we did a little of that," Vicki admitted sadly. "He wasn't very good in bed, so our relationship pretty much ended. I didn't even know at the time he was married because he never talked about Gina, but I got kind of suspicious because he never asked me to come over to his place. Then, Sherri Johnson pulled me aside one day after we broke up and told me Matt had a wife. I was embarrassed after being made the laughingstock of the musher community and I felt so sorry for Gina. You know, I never met Gina and I don't know if she knows."

"I don't know either," I lied. "When did this all happened?"

"Last year—you know I got into mushing about that time? I had show Siberians and I wanted to prove they could work." She laughed at what she saw was her own joke and then saw my reaction or lack thereof. "See, most show Siberians aren't good workers. They come out of the Monadnock and Chinook lines. Originally, these lines were racing lines, but show breeders have made them into show dogs, not working dogs. The Seppala, Sepp-Altas, Lombard, and Zero dogs are built for speed. It's almost as if there are two breeds within the Siberian Husky."

"So a show dog can't be a race dog and vice versa?"

"Well, there are show dogs that race and race dogs that show," Vicki said. "But the crossover is far less than you might think. Most show judges want these boxy, fluffy, small square dogs because they don't know what a good working dog looks like. And the working dogs are too lanky or too tall or don't have just the right markings for the show ring. Sure, the standard doesn't mention markings, but all the show judges want those little dots over the eyes and a conventional color. It's hard to win with a working Siberian, but not impossible, if you can find a working judge. So, the purebred folk are pretty much divided down the middle, between the working and show dogs.

"Anyway, here I show up with my little boxy champions at the Buffalo Creek training area and Matt just laughs. I was so mad I almost packed up my gear and left. But Matt apologizes quickly and suggests I buy some dogs from Alan and he'll help me train and get competitive. He had seen me at the Colorado Springs cart races where we came in dead last. Heck, somebody with this rag-tag team of pound mutts passed us! I couldn't believe it.

"So, he introduced me to Alan and I bought some better dogs and began gradually moving up. The problem has always been the Alaskans with their unlimited gene pool have always had the faster dogs. But Siberian mushing has grown in popularity and we're now nearly half of the teams. But we don't get nearly the recognition we deserve for beating nearly half the field."

"So, how does that relate to Matt?"

"Well, Matt was always telling us to bring faster dogs. If we can't make it, we ought to have our own little races and quit complaining. I always found that to be closed minded."

"But Matt got you started with faster Siberians."

"Ironic, isn't it?" Vicki took another gulp of the buttered rum. "If I had known he was such a jerk, I wouldn't have been so quick to hop into bed with him. I should've guessed he was a jerk when he turned out to be such a lousy lover."

I tried to keep from laughing, but instead managed a smirk behind the mug of hot cocoa. "So, you killed him for being awful in bed," I chuckled.

"I should have," Vicki admitted. "But I didn't. I felt like a fool, to be sure, but he wouldn't be worth the hassle of jail time, if you know what I mean. Besides, he introduced me to Alan." She let a little sly smile creep across her face.

"How are your and Alan's pups?" I ignored the implication.

"Oh, terrific! They're about five weeks old now. Alan says in a few more weeks I can come by and pick out mine."

"Haven't you seen them?"

"Oh yeah, I've seen photos."

"But not in person?"

"Oh no—Alan's funny like that. He doesn't like anyone around while the puppies are young because we can track in diseases. You know, like parvovirus and corona."

"Surely he and his dogs can bring that junk in from a race," I said. "My team always comes down with some sort of intestinal bug or kennel cough even though I have them vaccinated and keep them separate. It's the nature of the racing."

Vicki shrugged. "Alan thinks he can keep it contained. He limits visitors."

I drank the cooling hot chocolate and ordered more. Vicki ordered a beer. "So, who do you think killed Matt?" Vicki asked.

I shrugged. "I don't know. I suspect it's whoever stole my dog and cut my lines."

"Sam didn't like Matt."

"Sam Horton?"

She nodded. "He and Matt were always mouthing off."

I sat back and thought about this. Yeah, Sam and Matt were always talking trash. I filed that bit of information away. "Let's go back to the purebred thing. Or should I say Siberian thing? I've never heard Liz or any of the other purebred people complain about inequality."

"Well, they're not half the teams."

I let that go. "Matt was adamantly opposed to Siberian Huskies?"

"He didn't like us much," Vicki said. "He didn't want separate classes or special awards or anything. Here we've been fighting for special recognition and he constantly opposed us. Said we didn't need any recognition to have slow dogs. Told us we ought to get Alaskans if we wanted to win money."

I considered her statement. As much as I had disliked Matt, I had to concede he might have had a point. I had had my butt whooped plenty of times by top-notch Siberian teams. Heck, Alan Freeman had beaten my team on many occasions. If he had been an ISDRA member at the beginning of the season, he might have taken a silver medal.

But Alan's wasn't the only fast Siberian team out there. Other people have beaten Alaskan drivers and earned ISDRA medals. Sure, it was tougher, but it proved how these folks were top mushers and dog trainers. I idolized them.

"Your dogs are fast," I remarked. "A little attention to training and breeding and you'd be beating my Alaskans."

"But I've done everything I can. I just don't have the gene pool the Alaskan drivers do."

She hit a sore spot with me. "Really? Do you think Alaskan drivers just wantonly cross in a Greyhound or Saluki whenever we feel like it? And if we did, how many puppies would make the team?"

Vicki didn't answer. I continued. "The crossbreeds are rarer than you think. When we add an outcross like that, usually we have to breed back in the Alaskan lines to produce something worthwhile. Yes, my dogs have Saluki, Greyhound, and Borzoi in them but it's three generations back or more. The mathematics prove these dogs are only twelve point five or six and a quarter percent of whatever was crossed in originally."

"But we can't compete against that!"

"Why not? Other Siberian mushers have."

Our conversation was clearly at an end. I knew I had lost her. Little doubt she found me as insensitive as Matt had been. Maybe worse. We were silent for a while. As I got up to leave, Vicki laid a hand on my arm. "By the way, who told you about Matt's and my affair?"

I hesitated. "I'd rather not say."

She sighed. "It's probably for the best. I was just curious." She paused and smiled slightly as if she might disclose a secret. "You see, I wasn't Matt's first fling, you know. He played the field."

I sat back down. "Really?"

"Oh yeah—lots of women because he was kind of safe. I mean, he wouldn't leave Gina, so there was no danger of commitment. I mean, he already had a commitment with Gina."

"I don't understand."

"I guess if you're a married woman, you don't want a commitment—you just want a little fun. The last thing you want is some guy insisting you get a divorce."

"He liked married women? Didn't Gina know?"

Vicki shrugged. "Yeah, she knew, but I don't know if she knew how many."

The waitress came by and I ordered another hot cocoa and another buttered rum for Vicki. "My treat," I said.

"I don't think Gina cared much," Vicki said, once we received our drinks. "You've seen that big house they live in?" I nodded. "Why would Gina leave *that*?"

"She could've gotten that through a divorce."

"She could've gotten the *mortgage* through a divorce," Vicki remarked pointedly. "Alimony isn't much in Colorado—you know, this is a no fault divorce state. They have no kids, so no child support."

"It sounds like you thought it through," I said.

"No, Matt thought it through," she said. "Matt gave me the whole song and dance when I discovered he was married and confronted him with it. You know, Gina threatened to leave him once when she caught him and another woman in their bed once."

"Oops."

"Oops is right." Vicki sipped on the buttered rum for a minute or two in silence.

"What happened?"

"Nothing really," Vicki shrugged. "I heard Gina was screaming about divorce and taking the house and everything. Matt told her to shut up because all she'd get is a mortgage and would have to go to work. The best she'd be able to get is a waitress job."

"How do you know all this—Matt told you?"

"No, Sherri told me."

"Sherri?" I was confused.

"Yeah, Sherri Johnson—Lee's wife."

"How would she know?"

"Steph, you are so naïve," she said as she drank the rest of her hot butter rum. "Sherri was there. Sherri was the 'other woman.'"

Chapter Thirteen

My head spun as I walked back to the truck. The cold wind slapped me in the face. I climbed in and pushed aside my parka, gloves and hat when I found my cell phone. I had forgotten I had it with me. It had been a Christmas present from my folks this winter, but I still wasn't used to it. I had tossed it in my truck and left it. I pressed the button to turn it on and watched as the little symbol showed three lines. I assumed that meant I could transmit. I entered in my home phone number and pressed the SEND key.

Amy answered and I told her what I had learned.

"Lee was with Sherri—wasn't he?" Amy asked after I told her about Sherri and Matt's affair.

"Yeah, Sherri was. I'm wondering why Sherri told me about Vicki's affair and not her own."

"Lee was there—maybe Sherri didn't want to talk about it."

"Do you really think Lee wouldn't know?" I replied. I stare out into the gloomy afternoon. The snow was coming down harder and was starting to cover the windshield again. I started the truck and turned on the heater and the windshield wipers. The wipers squeaked annoyingly against the glass.

"Don't know," said Amy. "Do you think Lee and Sherri both killed Matt?"

I watched the clumps of snow slowly trickle down from the top of the windshield only to be gobbled up by the wipers. "I don't know. Lee has motivation: Matt had an affair with Sherri and Matt dragged up that steroid thing. Maybe Matt threatened to bring the steroid thing up to the ISDRA board again. Lee could lose his privileges and even his earlier awards."

"With Sherri he'd have the opportunity. Maybe together they took Matt out."

"Only…"

"Only, what?" Amy's voice crackled with static. I glanced at the battery indicator. It showed low.

"I don't think it's Lee."

"Why not?"

"I don't know. Something tells me it's not. Lee's not like that."

"How about Sherri?"

"She was with Lee, remember?" I said. "Anyway, Vicki gave me a couple of other names of women she knew Matt had affairs with."

"Who? Let me write them down." More fuzz.

"I'm losing you—I've got to recharge the phone and the cigarette lighter in the truck doesn't work," I said.

"Who are—?"

"Tami White."

"Tami White," she repeated. "She runs Alaskans."

"Right."

"Bev Long."

Fuzz. "Who?"

"Bev Long," I said. "She's a friend of Liz Smith. She runs Samoyeds."

"Samoyeds." Crackle. "Right."

The wipers were barely keeping up with the snow. "Look," I said, "I got to go. It's really snowing."

Crackle. "Okay. See you—on?"

"Got a couple of errands to run. Be home around dinner."

Crackle. Fuzz. "—en?"

"Dinner." I glanced at the phone. It had gone into "scanning" mode. I turned it off.

Snow was really coming down now and I dreaded taking I-70 home. Eisenhower Tunnel is notorious for skier backups. The only other way eastbound out of Summit County is Loveland Pass. It's a narrow two-lane road that runs under avalanche chutes and is closed much of the time. The sky above the southwest mountains was clearing. I made a decision to go home the back way.

The back way out of Summit County is Hoosier Pass. Highway 9 is a two-lane road that links Southpark with Breckenridge. I followed Highway 9 out of Frisco and began the long climb up the pass. Plows had already cut a path in the fresh snow. After I made the Hoosier Pass Summit, I could see Southpark stretch out before me. The snow had stopped not far down the other side of the pass—Southpark does not get as much snow as Summit County.

Matt Rayburn's murder was confusing. A number of people had motives but no one seemed to have good enough reasons. First, there was Lee and Sherri Johnson, who could've killed Matt because he brought up the old steroid rumor again and because Matt had an affair with Sherri. Then, there was Mary Palmer whom Matt bilked $500 from. Then, there was Gina, his wife, who hated dogs, had a money problem, and probably knew about the affairs. Cindy Travis had acted annoyed at the thought of Matt—maybe he had gotten a little too active in club politics. Vicki was Matt's lover—she could be lying about why she broke up with him. She had as good of a motive as anyone else. But then there were Bev Long and Tami White—both married, both of whom had affairs with Matt. Who else? I wondered. Alan Freeman, Sam Horton, and Ray Bryce. And two dozen other mushers. None of it made sense.

Highway 9 leads through Alma and then into Fairplay. Alma, once little more than a ghost town, now has experienced a revitalization due to the inflated housing prices in Summit County. Summit County, which boasts of ski resorts such as Keystone, Arapaho Basin, Breckenridge, and Copper Mountain, has become too expensive to live in. Most resort workers can't afford the half million and higher priced condos and homes, so they look for inexpensive alternatives, including Park County where Southpark, Fairplay, and Alma reside.

I recalled Alan Freeman lived in Fairplay, not far from the Fairplay Nordic Center. The town sits on the banks of the South Platte River. Fairplay is the quintessential mining town. In the mid-1800's, miners who came to Southpark, lured by its gold, received a tepid welcome at the town of Tarry-All. So much claim-jumping occurred at the Tarry-All site that a number of the new miners left to found a new town farther up the Platte River. They named their town, Fair Play because everyone would have a chance to establish and keep a claim. The Fair Play miners called their neighbors "Grab-All," and evidently, this was Tarry-All's demise. Fair Play is still in existence, but only the creek and the mountains near the ghost town's site are named Tarry-All. Fair Play was the first town with a miner's dole, of sorts, where down-on-their-luck miners could pan a little gold for their whiskey in Whiskey Hole.

The most romantic legend about Fair Play is that of the barroom dancer, Silver Heels. Silver Heels was a beautiful woman who stayed and cared for the miners during a smallpox epidemic when the other townsfolk left. Eventually, she contracted the disease herself. The disease scarred her beautiful features, forcing her to wear a veil. When the miners looked to repay her kindness with a collection of several thousand dollars, Silver Heels was nowhere to be found. Years later, so the legend goes, a woman dressed in black was seen at the Alma cemetery where many of the smallpox victims were buried. She would flee if anyone attempted to approach her. The townspeople of Fair Play named a mountain north of the town in her honor.

Fairplay's population has dwindled from ten thousand or more to just a few hundred residents. The Fairplay courthouse, library, and hotel are still there, as are many of the old homes, but most people hardly give the town much notice. In the summer, during Burro Days, you can "Get Your Ass Up the Pass" where there are real Burro races up Mosquito Pass. Other than that, Fairplay remains a sleepy little town.

I looked at my watch. It was two o'clock. I decided to turn into the historic Fairplay Hotel and grab a quick bite. Outside the hotel is the gravestone of Prunes the Burro, 1867-1930. Prunes worked the mines for many years with his owner, Rupert Sherwood. Prunes was evidently a popular sight in Fairplay, running errands alone for Mr. Sherwood. In his later years, Prunes would go house to house visiting for free handouts. Eventually, he died and was buried on Fairplay's main street. Mr. Sherwood died a year later and asked that he be buried alongside his faithful companion. His ashes were scattered on Prunes' grave. Many attribute Sherwood's last request to the strong ties the Fair Play miners had with their burros. It must have been cold and lonely up in the hills outside of Fair Play.

After eating the hamburger and fries, I borrowed the restaurant's phone book and looked up Alan Freedman. I remembered that Alan lived in Fairplay. I found his number and dialed it from the outside payphone. He was home.

"Hi, Steph, how are you doing?" His voice was strangely upbeat. "I'm sorry for grousing at you this morning—I didn't have any right to say the things I did."

"That's ok," I said, trying to sound just as positive. I decided to not tell him about Tasha or the cut lines. "I was in your area and wanted to take a look at the trails you're always boasting about."

"You're in Fairplay? Great! Come on over."

I got directions and hung up.

You can see Mount Silverheels if you follow the forest roads north out of Fairplay. Along Beaver Creek is where the aqueduct runs that provides Fairplay its water. Driving along the hard-packed dirt road, I passed two snowmobiles with skis tied behind their drivers, heading towards the Fairplay Nordic Center. The Nordic Center provides groomed cross-country ski trails. This year, Fairplay had enough snow—some years, there is almost none. The Forest Service had posted a new sign along the road stating "Watch for Moose" along with a silhouette of a large bull moose for emphasis.

I took the turn off to Alan's house and followed the Beaver Creek. Mounds of smooth rock from mine tailings, or maybe what the sluices dug up, choked the creek. Some mounds towered ten to fifteen feet in height. I continued down the road. I knew the way well enough—I had run dogs in the shadow of Mount Silverheels before. But Alan didn't know that, so I would pretend I'd never been around the snowmobile trails.

Alan's house was a new A-Frame with blonde wood, set back some 50 yards into the pine and aspen. I couldn't see the dog yard from the road—he had it situated behind the house and hidden from view by an eight-foot privacy fence. He had no garage—instead he had a carport-like pad under his deck. Wooden planks lined three sides like a slatted wall. A red Yamaha snowmobile sat just under the deck. Alan was working on the snowmobile.

A chorus of howling from somewhere behind the house greeted me. I parked my dog truck behind Alan's new truck and came out. Alan beckoned me, his hands black with grease. He was holding a wrench.

"Snowmachine broke?" I asked, using the Alaskan vernacular for snowmobile.

"Nah, just needs a tune up," Alan said. "Luckily these little four-strokes can take a pounding." He turned the key and hit the ignition switch. The snowmobile roared to life with its characteristic high-pitched whine. He gave a couple of experimental shots of gas with the accelerator and the engine responded.

"Sounds good," I said.

"Hang on a moment while I wash up and get on a parka," he said. He eyed me. "You got a parka?"

"Yeah, in the cab," I said.

"Get it—we'll take the snowmobile."

I watched Alan walk inside. Most mushers are "rugged" looking—meaning they're a little on the rustic side—windburned, weathered faces showing age a little prematurely. But on some, the look is handsome. Alan was one such musher. He was thirty-five—if I remembered correctly—six feet tall and muscular. I could see why Vicki thought him a fine catch. I found him attractive.

I walked back to the truck and pulled out my parka. I heard a dog stir in the front box—either Mocha or Sam—and peered into the box. Sam's fur was poking out of the grating so I tickled his back. He shifted and Mocha groaned, looking at me expectantly with bright eyes. "Not today, Mocha dear," I said. "You've already had your run."

Alan was waiting on the snowmobile. "Climb on," he said. "I'll show you the trails."

I climbed behind him and took the open-faced helmet he offered me and put it on. I then slipped my arms around his waist and we took off. The trail was a forest service road that followed Beaver Creek. To the left were coniferous pine, lodge pole, and blue spruce mingled with aspen that had long ago shed their fiery gold leaves. Beaver Creek—aptly named with its beaver dams—wound its way along the right. Old cabins and mines lined the road—a testament to Fairplay's mining heyday. Dense thickets over six feet tall choked the creek.

"It's great fishing here," Alan shouted above the snowmobile's whine. "I've caught some delicious pan-sized trout here."

"I bet," I said. "Where did you see the moose?"

"About a mile or two up," he replied. "It was something. I was driving dogs and the moose just popped out of the thicket. Damnedest thing I ever saw."

"Wow," I said appreciatively. "I've only seen moose in Rocky Mountain National Park or Yellowstone."

"Well, this one wasn't that big," he said. "But she was deep in the thicket."

About a mile up, another road split off to the right across the creek. The main road continued onward towards Silverheels to the north. He stopped the snowmobile and motioned to the thicket. "It was about here," he said.

"How far does the trail go up?"

"It eventually goes to a rough jeep trail that circles back to the main road," Alan said. "It's too rough for the dogs to run on but you can get about eight miles total up and back. There's a turnout a mile from here which will give you two miles." He pointed up the hill.

I was looking past him when he leaned forward and kissed me. I drew back in surprise and he turned around and drew me closer. Surprised at my own reaction to his closeness, I didn't resist.

"Alan…" I began. My throat was dry and his name came out raspy.

"Shhh," he murmured and pressed his lips against mine.

For a moment, I lingered in his embrace. Then, I thought about Vicki. I pulled away. "I'd love to see the trails."

"And I would love to take you back to my place," Alan said. "It's a little too cold out here."

My face burned red at the suggestion. "Do you always say that to women you show mushing trails to?"

"Only the pretty ones," he grinned.

"Like Vicki?"

A shadow crossed his face. "Vicki?"

"Yeah," I grinned. "You're dating her, aren't you?"

"Not exactly." He straightened up as I pulled away. An uncomfortable silence followed.

"So, which trails would you be interested in?" he asked finally.

"How about the main one? Where does it go?"

He eyed me for a few moments before looking up. "Towards Silverheels. It has quite a climb."

"That sounds good."

We rode up the hill past the Colorado Gold Miner's staked claims. As we wound our way up, the forest gave way to alpine meadows. The wind picked up and blew snow across the road in horizontal sheets. I squinted to avoid getting the blowing snow into my eyes.

Alan pointed to a nearby hill. "The trails fork here. The main trail becomes a Jeep road. It eventually winds its way back and connects to the main road out of the Fairplay Nordic Center."

I nodded. I had been on the trail before, but he didn't know that. "How long is the trail to here?"

"Roundtrip, it's about seven miles."

I nodded and looked back down the valley. The sun was sinking below the mountains, turning the snowcaps crimson in the waning light. I got off the snowmobile and Alan followed me. The snow here was hard-packed and crusted over from the wind. My boots crunched through the layers a couple of inches.

"So, what got you involved in Siberians?" I asked, turning to him.

Alan shrugged. "What got you involved in Alaskans?"

"No fair—I asked you first," I shook my finger at him.

"Well, my first sled dog was a Siberian," Alan said. "His name was Max. Typical pet Siberian with blue eyes and a stilted gait. I loved him anyway. I picked up Lee Fishback's *Training Lead Dogs* and the Bella Levorsen and Sierra Nevada Dog Driver's book *Mush!* and started training him. I bought a couple of other Seppala dogs from Utah and the rest is history. What about you?"

"I had Alaskan Malamutes. I went to a race and saw the Alaskan Huskies and just fell in love with their drive," I said.

"So, you abandoned the Malamutes?"

"No, I still have Winnie. I just don't run her. Why did you stay with Siberians? I mean, most of the top teams are Alaskans."

He sighed. "Yeah, I know. And everyone who has a Siberian wants it to run faster. It's tough, sometimes, because in order to breed faster Siberians, I have to sacrifice the standard. Did you know there's a disqualification in the show ring with dogs over 23 1/2 inches or bitches over 22 inches? Half my kennel wouldn't make it."

He turned to me. "Sometimes I envy you and the other Alaskan drivers. You've got no standard to breed to and an unlimited gene pool. The Siberian drivers have to stay within the breed. It's tough because the breed has been divided between the working dogs and the show and pet dogs. It's almost like we have two different breeds."

"You've got fast dogs," I remarked. "Faster than my Alaskans."

"Big fish in a small pond," he shrugged. "This line has gone about as far as it will go. I've had to make some tough choices and I'm breeding back into the lines I'm not thrilled about." He paused. "Don't get me wrong—I like Vicki and her dogs, but they are slow."

"Then why breed to them?"

"My lines are tightly line-bred. I need an outcross."

I nodded. "Alaskan drivers run into the same predicament with closely bred lines."

"Yes, but they can outcross anywhere." He smiled, but it was forced. "Don't get me wrong, Steph. I love the Siberians, I really do. I just wish there was more to go on."

We got back on the snowmobile and we drove down the hill,

the cold wind beating against our faces. When we arrived back at Alan's house, he parked the snowmobile under the deck and shut it off. "How about some coffee?"

"Not if you're going to hit on me again."

He laughed. "You can't blame me for trying."

"Oh I could, but I won't hold that against you."

He laughed again and led me inside. The home was an open A-frame design with blonde pine along the walls and ceilings. A carved log sofa and loveseat with red and green Aztec design upholstery sat in an "L" around a log coffee table and end tables. They faced a huge moss-rock fireplace. A number of trophies and ribbons sat on the wooden fireplace mantle. I looked at them in awe. Six dog purebred, 1st place, 1997. Four dog, 3rd place, 1999. Eight dog, 1st place, 1999. Ten dog distance, 2nd place, 2000. A large photo of Alan and his team sat on the mantle, partially obscured by ribbons and two other trophies.

"Wow! I didn't know you did so well."

I was interrupted by the tick-tick-tick of a dog's toenails on wooden flooring. A beautiful gray and white Siberian Husky came out of a hallway that I presumed led to the kitchen. "Arrr, Arrr, Arrrwoo!" the Husky said.

Alan must have seen my expression. "His name is Nanook. Call him—he'll come if you do."

"Nanook, come here!" I called, kneeling down. The Husky began howling and then, with a mischievous look in his eyes, bounded right to me. My arms went around his neck and he paused and gave me a tentative lick on the nose before wiggling out of my grasp and dancing between the two of us.

"He's a friendly old guy," Alan said fondly. He rubbed Nanook behind the ears. "He likes you, you know."

"He's not a race Siberian, is he?"

Alan shook his head. "No, he's a pet dog. Somebody found him about two years ago wandering around Fairplay. So, they left him tied to the gate with a note saying they thought he was mine. I didn't have the heart to turn him over to animal control. So, he's mine."

"Real shame," I said, shaking my head. "His original owner probably dumped him. He's lucky someone picked him up and you took him—otherwise he'd probably be dead by now." I walked over to the tan couch and sat down.

"Coffee or tea?"

"Tea," I said as Alan walked into the kitchen. Nanook snuggled up to me on the couch. I rubbed his head gently. "So many people think they're doing these guys a favor by dumping them out in the country. Problem is these dogs don't know how to fend for themselves nor will the ranchers or people out in the country take them. They end up running livestock or game and getting shot by either the ranchers or the game wardens. Those are the lucky ones. Many die of starvation or are hit by cars or become prey to a hungry bear or mountain lion. It's bad news."

"Yeah, it is," said Alan as he brought me a cup of hot tea. He sat down in the cushioned chair hewn from pine in a rustic style.

"So, tell me: have you heard when Matt's funeral is?" I asked.

Alan shook his head. "Have you asked Gina? I didn't really know him that well. He hung around the Alaskan mushers' circles."

"No, I haven't talked to Gina," I lied. "I don't have her phone number and I was hoping to attend. Do you have her number?"

Alan shook his head. "No, I don't. But wasn't Matt a Director at Large or something for the club?" He leaned over and dug through a small stack of papers on an end table, and pulled out the club's newsletter, *The Howling Husky.* "Yeah, here it is." He handed me the newsletter. "I didn't know you and Matt were friends."

"We weren't close or anything," I said. "I just felt bad for him and for Gina. I mean; to be murdered? The whole thing is so weird."

Alan shrugged indifferently. "Matt wasn't popular. You heard him and Lee go at it Saturday night at the banquet."

"Yeah," I said. "But who would do such a thing?"

"I don't know," Alan said. "It does seem pretty senseless."

"I know you didn't know Matt well, but I figured maybe you might know who among the purebred folk didn't like him."

"Doing a little extra-curricular sleuthing, are you?" Alan eyed me appraisingly.

"You could say that," I shrugged. "Matt was an Alaskan musher."

Alan nodded as he leaned back into the cushions. He pondered my question. "Well, Vicki Thompson didn't get along with Matt."

I nodded. "And?"

He shook his head. "I don't know—all the Siberian racers didn't like Matt. It took an awful lot for Vicki to push through Siberian awards and purses."

"What about you?"

"Me?" He chuckled. "Steph, I ran distance last year and started training distance this year. As I said, I hardly knew Matt, other than his reputation."

The clock in the hallway began to chime. I looked at my watch. It was five o'clock and it was getting dark. "Well," I said, finishing the last of my tea. "Thank you for showing me the trails. I better be going." I stood up.

Alan stood too. "Why don't you stay and have dinner?" he asked, again eyeing me appraisingly. "I have extra stakeouts if you need them for the dogs."

I could feel the heat as it crept into my face. I'm sure I was blushing. "Thank you for the offer, but I think I'll decline at this time." I walked to the door. Alan was right behind me.

He leaned against the door and smiled. "Think about it, Steph," he said. "I've admired you for some time and I think you're a very beautiful woman."

"Thanks," I said. "Could you please move?"

"Think about it. We can go slow, if you want." He opened the door and with a roguish grin, performed an exaggerated sweeping bow.

"I'll think about it," I said as I left.

Chapter Fourteen

"Alan kissed you and you didn't do anything?"

I shrugged and dug into the chicken fried steak and reconstituted mashed potatoes on my plate.

Amy hrumphed and fixed her own plate. "Honestly, Steph, you just had the biggest romance of your life knock on the door and you just slammed it shut."

"He's romantically involved with Vicki."

"Does she have a ring?"

"Anyway, Alan wasn't looking for romance. It was more a one-night-stand."

"It was afternoon."

"Whatever." I dug into the potatoes and buried the forkful into the brown gravy. "It doesn't matter anyway. We still have a murder to solve."

"But Tallon told you that you're no longer a suspect—you've got an alibi."

"True—but I've got to find Tasha," I said. "The murderer has got her—I'm sure of it." I paused. "Damn! I should have told Jack about the snowhook."

"Jack?" Amy raised an eyebrow.

"Would you quit playing Yenta for a moment and hand me the phone?" I pulled out the card Jack had given me and dialed.

"Frisco Sheriff's Department," a man's voice answered.

"This is Stephanie Keyes, is Officer Tallon available?"

"Sorry, he's on patrol right now. Can I take a message?"

I gave him my name and number and told him that I had more information concerning the Matt Rayburn murder.

I hung up the phone and called Mary Palmer. She wasn't there, so I left a message for her telling her my dilemma about the truck stakeouts and the urgency to have new ones made. I gave her the lengths and hoped that they would be ready by Granby.

My next phone call was to Sherri Johnson. "Sherri, I'd like to talk to you about Matt Rayburn."

"I told you what I know…" Sherri began. I detected a bit of cautiousness in her voice.

"I don't think you have," I said. "Not about you and Matt."

There was silence at the other end.

"Look," I said. It was evident she wasn't going to say much. In truth, I was surprised that she hadn't hung up. "I know you can't talk there with Lee around. Let's meet at the Crow's Foot tomorrow at ten over coffee. Can you talk then?"

"Yes," Sherri said softly. "I'll meet you there."

~ * ~

The Crow's Foot is the restaurant in Bailey that sits at the foot of Crow Hill. Crow Hill is an awesome south-facing hill that Highway 285 runs down. It has a 7% grade and in the wintertime is usually covered with snow and ice, inspiring the restaurant to print their own bumper stickers proudly proclaiming "I Ski Crow Hill."

The Crow's Foot is rustic in its own right. The restaurant serves almost anything, but specializes in pizza and Mexican dishes. They have an excellent chicken fried steak, if you care for country cooking. They have the largest selection of cakes and pies on the planet. They're also open for breakfast.

Sherri was sitting at a table with a cup of coffee when I walked in. I ordered some hot tea and sat down. Sherri's face was red. She chewed her lip and gripped the coffee mug tightly.

"If you're thinking you're going to blackmail me about Matt, you'd better think again," she said without preamble. "Lee already knows about it and knows it's been over for some time."

"Whoa! Sherri, I'm not looking to blackmail you," I said, taken aback. "I just wanted some information—that's all."

"What kind of information?" she asked warily.

"How long ago did you and Matt...?"

"What has this to do with anything?"

"It has to do with the murder," I said.

"Why should I answer you?" Sherri said. "You're not the police."

"I'm not," I agreed. "And I can get the information from anyone else who knows about the affair. And then, I could go to the police with what I had learned and tell them you and Matt had an affair and that it's funny that both you and Lee have no alibis."

"So, it is blackmail."

"I wouldn't call it that. I have no desire to do that."

She met my gaze. Her jaw was firmly set, but I could see a slight twitch in the muscle. "Then, why are you asking?"

"Because—because somebody killed Matt and the police still think I'm a suspect," I lied. "Somebody just destroyed hundreds of dollars of my equipment and I'd like to know who. That someone stole Tasha, my Alaskan Husky. Maybe something you know can help vindicate Lee." I paused. "Or yourself."

"That's it, isn't it?" she said, setting her jaw again. "You think I did it."

"Not necessarily, though you have to admit having an affair with him might give you probable cause…"

"Oh, cut the bull shit!" she snapped. "Look, the last time I was with Matt was over two years ago. We had a fling, okay? It was stupid. It was wrong. Lee almost divorced me over it and threatened…" She stopped, realizing what she was saying.

"Threatened?" I raised an eyebrow.

She hesitated. "Lee was mad and said a lot of things he shouldn't have. Lee has quite a temper. You don't want to get him angry."

"I'm sure."

"But you know, Lee really didn't mean anything he said. He wouldn't hurt anyone—even a slime like Matt Rayburn."

"What did Lee threaten?" I asked.

"Nothing! Lee just made the typical angry comments that someone who just found out his wife cheated on him would say, okay?"

"Like he would kill Matt?"

"No!"

"Then what?"

Sherri exhaled loudly in exasperation. "I don't know! Lee said a lot of things he shouldn't have, in retrospect." She fell silent and sipped some of the coffee.

I decided a different approach. "What about the steroid thing?"

"Oh, Lee was just mad because Matt was trying to weasel some better dogs out of him," Sherri sighed. "Matt was goading him, and poor Lee just wasn't in the mood for that. You have no idea how sorry Lee is about that outburst—the police have really been bothering him about it."

"So, Lee was with you the entire time since you left the restaurant?"

"Yeah. We went to get some sandwiches at Arby's."

"Did you go through the drive-through?"

"No—we had the sleds on top. The overhang would have taken them right off."

"Does anyone remember serving you?"

"No, but the officer involved in the investigation is asking Arby's to check the security tapes. We sat down for a few minutes to eat the sandwiches and then drove back to the motel. That's when we saw you."

I nodded. "Do you know who was Matt's latest girlfriend?"
Sherri shook her head.

"Do you know if Matt ticked anyone off enough to kill him?"

"Gina has no love for him," Sherri mused. "With Matt gone, she's got the mortgage paid for."

"What about Tami White or Bev Long? They were former girl-friends."

She chuckled. "I knew about Tami, but Bev? That's news to me."

"Would they have any reason?"

"Tami moved back to Minnesota in September. She got divorced soon after. I think she's going by her maiden name of Prickett. I hear she's been doing pretty well out there."

"Okay," I nodded. "I've seen her name. I didn't realize who Tami Prickett was."

"Bev has been taking a low profile. I think she's going to be getting out of dogs soon. You'd better ask Liz Smith about her."

I nodded and made a mental note to visit Liz.

"Who do you think would have a reason to kill Matt?"

Sherri took a sip of her now cold coffee. "I don't know, Steph, I really don't. Matt was a pain in the ass and I have no idea why I even fooled around with him. I guess it's because he was younger and good-looking. But, he was manipulative and devious. I won't say I'm sorry to see him gone, but I wouldn't have been the one to do it. Nor would have Lee, not after all this time. Thankfully, I can say this because I was with Lee the entire time. He didn't do it."

~ * ~

I finished my tea and went to the payphone in the Crow's Foot near the bathroom. A quick call to information yielded Liz's number.

"Hey, Liz, this is Steph," I said as soon as she picked up the phone. "I got a favor to ask you."

"I've got one too," Liz said. "Sasha just had the litter this morning—I was wondering if you could come by in the next three or four days and clip dewclaws?"

"Congratulations," I said. "How many pups?"

"Six—two females and four males."

"Nice litter."

"They're all placed out too," Liz said smugly. "I'm keeping a female and the rest have good homes."

"Great!" I said.

"So, did you find your dog yet?"

"No," I said ruefully. "I'm trying to find out if anyone saw anything." I paused. "You know Bev?"

"Bev Long? Sure. Why? You don't think Bev took your dog? She's getting out of dogs."

"Really? I didn't know that," I said.

"You didn't see her at Frisco, did you?"

"No, but I wasn't looking for her."

"It's the money thing," Liz said. "She's keeping Niki and Shadow, but has sold the rest."

"Did she know Matt at all?"

"Oh yeah, she was seeing him behind Gina's back," Liz said.

I must have gasped because Liz laughed. "God, Steph, you are so old fashioned!" She paused. "Wait, are you thinking she might have off'd him?" Liz laughed again.

"What's so funny?"

"Oh Steph, you're too funny! She dumped him. She told me 'good riddance to the lout!' Her exact words, I swear. Besides, she was in Denver. Her mom's at Swedish Hospital—just had an emergency quad by-pass on Friday. She had more on her mind than driving up to Frisco on Saturday night and killing Matt."

"Okay," I said sullenly. Dead end.

"Hey, don't be glum—come see the pups. When will you be able to clip dews?"

"This weekend is the Granby race," I said. "Would Monday be too late?"

"Hmm, four days. Should be okay."

I looked at my watch. It was eleven o'clock. "Got to run— Rachel is expecting me at noon."

Before I left, I made one more phone call to Jeff Dreyer, Gina's accountant. He had a cancellation in his schedule tomorrow and was happy to see me that morning for tax advice.

~ * ~

The clinic proved busy this afternoon. We were short-staffed today. Only another vet tech named Claudia and I were there. Sandy had called in sick and there wouldn't be a relief vet in until tomorrow. I checked the list of appointments to pull the files for the up-coming patients and paused when I saw the name "Buster." His owners were Joe and Cindy Travis. The appointment was for two-thirty—it was already two-fifteen.

I pulled the chart and flipped through the records. Buster, it seems, was not an Alaskan Husky, but a Parson Russell Terrier. I had just enough time to look at the chart when Rachel called me over to hold a cat for its nail clippings.

Cindy came in with a little brown and white terrier in her arms. The waiting room was already full with a Labrador, two domestic shorthair cats (in crates), and a German Shepherd with their respective owners. The German Shepherd was a walk-in, but the others had appointments and Rachel was short-staffed and running behind. I led the chocolate Lab and his owner into an examination room and waved hello to Cindy. She was busy weighing Buster on the floor scale.

"Hi Cindy, we'll be with you in a moment," I said.

"No problem, Steph," she said. "I can see you're busy."

A few minutes after some clients left, I was able to put the two cats in their own exam rooms. I sat down next to Cindy.

"You look tired," she commented. Buster took a couple of sniffs at me and wiggled in her arms.

"Yeah, it's been a long day already," I admitted. "Can I pet him?" She nodded. I petted the Parson Russell. Beneath the short coat, I could feel the muscle on the sturdy little dog. "He must get a lot of exercise with the huskies."

"He keeps the huskies in line," Cindy said. "He's boss dog at home."

"I don't doubt," I laughed.

"I heard about the missing dog," Cindy ventured. "Vicki told me," she added after seeing my surprise. "You better watch yourself," she said. "I heard about the officers searching your truck."

"Who told you that?"

"Lee saw the whole thing on Sunday."

"Great."

"And now someone stole your dog?"

"They vandalized my truck too. I searched everywhere for Tasha, but couldn't find her."

"What does Tasha look like?"

"She's a red husky about forty pounds."

Cindy frowned and shook her head. "Steph, I don't like this. Not one bit. Why would someone take your dog? That had to be a threat and you know it. Next time, it could be your brake lines instead of your ganglines or he could put poison in your dogs' food."

"Or she."

"Or she," Cindy sighed. "Listen, you're a good person—I know that. You can stop being a hero and let the police handle it."

"You'll have to make a follow-up appointment to get those stitches out," Rachel was saying as she walked out of an exam room. The owner, a small woman with dark hair, was being dragged by a Golden Retriever with an Elizabethan collar on its neck. "Careful!" Rachel said, "or she'll pull out the stitches. Steph! Can you get her about ten Acepromazine?"

I stood up. "That's my cue," I said to Cindy. "Ten Acepromazine?" I asked Rachel as I walked over to the counter.

"And set up an appointment in ten days to have those stitches removed," she added. I nodded.

After I was done with the Golden, I checked on the cats and then slipped into the room where Claudia had put Cindy Travis and Buster.

Cindy was sitting down, reading a dog magazine with Buster snoozing at her feet. She looked up.

"I don't have much time to talk," I said. "I'd like to know what Matt was doing to shake the club up."

Cindy frowned. "What does this have...?" She paused. "Oh, still snooping around?"

"Yep," I said. "And don't give me this crap that I should stop investigating. If I don't, Matt's murderer may try something else on me."

Cindy sighed. "Oh, very well. Matt was angry about the way the club was handling the whole Siberian issue. He threatened he was going to run against me for president of the Western States Sled Dog Club."

"What did you say?"

"I said 'Be my guest.' He didn't have the support, you know."

"Half the club is some sort of purebred," I remarked. "I can't imagine him winning."

"He was starting to garner some support among the Alaskan drivers. Lee, for example, might have voted for him. Lee's pretty tired of the concessions we've made."

"Would it have been enough?"

She shook her head. "No, I don't think so. Especially after the banquet when Matt brought up the steroid incident. He lost a number of supporters that night."

"Right," I said.

"Does that help?" Cindy asked. "You know, I founded this organization back in nineteen eight-two, but even I am getting tired of the politics. In some ways, I wished he had been able to run against me and win. That way, I could walk away from the whole Siberian/Alaskan issue."

"Thanks," I said. "I appreciate it. I've got to go back to work," I added as I left the room.

~ * ~

Friday morning, Rachel didn't expect me into work until noon, but I couldn't afford the luxury of sleeping in. My appointment with Jeff Dreyer was at eight o'clock. His office was in downtown Evergreen in the little mall by Bear Creek. There's a bar and some New Age and gift shops, but not much else. As I entered the glass doors of the two-story pine mall, I was quickly reminded how quaint and rustic Evergreen could be, in spite of the high prices. Evergreen was originally the mountain retreat for the affluent. While Morrison, Nederland, and Indian Hills became havens for flower children in the sixties and seventies, Evergreen attracted those with money. Famous music stars owned multimillion-dollar ranches along Upper Bear Creek. Its proximity to I-70 made it the ideal mountain getaway for the rich who didn't like driving up the narrow lanes of Highway 285 in Turkey Creek Canyon.

Jeff Dreyer's office consisted of two small rooms: one, the waiting area with a well-worn brown leather couch and a surplus secretary's desk. Black filing cabinets, four drawers high, lined the walls to the left. The secretary's desk, now empty, had stacks of unfinished work piled on it. A standard black and orange "Help Wanted" sign on the door, just under the gold lettering that said Jeffery S. Dreyer CPA, suggested that perhaps it would be a while before the work actually got done.

The second room was not much bigger than the first. Jeff Dreyer sat at a wooden desk with a phone handset cradled on his shoulder. He was furiously scribbling on a yellow legal pad. His in-basket was overflowing; his out-basket held mail. Files were strewn across the desk. He had pushed the black rimmed glasses almost to his forehead when he saw me. He straightened them back in place on his hawkish nose. He motioned me into the second room and waved me toward one of two mahogany, genuine distressed leather, winged-back office chairs. I sat down.

"...so you do want to take the in-home office deduction," he was saying. "That should save you a bit on taxes..." He paused. "Yes, I know. Look, I've got a current client here—can I get back with you? Great. Good-bye." He hung up the phone. "Ms. Keyes?" he asked pleasantly. He was a small, thin man around forty-five wearing a southwest print Buffalo shirt, Wranglers jeans, a five hundred dollar pair of ostrich-skin cowboy boots, and a silver and turquoise bolo tie with a Kokopelli design.

"Uh, Stephanie," I said. "I'm awfully glad you could take the time to take a look at my taxes."

"I had a cancellation—I'm glad you called. I so seldom get cancellations," he said, wringing his thin hands together. "Now, how did you find out about me?"

"Gina Rayburn recommended you," I said. "She said you were a real whiz with numbers."

His chest seemed to puff with pride. "Gina's in a terrible pickle, what with Matt getting murdered," he said.

"She told me Matt did all the finances."

"That he did. That he did." He eyed the packet in my hands. "Are those your returns from previous years and your W2s?"

"Yeah," I said. I handed the packet to him.

He opened it up and began tsking almost immediately. "So, how do you know Gina?" he asked. "Are you her vet tech?"

"Yeah, but I knew her through Matt," I said. "I'm a musher."

"Oh, another one!" He smiled. He leafed through the documentation. "But I don't see any deductions for the business."

"Business?"

"Do you run this like a business or is this more of a hobby?"

"I was thinking about setting myself up as a business—like Matt did," I said, thinking on my feet.

"How many dogs do you sell a year?"

"Five."

He looked disappointed. "I might be able to do something with it."

"I could sell more."

He frowned as he looked at the return. "Do you always get money back?"

"Usually," I said.

"Well, you shouldn't. That's your money, you know. The Government is making interest off of that, not you."

I nodded. "Okay, I had heard that before. How many deductions should I consider?"

"I don't know—I'd have to calculate that out. Also, that will change if we set you up as a business."

By the end of the hour, he was ready to sell me his business incorporation package for a thousand dollars. I guess that's how he pays for his boots. I asked him if he could do my taxes and then we'd talk about the business. For some reason, a hundred and twenty dollars for the tax return was disappointing to him. His next client was waiting patiently out in the reception area when we shook hands and he promised to mail the return by April 1.

His next client was a tall blonde woman in a business suit. He ushered her in and shut the office door. Unlike the door to the mall, this door was solid pine and afforded some privacy. The window in the office had mini-blinds that were already lowered and closed. I was alone.

My first thought was to leave, but curiosity got the better of me and I walked quickly over to one to filing cabinet marked "P-Q-R" and opened it. Skimming down the files, I quickly located "Rayburn." At this point, I wished I had one of those tiny cameras that you see in all those spy movies. Instead, I opened up the file and stared at the return.

Matt Rayburn made $37,000 as a medical technician. Last year, his "business" grossed $24,872. Almost twenty-five thousand? I blinked. Was that right? I did the math—twenty-two dogs in four years was roughly five dogs a year. Those dogs would have run five thousand dollars apiece—ludicrous! Unless, Matt had bought and sold more dogs than he had brought to Rachel. For all I knew, he could have been an animal broker licensed with the USDA. I started looking for proof of brokering when I heard the unmistakable screech of a chair being pushed back. I grabbed the documents and shoved them back in the file drawer and shut it. At that moment, Jeff Dreyer came out.

"Ms. Keyes?" he asked, obviously puzzled. "Do you need something?"

"I thought I had left something," I said, scrambling for a moment. "I think I lost your business card and I wanted to get another one."

Jeff smiled. "Here," he said, taking several from the desk. "Give them to your friends and relatives too."

I smiled back. "Sure will," I said as I left.

~ * ~

When I returned home, the message light was blinking on the answering machine. I pressed the play button. "Hey, Steph, this is Mary," Mary Palmer's voice came over the speaker. "Got your message. Your lines are ready for you, if you want to pick them up. I've also got that Risdon, if you're interested. I'll be around until one, so stop by if you can and I'll make sure the lines fit."

I checked the time. It was almost ten. I had just enough time to get the lines fitted. I hopped in the dog truck and drove down to Mary's.

Mary lives in a little red cabin just off the main Pine Road. There's no real driveway, just a dirt turnout large enough to park cars on so I parked there and walk up the well-treaded path. Five Huskies twirled around on their stakeouts and barked in greeting. I walked up to the door and knocked. "Come in!" Mary's voice rang from inside.

I opened the door and stepped in. Brightly colored harnesses, ganglines, and other mushing gear hung from the ceiling and the walls. Tables filled with spools of cable and polyethylene rope, bolts of cordura and polar fleece, and dog coats, booties, and various other projects, filled the tiny room. At the far end of the room was an industrial-quality sewing machine. Mary was sitting at the sewing machine, piecing together a blue dog jacket. She waved me in.

I carefully picked my way through the sea of equipment. "You look busy," I said as I stepped over bags of blue cordura booties lying on the floor.

Mary sighed in disgust. She waved her hands over to the pile of harnesses. "Jim Felton called last week—needed twelve lightweight racing harnesses immediately. He couldn't have my standard sizes, so I had to go out and measure his dogs. He then asked if they'll be ready next week. Christ, like I'm not backordered 'til spring? Everybody wants something. I'm lucky I've got Ken helping me out at least part time, otherwise I'd never get anything done."

"I'm sorry about the stakeouts…" I began, shifting uncomfortably.

"Oh no!" Mary said. "It's really no problem with those. I give Kenny the measurements and he measures and cuts them while watching TV at night. He's a good kid and he likes doing cable. Anything to help his mom out when he can."

"Well, thank him for me," I said sincerely. "I know this was such a rush job."

"Couldn't be helped." She stood up and looked around. "Where did I put them?" She waded through the bags and then settled on sorting through a pile. "I put them somewhere…"

"Kenny has been doing really well in the junior class," I ventured. "How old is he now? He must really enjoy being in the adult classes now."

"He's fifteen," she said absently. "He's already saving money for a faster team." She paused. "Ah, here they are!" She pulled out two coils of cable stakeouts. "Let's try them out."

I backed out a few steps and then turned around and picked my way through the equipment labyrinth.

"You know," said Mary, "I'd say whoever cut your lines was trying to scare you."

I grunted noncommittally and opened the door.

She met my gaze. "This is about Matt's murder, isn't it?"

"Maybe," I said. "Maybe not. Maybe I should have kept my

equipment locked up." And my dog at home.

"And maybe someone would have cut something else if they hadn't had your equipment to mess with. A brake line, perhaps, or something worse."

"Are you going to check to see if the lines fit or not?" I asked, my hands on my hips.

She nodded. "Yes, yes. It's just that I'm worried for you."

"I can take care of myself."

"Matt could take care of himself and he's dead."

I didn't say anything. Mary continued.

"Matt must have pushed at something he shouldn't have," Mary commented as we stopped before my truck. Cars whizzed along the highway towards Pine about ten feet away. I knelt down and opened one of the telescoping stakeout bars that I had attached to the front bumper. "He pushed someone a little too far this time and they killed him for it. Now, you're swatting at the same damn hornets' nest like a piñata." She clipped the end of the line to the open stakeout and stretched it across to the other side. I opened the other stakeout and we clipped it together. "See, it adjusts through the turnbuckle here," Mary said.

"Why the warning?"

"Everyone knows you're investigating Matt's murder—it doesn't take a detective to figure that out. The murderer knows too—he'd have to with this community. Everybody talks, see? There aren't any secrets."

"Just one—who killed Matt," I said.

"Why are you so damn interested?" Mary asked as she unhooked the stakeout cables from the poles and began coiling them up again. "He wasn't you're friend. Hell, he wasn't anybody's friend, except perhaps Sam's. In some ways, it's better he's gone."

"You really think that?" I asked. "He was always bouncing checks on you."

"Yeah, he was," Mary said. "But he always ended up paying me in the end. The Risdon sled was just another bounced check he'd make good on eventually. I threatened him with repossession because I was tired of it. I don't know if I would have carried through on the threat, though. By the way, I have the Risdon, if you're interested. Gina returned it after Matt's death."

"I'd love it—can you hold it for me until next payday? You said five hundred, right?" I asked.

"Why don't you take it now and use it at Granby?"

I shook my head. "This is going to set me back a small fortune and anyway, Gina may be selling the dogs. I want enough cash in case she does."

Mary shrugged. "Suit yourself—I know you're good for the money."

We test fitted the other side. Ken's workmanship was impeccable as usual and the stakeouts fit perfectly. Three hundred and twenty dollars later, I was the proud owner of two sets of stakeouts, another eight-dog gangline, and a mega-brake to replace the one that busted in the race.

As I drove to the vet clinic, Mary's words echoed in my mind: *Why are you so damn interested? He wasn't your friend.*

"No, he wasn't," I admitted aloud. "But nobody, *nobody* steals a dog from me. Murderer or not, no one scares me away."

Chapter Fifteen

The next day was the third of the Triple Crown Races in Granby, Colorado. Granby is nestled in an area known as Middle Park. It isn't much of a park, if you compare it to Northpark (around Walden), Southpark (around Fairplay) or the park surrounded by the San Juan Mountains. But since it is a grassland that stretches from the south side of Berthoud Pass (near the Winter Park/ Mary Jane Ski Areas) to Kremmling, it makes sense to name it Middlepark.

The fastest way to get to Granby, Colorado, is over the infamous Berthoud Pass. It rivals all other passes in Colorado, with the possible exception of Monarch Pass and Independence Pass as being the most daunting. Before I-70 was built, the only way west to Salt Lake City was on US 40, which takes you over Berthoud Pass, with all its avalanche zones and precarious overhangs. There is now a longer way to Granby which takes you through the Eisenhower Tunnel to Silverthorne (near Lake Dillon and Frisco), north on Colorado 9 to Kremmling, and then east to Granby. That takes an extra two hours, which nobody wants to drive. There has been talk for years about running a tunnel between I-70 at the Berthoud exit to Winter Park, but the money just isn't there. So, the prices in Grand County are not the prices of Summit County. You can stay in a motel for anywhere from $25 to $50 a night, double occupancy. The $25 a night guarantees a bed and maybe hot water.

Hunters, mushers, skiers, snowmobilers, and other outdoor enthusiasts enjoy the lower prices and less crowded recreational areas than those in Summit County. Fraser, Colorado, which lies between Winter Park and Granby, vies with International Falls, Minnesota, for the dubious honor of being called the Icebox of the Nation. Granby is relatively warmer than Fraser, but is closer to the train tracks. On a cold night when the temperature inversions hit, you can really smell the diesel exhaust from the trains and the long haul truckers. Granby is not the place to stay if you are a light sleeper either. The rumble of the highway and the locomotives will keep you up all night.

There are some great mushing areas that come out of Grand County. An area less traveled is Church Park, along the Big Muddy

River. In good snow years, that area can get more than six feet of snow. The forest roads run from Fraser to Hot Sulfur Springs some forty miles away. I've never run out of snow there.

These trails are usually forest service roads. They're nice and wide and heavily wooded with pinon, lodgepole, blue spruce, and other coniferous trees. When you're out there alone with your team, it can be so quiet—at least until the next snowmobile tour comes by.

The Rocky Mountain Sled Dog Club (RMSDC—a sister club to the Western States Sled Dog Club) holds the two Granby Races, the Ididarace (near Kremmling), and the Grand County Race. This year, to avoid conflicting with the new Frisco Races, RMSDC decided to run their races on opposite weekends. The Colorado Mountain Mushers, now primarily running distance races, didn't care if they held their races at the same time, since their venue was different. The RMSDC holds the Granby race in the Granby Sports Park, just opposite of the Silver Creek Ski Area. RMSDC does an excellent job of grooming a good trail. You can usually see these races during the middle to the end of February on the weekends.

These races are big—over eighty teams compete in any given race—and it is not uncommon for the number to be well over one hundred. The money is good in these races; combined they can top over $20,000. Most mushers who race here are from the Rocky Mountain region, but it isn't that unusual to have competitors come from as far away as Canada, Minnesota, or Washington. In recent years, RMSDC has added ten-dog to the sprint race.

Amy and I drove into the Granby Sports Park at eight o'clock. Already, the parking lot was full of dog trucks. We parked beside a dauntingly professional rig with Ontario license plates. It was a new dark blue Ford 250 with a newly painted double-decker dog box and two Risdon composite sleds on top. "Howlin' Husky Racing Team" was painted in six-inch letters on the back. My own dog box sported "Screaming Weasels Sled Dogs" with a long weasel-looking husky howling at the moon.

As cold as Granby normally is, today it was sunny. Without clouds, the race promised to be warm. I walked across the parking lot towards the registration and staging area, taking a few detours to check out the dogs. Although the other mushers thought I was checking out the competition, I was actually looking for Tasha. I saw several red huskies, but none were Tasha. I didn't really expect the murderer to have her in full view, but I wasn't going to lose the opportunity.

Already officials were checking stopwatches and writing up the running order on large whiteboards. I approached the registration table. Cindy Travis stood in line in front of me. She was scowling.

"Did you hear? They're not seeding. It's going to be a God-awful mess," she turned to me. Seeding is the practice where the club takes your current standings and determines your race order. Fastest teams go first.

"Really? How many teams?"

"Oh, it probably won't affect you—you run eight-dog, right?" I nodded.

"They have only thirty teams registered."

"Only?" I said. "That's huge."

"Check out the stats," Cindy replied. "Forty-seven four dog teams. Twenty-nine three dog. Nineteen skijorers. This race keeps getting bigger every year."

"Wow, that's going to exceed their record."

"It's the weather," Cindy sighed. "That heat-wave in the Midwest has caused the cancellation of more races. They don't have any snow. I heard Neil Swenson may be getting out of dogs if this weather keeps up."

"No!" I said. "Not Neil. He's been in dogs for ages."

"Talked to him this week—he's getting old, you know. He slipped in places this year. He says it's not the dogs; it's the driver."

"He took silver last year in Open, didn't he?"

"Yeah, the first time he hasn't been a serious contender for gold. I heard he'll be lucky if he gets a bronze. Derek and his pointer crosses are giving him something to think about."

"Doesn't he have a kid into dogs?"

"John? Yeah he ran as a teen, but he's in college now. Not interested in the old man's sport anymore. Hear he wants to be a vet."

"Speaking of getting out of dogs, have you heard anything from Gina?" I asked.

Cindy gave me a long look. "Interested in some of Rayburn's dogs?"

"Maybe," I hedged. "I was wondering if you heard anything."

Cindy shook her head. "I don't even think Gina knows my name, much less the name of WSSDC. You might want to ask Sam

Horton. He and Matt were pals. I'd suspect if Gina were selling, he'd know. She really wasn't interested in the dogs."

"No, it didn't strike me that she was interested," I said. "Though Matt sure was. He was a Director-at-Large."

"He was definitely At-Large," Cindy smirked. "Somebody should have reined him in."

"You weren't fond of him, I take it."

Cindy eyed me appraisingly. "After the stunt he pulled at the last race, I'd suspect you wouldn't be fond of him either."

"Not fond, certainly, but he didn't deserve to die," I said.

"No, he didn't, though things are a bit quieter now that he's gone."

"Next!" said the woman at the registration table. She was a largish woman in a thick red down parka with a pink musher's cap and dark rimmed glasses. "What class?"

"Four dog," said Cindy. "Joe Travis."

"Your name is Jo?"

"No, it's for my husband, Joe," Cindy explained. "I'm Cindy Travis."

The woman looked down at the sheet and shuffled through a few pages with fingers firmly ensconced in rag wool gloves. "Travis—running four-dog. Purebred or mixed?"

"Alaskan Huskies," Cindy said with a sly glance at me. I grinned back.

The woman looked through her paperwork and then met Cindy's gaze. "Is that purebred?"

"Do you think I would want a handicap?"

The woman chewed her lip and gave Cindy the bib and starting order sheet. The Rocky Mountain Sled Dog Club had printed each team's starting order and handed it out with the bibs.

"Next!"

"Stephanie Keyes. Eight-dog. Alaskan Huskies."

The woman didn't blink and gave me my bib and start order. I looked for my name. I was fifth out.

"Damn!" said Cindy. "Joe'll be mad. He's twenty-third out. How'd you do?"

"Fifth out," I grinned.

"There's no head-on passing like Frisco, so you should have a clean run," Cindy observed. She paused. "Say, I have to get back to the bus and get Joe ready for his run, seeing as four-dog goes out early. Sam Horton should be available—I think he's running six-dog and maybe ten."

I felt my stomach knot. I really had no desire to talk to Sam, given his reaction to me when I found the body. "I don't know."

"What?"

"He nearly strangled me the night Matt was murdered," I said. An image of Sam coming towards me filled my mind. I shuddered. "I don't want to be the next body found."

Cindy smiled. "Don't worry—Sam's bark is worse than his bite. He's really a nice guy—once you get to know him."

Somehow, I couldn't imagine anyone who hung around with Matt as being "a nice guy." Especially one with big meaty hands that could choke the life out of you.

Cindy must have guessed what I was thinking. "I really wouldn't worry about him, Steph. He was actually asking about you earlier."

"About what?" My voice sounded shrill in alarm.

"Calm down," she patted my arm. "He wanted to know how you were coping with the shock of finding Matt first. He told me he behaved badly and he wanted to apologize."

"He did?" I said in a small voice, still in disbelief.

"Go talk to him. He's parked towards the front."

~ * ~

Part of me wanted to go back to my truck and prepare for the race. But I knew I had been putting off talking to Sam Horton too long. I walked along the dog trucks until I spied Sam's large frame towering over his Alaskan Huskies that were staked out on his truck. He drove a green Ford F250 with an older dog box painted white that sat on top of the truck's bed. He had the tailgate open and was stirring up some warm water mixed with something that looked like bits of meat and beef broth. He then took the five-gallon bucket and ladled the water out with a scoop made from an old one-quart pan with a wooden handle strapped to it. His dogs danced as he approached and he poured the water into bowls he set in front of them.

"Hi, Sam," I said.

Sam had been kneeling down to pet an Alaskan. The sun was behind me, so he had to squint to look at me. "Hi, Steph," he said.

He got up and moved to the next dog, a classic gray and white husky, and gave him a scoop of baited water.

"Sam, look, I know we don't always see eye-to-eye..." I began and then faltered.

Sam seemed to not hear me and continued on his rounds.

"I didn't kill Matt—you must know this by now."

"No," he said slowly. "I didn't know. But I'm glad you said it." He didn't look at me. Instead, he ran his hands down a brown and white Alaskan Husky's legs to check for injuries.

That's it? I wondered. I stood for a while in silence watching Sam check his dogs over. "Vicki says you and Matt weren't on the best terms," I ventured.

Sam looked up, a puzzled expression on his face. "What would Vicki know? She's a Siberian driver."

"She made some comment about you mouthing off."

Sam shook his head. "We ran Alaskans and drank beer. That's all."

"Matt had a lot of Alaskan Huskies come through his yard, didn't he?" I changed my tact.

"Now that you mention it, yeah. He always had new dogs."

"Who bought his Alaskans?"

Sam paused for a moment and looked thoughtful. "I don't know. He had a 'for sale' sign out a lot, but I don't remember any buyers."

"Nor do I," I mused aloud. "Isn't that curious?"

"Well, people always knew he had Alaskans for sale—it wasn't a big secret," Sam remarked.

"Who did he buy from?"

"I don't know."

"He bought from Lee," I said. "I think I've seen some of Bruce's dogs. Matt must have bought them back when Bruce got out of mushing."

"Maybe he got dogs from Alaska or the Midwest."

Sam turned and opened up a dog box. A familiar snarl came from the box and he lifted out a brown and black spotted Alaskan Husky.

"Is that Poco?" I gasped. "Matt's Poco?"

Sam turned to me. "Yeah, why? Didn't you know? Gina sold the dogs."

My mouth grew dry and my throat felt like it was closing up. "No," I said. "Gina promised me she'd call if she decided to sell Matt's Alaskans." I paused and looked at the dogs staked-out. "What other dogs did you get?"

"Max and Penny," Sam said. "They're just team dogs. Most of the good dogs were already picked over."

"Damn! What about Blue and Shep?"

"They were already gone."

"Damn! Do you know who else might have bought dogs from her?"

Sam shook his head. "Gina didn't say," he said. "I don't think she knows everyone's name."

"Look, I run eight-dog. If you need handlers for six and ten come get me and Amy. We'll help you to the line."

Sam grinned. "Thanks."

I ran back to my truck as fast as my Sorrels would take me. I turned the corner of the truck, nearly tangling myself up in the stakeout lines and tripped over Jasmine. The husky made an indignant cry as I tumbled onto the hard ice next to her and almost cracked my skull.

"Well, that was graceful," Amy said at the tailgate.

Jasmine looked down at me reprovingly. Her blue eyes met mine and she made a small noise that echoed her annoyance.

"Damn it, Amy, Gina sold Matt's Alaskans."

"Well, they're hers to sell." Amy took the pooper scoopers out of the truck and started picking up after Lightning.

"Yes, but she promised she call me if she was selling out." I got up and brushed off the snow. I opened up the truck door, carefully dodging Mocha's attempt at trapping me in the stakeout line. I rummaged in my backpack. "Where's my cell phone?"

"In the glove compartment—dead," Amy remarked. "You never recharged it."

I peeked out of the door. "You have yours?"

"Yeah, why?" She crossed her arms.

"I need to call Gina."

Silence.

"I'll pay you for it."

Amy pursed her lips. "I don't know."

"Come on…"

"Oh, Okay," she sighed. "It's in my backpack." I was already diving into it. "Promise me you'll recharge your phone."

"Yeah, sure, whatever," I said as I dug out the phone and dialed Gina's number.

The phone rang once, twice, three times. "Come on," I said. "Answer it."

Fourth ring. "Hello?" Gina's voice answered sleepily.

"Hey, Gina, this is Stephanie."

"Stephanie?" Her voice was groggy. "Do you know what time it is?"

I glanced at my watch. "Eight-forty-two, why?"

"Are you at a race?"

"Can you hear the dogs in the background?" I asked. OK, I tuned it out. Now I realized what a cacophony the dogs were.

"Jesus, Stephanie, the rest of the world doesn't get up this early on a Saturday! Why'd you call?"

"Gina—I just ran into Sam Horton. He has Poco. I thought you were going to call me when you were selling the Alaskans."

There was silence at the other end.

"Gina?"

"Is that what you woke me up for? Dogs?"

"I'm sorry—I assumed you were up."

A long drawn-out sigh. "I swear you mushers are all alike. Matt was the same damn way. 'Come on, Gina, time to get up!' It was five-frickin-thirty in the goddamn morning!"

"Look, Gina, I'm sorry. It's after eight. I assumed you'd be up."

"You assumed wrong."

"Look, don't hang up. Why didn't you call me?"

"I forgot. Okay? I'm an idiot. So sue me."

"Do you know who you sold Blue and Shep to?"

Another exasperated sigh. "Which ones were Blue and Shep? Honestly, Steph, I don't know which dogs were which. I sold them because I had no idea how much work they were."

"Are they all gone?" I pressed

"I've got an old one left. I think his name is Pete."

"Who did you sell the dogs to?"

"A few mushers."

"Names?"

"Well, there was Sam." Gina paused. "I don't remember anyone else's name."

"Receipts?" I asked hopefully.

"No, I don't want them back. A few wrote me checks, though. I haven't deposited them yet."

"Can you look on the checks and find out?"

"Not now," Gina said. "I guess since I'm awake I could, but after my coffee. What's your number, I'll call you back."

I gave her Amy's cell phone number and pressed END.

"Gina wasn't awake, was she?" Amy asked.

I shook my head. "Gina wasn't too happy about it either."

Before Amy could respond, the familiar call echoed through the staging area. "Driver's Meeting!"

I looked at her quizzically. She nodded her head over to the officials. "Go on!"

I handed her the phone and walked over. Lee Johnson caught up to me and walked next to me. "Lee," I said. "Gina sold Matt's dogs."

Lee looked startled. His brow furrowed. "Gina sold the dogs? Damn! I had contracts with Matt for Right of First Refusal."

"I don't think Gina knew that," I said as we walked towards the gathering crowd. "Matt bought a lot of Alaskans from you, didn't he?"

"Yeah, he did," Lee admitted. He paused and considered me. "Why?"

"Who else did Matt buy Alaskans from—do you know?"

"He bought a lot of dogs out of Alaska," Lee said. "I think Matt got his pointer-crosses out of Heikki Seppanen."

"North American stock?"

"Yeah."

"What about the huskies?"

Lee shrugged. "Matt asked me one time if Shawn Bailey had good Alaskan Huskies."

"Shawn is in Minnesota, right?"

"Yeah—Shawn might actually be here in Granby. They've had no snow except where they've been able to get lake effect."

"Everybody listen up!" Kirk Shaffer, the race marshal shouted. He was a big man with red unruly hair and beard. He wore a Purina Pro Plan cap and a dark blue snowmobiler's suit. He stared momentarily at the papers in his hand through thick glasses and then looked up. "We've got a really good trail laid in. The trail is hard and fast with about four inches of powder from Wednesday night…"

I wasn't really listening. I was thinking about Matt. Maybe this wasn't about sex. Maybe this was about dogs. Dogs and money. But who would kill Matt over dogs and why? Was Matt buying dogs on promises of payment and failed to pay? Why wouldn't the owner just take the dogs back? Unless Matt couldn't give them back because he sold them…

"…All of you have a good run!" Kirk finished.

"What'd Kirk say?" I nudged Lee.

"What?" Lee stared at me.

"I wasn't paying attention."

"The trail's good—I got to get back. Sherri is going out four-dog." He left me standing alone.

I scanned the parking lot. People were scurrying back to their trucks to begin hooking up for three-dog. I walked back to the registration table and looked over the listings. Kirk Shaffer walked up and looked over my shoulder.

"You need help, Steph?"

"Yeah," I said. "Do you know if Shawn Bailey made it in?"

"Shawn Bailey…Shawn Bailey…" He paused. "He's from Minnesota, right?"

"Yeah, from Ely, Minnesota," I said.

"Shawn drove in last night," Kirk said. "He's got the big rig on the end."

I looked up and grinned. "Thanks!"

~ * ~

I walked along the trucks towards a white one ton dually with a large flatbedded dog box made from fiberglass. A green logo with sled dogs and shamrocks ran across it saying "Luck of the Irish Kennel. Shawn Bailey, Ely, MN." Walking around the truck, I noted the generous list of both local and national sponsors. Alaskan Huskies cavorted on stakeouts around the truck. One brown dog looked like a pointer cross. She playfully reached for me with her dainty paws.

A man with blond hair and blue eyes and a red and black checkered huntsman cap peeked around the corner. He was wearing black arctic weight Carhartt overalls. "Can I help you?"

"Hi! You must be Shawn Bailey," I said extending my hand. "I'm Stephanie Keyes."

Recognition entered his eyes. "Ah, the one to beat in eight-dog, or so I hear." He took my hand. "Glad to finally meet you, Stephanie. I've heard a lot about you and your team."

I laughed. "My reputation is a bit unfounded."

"So, checking out the competition?" he grinned. "Or just being friendly."

"A little of both," I said. "I didn't see you last weekend at the Frisco race."

Shawn shook his head. "Couldn't make it. We had the Macninaw Mush in Michigan. There wasn't much snow, but it's been a tradition there. Came in first in eight-dog."

"Congrats," I said. I walked around the truck, considering his dogs. They were houndy things; they looked like greyhounds with double coats. Mushers use the terms husky and hound to describe Alaskan Huskies. "Husky" means that the dog resembles a Siberian; "Hound" means it favors anything other than the Siberian. A dog can be called "Houndy" if it looks to be part German Shorthaired Pointer or Greyhound. My Alaskans are typically a mix of both, but tend toward the hound or "screaming weasel" side. "Nice dogs" I said. "Are you selling any?"

"You like them?" Shawn asked, obviously pleased. "They're out of Champaign stock originally."

"They're nice—I hear Matt Rayburn bought some of his dogs from your kennel."

He grinned. "Matt always said it made the difference in his kennel."

"I bet." I stopped in front of a beautiful gray and white bitch. "Can I pet her?" Shawn nodded. The little dog was about 40 pounds and had the build I was looking for. She looked up at me with a soulful expression; her deep brown eyes accentuated by the gray mask. I knelt down. "Hi, little one, what's your name?" She hopped all over me and gave me rapid-fire kisses.

"You have a good eye," he commented. "Her name is Shelly. She's running on my eight-dog team."

"She's beautiful," I said, and I meant it.

"She's getting up in years. She'll be turning five this spring."

I nodded. Sprint dogs lose their speed as they grow older. Although the dog was not that old, a sprint dog loses its competitiveness when it matures. Most Alaskan Huskies live over ten years old; some as high as fifteen. At five, she'd be good competitively for another couple of years. "What's she out of?" I asked.

"Oh, she'll make an exceptional brood bitch," he said. "She's linebred Saunderson. I've got her sister, so I don't need her for the lines. I was going to offer her to Matt, but if you're interested…"

"How much?"

"A thousand."

I whistled through my teeth. "Awfully high buck."

"You get what you pay for."

I nodded but said nothing. I went back to looking at her and mentally calculating how many weeks of eating nothing but hotdogs and beans would buy me.

"By the way, I don't see Matt's truck around here," Shawn said. "I had a couple of Alaskans Matt said he wanted to buy…" He paused and stared at me. "What's wrong?"

I must have shown my dismay. "You don't know? Nobody told you?"

"Know what? Told me what?"

"Matt's dead. Somebody killed him in Frisco."

I watched Shawn's reaction carefully. The blood seemed to drain from his face. He caught his breath and ran a hand through his blonde hair. "Whoa! You had me going for a second—you're joking right?"

I sighed. "I wish I were," I said. "Look, I'm sorry. I shouldn't have been the one to tell you. Do you want to sit down?"

"Yeah, I do," he said. Shawn walked around to the back of his dog box, which opened to a storage area and sat there. "Wow! That is something. I just spoke to Matt two Fridays ago." He opened a metal thermos and poured some hot coffee in a cup.

"Really?" I said.

"Yeah." Shawn took a sip of coffee. "Where's my manners?" he said. "Would you like a cup? I have Styrofoam cups here."

"No, thanks," I said. "What did you talk about?"

Shawn shrugged. "It was nothing really. Matt just asked me about some of my Alaskan Huskies. I was pretty aware of what type he was looking for, so I made recommendations."

"What type?"

"Like Shelly—you know, the more husky looking dogs. Matt really seemed to like them."

"That's odd," I mused. "Matt bought dogs from Heikki Seppanen too."

"Really?" Shawn leaned forward. "Pointer crosses? They'd be houndy. Well, that's unusual. You don't go buying huskies and pointers. Not unless you have a big operation and are planning a breeding program."

"Matt didn't have either," I said. "Sure, he had a litter here or there, but not what it would take to have a real winning team."

"Matt didn't strike me as the type to experiment."

"Me neither." I paused. "Can I see those huskies?"

"Sure," he said. "I've got two on the other side."

We walked around the truck. A larger Alaskan Husky with black fur, a mask, and blue eyes considered us thoughtfully. "That's Thunder," he said and then pointed to a red and white female beside him, reminiscent of Tasha. "That's Fox."

"How do they do on your team?" I asked.

"Now, that's the strange thing—I've got faster dogs for sale, like Shelly," he said. "But Matt usually was very much set in a certain type."

"Did Matt say anything unusual about what he wanted the dogs for?"

Shawn shook his head. "Nothing seemed out of the ordinary, if that's what you mean."

I paused and considered Thunder and Fox and then shook my head. "I don't know, they're nice looking dogs, to be sure, if a little husky. I like a little more leg and a bit more angulation."

"My thoughts exactly," Shawn said. "They run good. Fox made my six-dog team this year."

I knelt down and gently called Fox to me. The red bitch hesitated for a moment and started to cautiously approach me. I offered my hand slowly, but she skittered away. "A little shy," I commented. I turned and looked up at him. Out of the corner of my eye, I could see Fox's ears prick and she cautiously approached. I pretended not to notice.

"That didn't seem to bother Matt," Shawn shrugged. "Now, I can see it would bother you, so I wouldn't offer her to you. You're also looking for a different body—something more houndy."

"Right," I said, as I felt a curious nose touch my forearm. I stayed perfectly still, letting the timid husky explore me. "Did you raise her?"

Shawn shook his head. "Nah, she came from Tim Jackson's kennel. Tim runs a big operation and a few years back, he lost his handler. So, he had a lot of pups and almost no socialization. That's why she's so skittish. Tim has handlers now who play with and train all the pups, but that one summer, he was doing everything he could just to keep a clean and well-fed kennel. All the pups came out okay—just some of the shy ones followed their natural tendencies, like Fox here."

I nodded. "It's too bad. If you just miss that window for socialization, it's gone."

"Yeah, it is," Shawn admitted. "But, Fox is happy enough. She loves to run in harness with the other huskies. She's lead potential, even—I've had her up front a few times and she really turned on."

I stood up and Fox bolted, zipping underneath the truck. Wary eyes considered me again. "Well, thanks," I said. I turned to Fox. "Sorry, Sweetheart, didn't mean to startle you."

"No problem," Shawn said. He held out his hand. "It's good to finally meet you. Bruce Swenson used to complain about you every time he came back from Colorado."

I laughed. "Oh, *that's* where you heard about me. Poor Bruce, he always got so sick from the high altitude he'd swear he'd never come back to Colorado. Yet, there he was back in Granby every year. I swear, you could set your clock by it. What's been happening with the old cuss?"

"Bruce got out of dogs last spring. Decided he had enough."

We talked for a long while until I checked my watch and realized that I had wasted an hour at his truck. "Look, got to go take care of dogs," I said. I paused for a moment. "One more thing, if you don't mind me asking."

"Sure," said Shawn.

"What do you get for dogs like Thunder and Fox?"

"Thunder is a steady wheel dog, but he's almost five. I'm asking six hundred. Fox..." He paused and thought about her. "One thousand even. She's a lead prospect, you know."

"Are those the prices you'd offer to Matt?"

"Yeah," he said. "Why, are you interested?"

I shook my head. "I was just curious."

I returned to my truck to find Amy collapsed on the front seat. All the dogs were back in their boxes looking out at me expectantly. I pounded on the glass, startling her. She stuck out her tongue and closed her eyes again.

"Hey, Sleepy-head, we have a race to run." I opened the door. Amy stirred slightly and opened one eye.

"You have a race to run," Amy corrected. "The dogs were all dropped and they all drank water. Where have you been?"

"Talking to Shawn Bailey."

"Who?"

"A guy who sold some dogs to Matt."

Amy sat up. "Really? What did you find out?"

"That Matt liked different types of dogs."

"And we care about this because?"

"Because it doesn't make sense," I said. "To have a competitive sprint team, you have to have matched dogs. Now, I liked a lot of Matt's dogs that I've seen on his team. They're built like mine: houndy. The dogs Shawn says he was interested in were husky. What's more, Lee says Matt bought a few dogs from Heikke Seppanen, who ran pointers. Those are hounds."

"Maybe he was buying them to sell them," Amy suggested.

"That would coincide with the large number of Alaskans cycling through his kennel," I agreed. "But who would want husky-built dogs?"

Amy shrugged. "Is there any application for them?"

"Distance maybe," I said. "Recreation or freight racing. Maybe if Gina had those names…"

Amy snapped her fingers. "That reminds me! Gina called back with the names." She pulled out a notepad and flipped through. "She said that some of the people paid cash, but she had the names of a couple of mushers who paid by check."

"Who?"

"Sam Horton."

"Already knew that."

"And a Jesse and Tami Brown."

I paused. "Who?"

Chapter Sixteen

"Jesse and Tami…"

"I've never heard of them," I said.

"Really?" Amy mused. "Could they be new?"

"You'd think I would have heard of them," I sighed. I looked over. The three-dog teams were coming back. We had time. "Let's leave the dogs in their boxes for the time being. If it gets too hot, we'll drop them, but I don't need them to get stressed out. I'll do some more snooping around and see if I can find out more about Jesse and Tami Brown. With over a hundred teams, you'd think that someone knows them."

~ * ~

I returned to Lee Johnson's truck. Lee was gone, but Sherri was there. I hesitated as I watched her ladle warm broth to the awaiting huskies. She looked up, saw me, and stiffened. She turned her head quickly and with rapid movements that belied the Carhartts, she scurried to the cargo box.

I stepped behind her. "Hi, Sherri," I said.

She stiffened again and slowly turned around. "Look," she said. "I really don't have time to talk I'm eleventh out in four-dog."

"Listen, Sherri, I'm sorry," I said. "You know why I had to ask."

"No, I don't," she said, pushing the bucket and ladle into the cargo box. She pulled out several black X-back harnesses that hung on a hook and looped them over one of the truck mirrors. "All I know is that you poked your nose where it has no right to be."

"Fair enough," I said. "I'm looking for a dog."

"We have none for sale."

"It's a couple of Matt's dogs that Lee sold him: Blue and Shep. Gina sold them."

Sherri turned around. Her blue eyes were hard. "Is this part of your 'investigation?'"

"It might be," I said.

"Then, I want no part of it."

"Have you ever heard of Jesse and Tami Brown?"

A silence ensued. I waited. She pulled out the lines for the next class. I still waited. She walked around and began harnessing dogs. I followed her.

She looked up. "They're distance mushers," she said finally. "Now, go away."

"Thank you," I said.

~ * ~

The four-dog teams went out and even before the last four-dog team left the starting line, frontrunners like Sherri Johnson were returning to the staging areas. I helped bring Sherri's team back to her truck and returned to my own truck to prepare my dogs for the eight-dog class. Six-dog would be out next. If Sam Horton needed my help, he would most likely come and get either Amy or me.

Amy and I opened boxes and unloaded dogs. Sam and Mocha shook themselves and stretched sleepily. They were warm and comfortable in the box. Even in the warm sunshine, the air was crisp. Sam twirled once on the stakeout before curling his big paws around my calf and grasping me. He tugged me towards him.

I laughed and obliged him. He hopped onto his back legs and peered intently into my eyes. His yellow-brown eyes searched my soul. I rubbed his head and petted the luxurious wolf-gray fur. "You gonna run for me today, Big Guy?" I crooned. A quick pink tongue darted out and he quickly planted a kiss on my lips. He pushed off as Mocha, who was staked out right beside him, snarled in jealousy. "Hey! Hey! Enough of that!" I snapped. Mocha's ears laid back and he glanced at Sam accusatorily.

"Hey, do you mind?" Amy asked from the other side. "We still have to get out Lightning and Skye."

"Okay." I gave Mocha a quick pat and walked over to the other side to help her.

~ * ~

Eight-dog started late at two o'clock. The sun was dipping behind the mountains that ringed Granby's narrow valley, when Amy and I hooked up the last of the team. The sun had made the parking lot slush and the runners scraped against dirt. In an hour or so, the slush would turn to lumpy ice. It wouldn't be fun going across that either.

Being fifth in line meant I didn't have much time after the first eight-dog team cleared the starting chute—a mere four minutes. If you've ever had the chance to hook up a large sled team, you know it isn't much time. Yukon, Lightning, Dancer, and Jasmine were all pounding the lines and barking wildly. Skye stood stoically placid, but I caught her make a small whine in excitement. Spice too, was remarkably calm. Mocha watched me with those strange blue eyes from his dark brown face. Sam was too busy pounding the line. I waved at Amy to lead us to the line.

I could see Shawn Bailey's big frame and checkered hat ahead. By his placement in line, I knew he drew third. Liz Smith, running her own Samoyeds and some she borrowed from Ken Mills was in fourth place. This was shaping up to be a very interesting race.

Liz glanced back at me and winked. She turned to Amy and said something, but there was no way I could hear it above the racket at the starting line. Hell, an atomic bomb could detonate in front of us, and we wouldn't hear it. Go to a race—you'll see what I mean.

Shawn's team was in the chute. I glanced back to see if I could pick out Lee behind us. I couldn't. Poor Lee—he must have gotten stuck with some high number. It was lucky for me—if the teams before Lee were lousy at letting other teams pass, they'd slow him down. All I had was four teams between me and an open course—assuming I could pass Shawn.

We moved up again as Shawn's team exploded from the chute. I watched breathlessly as his Alaskans charged out of the chute like Greyhounds. Liz's white dogs made an interesting contrast to those long, lean hounds. I watched her fluffy dogs lope out of the chute at a not-so-blistering pace.

My team practically dragged Amy into the chute. Amy handed Sam's and Mocha's neckline to a course worker to hold my two lead dogs. She ran back to me.

"Thirty seconds," the timer said.

"Liz wished you a good run," Amy said, practically shouting over Jasmine's and Lightning's screams. "She says she'll let you pass clean."

I nodded.

"Fifteen seconds," the timer shouted.

"Liz said 'Get Shawn Bailey,'" Amy grinned.

"I'll try my best."

"Ten, nine, eight…"

"Get out of here!" I good-naturedly slapped her on the shoulder.

"Four, three, two, one, go!"

The dogs charged from the chute, energized with the new trail. I hung on, hoping they looked as crisp as Shawn's dogs. We ran across the first flats and took the hill at full speed. As jaded as I am about my own team, even I had to admit they looked good. A mile into the race, we caught up to Liz's team.

Liz jumped off the runners and hooked down. She grasped her two lead Samoyeds and pulled the team over.

"You don't have to do that!" I shouted.

"Yes, I do!" Liz shouted back. "Give you a clean run—go get Bailey!"

"Thanks!" I waved as we passed the fluffy white team by. The dogs, energized by the pass, flew up the second hill. As we crested the hill, I could see two teams, maybe a mile out or more. "Go get them!" I shouted to Sam and Mocha. The lead dogs, filled with the desire to chase, were willing to charge down the hill full speed. I held them back, dragging my foot. Dogs can seriously injure themselves going downhill and on a fast track like Granby, it's imperative to play it safe. Once the team bottomed out on the hill, I let them fly.

Three miles into the course, I passed a musher, whose name I didn't know, but who had slower Alaskans. The pass was clean: I wave him my thanks and urged my dogs on. For a while, he drafted me—dogs will often pick up speed by following a faster team. It's a great way to improve your time. After a few minutes, his dogs grew slower and my team pulled away.

Somewhere on the hill into the fifth mile, I first caught sight of Shawn Bailey. His team had slowed considerably: they were trotting instead of loping. Sometime during the race, Shawn had stripped off the hat and black Carhartts and was down to jeans and a flannel shirt with a light windbreaker. Shawn's face was red as he puffed mightily and pedaled.

"You okay?" I shouted as we flew by his team.

"Goddamn altitude!" Shawn swore. "Come on, guys, get up!"

Shawn's dogs picked up the pace; some actually began loping after my team passed him by. Neither Shawn nor I counted on the altitude to wreck his run. Minnesota is about as close to sea level as you can get and Granby sits at 8200 feet. Of course, altitude would be a factor at nearly a mile and a half above sea level. We passed a pure-bred Siberian team and then raced for the finish line.

Amy was waiting at the finish and grasped my leaders' necklines as they came in. "They look great," Amy shouted to me as she led them towards the truck. I nodded in agreement. They were better today than I had seen at Frisco. Only Lee could touch us in eight-dog.

Amy led the Alaskans back to the truck. It was only two forty and I still had some investigations to do before the evening. We quickly watered and snacked the Alaskans. I let them stand outside until about three o'clock and then started putting them up.

"What's the hurry?" Amy asked as she put Jasmine in one of the boxes.

"I've got some investigating to do before tonight," I said. "Pack up the dogs, we're leaving."

"Aren't we going back to Granby?" Amy asked as she took Skye's harness off and gave the little Alaskan a quick rubdown.

"Nope," I said.

"Is this about Jesse and Tami Brown and those dogs?" Amy asked.

"Yeah, Gina sold Matt's Alaskans to the Browns in Nederland."

"Oh great!" Amy groaned. "Steph, you've got to be kidding! Nederland is two hours away."

"Don't worry, we're not going that far," I assured her. "We're just going to Frazer."

"Frazer?"

"Yeah, Jesse Brown is a mid-distance musher. There's a mid-distance race over on Corona Pass to the trestle—I'd bet anything Jesse is entered."

We finished putting up the Alaskans and equipment. I motioned Amy to get in the truck.

"Aren't you going to check your placement?" she asked incredulously.

"They'll have the placements at the banquet—I'll check there. I want to catch Jesse before he leaves the race." I gave the Dodge a few quick shots of fuel and turned the ignition. The engine roared to life.

"Lucky us," Amy grumbled as she climbed in and fastened her seat belt. "I'm hungry."

"Look, we'll have plenty of time to catch dinner at Little Joe's." I pulled out of the parking lot and paused to look both directions on Highway 40. "Besides, it might give us another clue as to who killed Matt."

At that suggestion, Amy brightened considerably. "Do you think the murderer might have bought one of Matt's Alaskans?"

"I don't know," I shrugged. "The affair thing doesn't seem to be netting any leads."

"Well, maybe you aren't looking at the obvious."

I glanced at Amy. "What do you mean?"

"Well, if Matt were *my* husband, I'd kill him."

I chuckled. "Yeah, you would."

"No—think about it: Gina gets squat if she divorces the bum…"

"Matt didn't have much of a life insurance policy."

"That you know of."

"Ok, you have a point."

"And Gina gets rid of the dogs…"

"Who would kill to get rid of dogs?" I asked.

"Any sane human on the face of the planet," Amy remarked drolly.

I chuckled. "Gina's still going to have to work."

"Minor inconvenience. I bet the house is paid for."

"Major inconvenience," I remarked. "You don't know Gina. Anyway, I doubt Gina could have done it. She doesn't strike me as the type physically capable of killing Matt."

"Good point," Amy said. "Gina could have had a lover do it."

"Right," I said. "Who?"

"I don't know," Amy groused. "It's better than the dog theory."

"Why?"

"Because people kill for love all the time."

"People kill for money more often," I said. We now slowed as we drove through Frazer. The one of two stoplights turned red. I stopped the truck.

"Why do you think the murderer might have bought one of Matt's Alaskans? I mean, we know the murderer would steal one—like he stole Tasha from you."

"And why buy the Alaskan now, when he could have bought the dog from Matt?" I mused.

"Maybe Matt didn't want to sell the Alaskan."

"Hard to believe," I smirked. "For the right price, Matt would've sold his mother. Matt was dog broker central." The light turned green. We drove on towards Winter Park.

Corona Pass is due east of Winter Park. The pass road is poorly marked and you'll miss it if you drive out of Winter Park. Corona Pass is also called Rollins Pass, depending on which side of the pass you're on, heads east towards Nederland and Boulder. It gets its name Rollins Pass from Rollinsville to the east. Eighteen miles up, you can hear the trains in the Moffat tunnel. I've run dogs to just below the old unused railroad trestle. At 11,671 feet, you feel like you are on the top of the world. Guaranteed. Just you, ten of your closest friends, and a billion snowmobilers. You can see all of Grand County below.

As you can surmise, this is a popular place for snowmobilers. Although this is National Forest, guided snowmobile tours run up and down the pass road in the winter. In the summer, Corona Pass is a mild jeep road. These old pass roads always amaze me. At one time, these jeep trails were the only way to traverse the mountains. People back then put up with a lot more and without much complaint, because, quite frankly, they didn't know any better. I know better and put my Dodge into four-wheel low as I climbed up the plowed section.

The pass road goes up a ways before it widens into a parking area, ringed with tall lodge pole pines. To my surprise, about 15 dog trucks filled the parking area. Some actually had to park alongside the lower portion of the pass road. I slowed and parked behind the last dog truck—a white Chevrolet half ton.

"Wow, I didn't know mid-distance was so popular," Amy commented.

"Neither did I." I surveyed the trucks. It was relatively quiet: I could hear a few dogs barking, but it was nowhere near the din I expected in a race paddock. "The teams must still be out. I may be able to catch Jesse and ask him a few questions when he comes in."

"I'll stay here," Amy said.

"Chicken," I replied, but I couldn't blame her. It was late afternoon and the sun was dipping behind the mountains. The wind had picked up too, blowing the dusting of snow off the tops of the trees. I opened the door. Far off in the distance, I could hear a train wail.

As if on cue, a husky took up the song and howled mournfully. I stepped out and listened to the song as other huskies took up the howl. Their voices blended with the sound of the wind in the trees. I closed my eyes and listened. In the dimming light, their voices seemed surreal.

I walked towards the front trucks, listening to the snow crunch under every step. Although it had been as warm as the Sports Park, the trees had provided some shelter against the relentless sun. A table was set up behind a '78 green GMC truck near the starting line. A woman sat on the tailgate, swinging her legs in boredom. Her heavy white Sorrel snowcats seemed to propel her legs on their own, their very weight causing her legs to swing back and forth like a strange perpetual motion machine. She wore a tan parka, overstuffed with down. A brown knit cap with white huskies or Samoyeds running across it sat atop short brown hair. The parka was unzipped, revealing brown polar fleece and black Gore-Tex underneath. She had long ago tossed the mittens aside. Even in the shade, I knew she was sweating.

"You're a little late—the ten dog teams are already coming back," she said without preamble.

"That's okay—I'm not looking to run. I'm a sprint musher," I said. "I thought I'd come over from the Sports Park."

She grinned. "Interested in going mid-distance?"

I paused and looked around. "You know, I haven't really thought about it," I admitted. "How many miles make up a mid-distance race?"

She laughed. "It depends. Most of the races here in Colorado are twenty to thirty miles a day for two days. We don't have many usable trails, so we take what we can get. In Montana, Wyoming, and Idaho, they can get longer distances. The Race to the Sky, for example, is three hundred and thirty miles. The Jackson race, the Stage Stop, is over five hundred miles in Wyoming."

"How many dogs?" I asked. "Ten?"

"In the Stage Stop or Montana—oh, no! They have fourteen or sixteen dogs in those."

"What about this race?"

"We have a ten dog class and a six dog class. Both go the same mileage."

"Wow—six dogs going twenty or thirty miles a day?"

"What's so odd?" she asked. "Lots of races run six dogs forty or fifty miles in a day." She paused. "By the way, I'm Sue McElhenney." She extended her hand.

"I'm Stephanie Keyes," I said, shaking her hand. Her shake was firm. "It's good to meet you."

"Anyone we can steal from the sprint side," Sue said. "You see, there's some interest, but not enough for a real purse or points. We have a good time."

"Seems like," I said.

"Take a look around—you'll find we're a much more laid back group." Sue leaned forward conspiratorially. "We're less stuck up than the sprint crowd."

"That's good to know," I said. "By the way, a friend of mine recommended I talk to a distance musher about some dogs. I was wondering if he was here."

"Who?"

"Jesse Brown."

"Jesse? Yeah, he's here. Both he and Tami are out on the trail."

"They're both running ten dog?" I sounded surprised.

"No, Tami is running six, so she'll still be out a little while. Jesse should be back any time now." She motioned at the row of trucks parked alongside the GMC. "The red Ford is Jesse's. You might want to keep an eye on it to see when he comes back."

At that moment, two teams came into view. Sue pulled a small pair of Bushnell binoculars out of her parka and peered out. "Speaking of which, that's Jesse, and the other team is, Rick Howe's."

Sue jumped up and motioned me to come with her. She ran to the finish line. "Go, Jesse! Go!" Sue shouted. The other handlers, present at the finish line, cheered, whistled, and clapped, some for Jesse, some for Rick.

"Which is Jesse?" I asked, watching the teams in admiration as they sprinted to the end.

"He's in the red parka." Sue paused. "Come on, Jesse!"

The dogs, energized by the sheering and the competition, flew into a lope. Rick Howe, who wore a blue parka, took out a cross-country ski pole and began poling.

"Can he do that?" I asked, startled.

Sue didn't respond or didn't hear me. Jesse pedaled hard, but it became clear Rick's dogs were slightly faster. Rick's team crossed the finish line first, amid cheers. A woman at the finish line, presumably Rick's handler, grasped the leader's necklines and led the team to a white one ton Dodge nearby.

Jesse's leaders crossed the finish line and Sue ran over and grasped the necklines. Sue brought the team to his truck.

"Thanks, Sue!" Jesse was saying as I approached.

"How'd they run?" Sue asked.

Jesse pounded the snowhook into the ground and stepped off the runners. That was the first time I got a good look at him. Jesse was a Native American or at least part Native American. I thought maybe Cherokee or Blackfoot, but later learned he was Athabascan. Jesse's skin was tanned and he wore his dark hair long and tied back in a ponytail. He looked in his late twenties or early thirties. Jesse's dark brown eyes seemed to take in everything they saw. He met my gaze.

"They ran really well," Jesse said, turning to face Sue. "The new dog, though, I don't know. I'm not sure if he'll fit in."

I looked down at the dogs. They were bigger Alaskan Huskies than I was used to. The point dog seemed familiar though. (Point dogs are those dogs behind the lead dogs). I stared at the brown and black Alaskan Husky. "Shep?" I asked. "Shep!"

Shep looked up and crooned at the sound of his name. I resisted petting him, knowing well Shep was working while still in harness. I stared at the beautiful lead dog, wishing Shep were in my team and not Jesse's.

"You know Shep?" Jesse asked.

"Yeah, that's Matt's old lead dog, Shep," I said. "Why do you have him in point? Shep's a dynamite lead."

Jesse shook his head. "Shep's a trail lead," he said. "This course requires a command lead. I had him in lead until we hit the crossroads. Then, Shep became confused and I had to hook down." Jesse paused and studied me. "I'm afraid we haven't met."

Before Sue could reply, I spoke up. "I'm Stephanie Keyes—I'm a sprint musher."

"Ah, the famous Stephanie Keyes," Jesse said in a tone that I wasn't sure if he was serious, joking, or being sarcastic. Jesse stepped off his sled, began picking up each foot on the wheel dogs, and examined them. "I've heard quite a bit about you."

"Hopefully good."

He didn't reply. "So, what brings you to the distance world? Interested in running longer than fifteen minutes? In these smaller races, there isn't much of a purse and we don't compete for ISDRA points."

"Shep brought me here," I said. "I was told you bought some dogs from Matt's widow, Gina."

"Yeah, I did," Jesse sighed. "Only now I wished I didn't. They aren't as good as they were touted to be."

"Really?" I said. "I always thought they were good."

"Take Shep," Jesse said as he opened up the cargo box and pulled out a bucket of baited water. He took out some brightly colored plastic dog bowls and handed them to me. "Could you give each of them a bowl? They need water."

"Sure," I said. I started distributing the bowls. "What about Shep?"

"He was necklining all the way." Necklining—a musher's term for lagging behind and not pulling.

Sure, he was, I thought. *He's only been running eight miles at a time.* "Typical sprint Alaskan," I said lightly as I laid down the last of the bowls. "They're only good for so much."

Jesse snorted. "I'll say." He walked around the team, pouring what looked like meat-baited water in each of the bowls. The dogs quickly slurped it down.

"So, how long have you been in mid-distance?" I asked.

"This is my second year mushing," he said. "You know, Gina said these Alaskans were trained twenty miles a day."

"Really?" I said. "I doubt Shep has ever seen over ten a day."

Jesse nodded. "That's what I thought." He paused and studied me for a moment. "Look, I don't know you well, but you have a reputation in the sprint community that even us mid-distance drivers have heard about. I know you take good care of your dogs and you don't dump them. I bought three Alaskan Huskies from Gina, and this past week, I haven't been too impressed. They may be more trouble than they're worth. I'll offer them to you at the same price as Gina sold them to me."

"Which Alaskans did you get?" I asked, my heart pounding in my ears. I could scarcely believe what I'd heard.

"You already know Shep. I bought Junior and Cindy as well."

I shook my head. "I don't know those dogs."

"Hang on a moment," Jesse said, pulling out a box of large dog biscuits from the cargo area. He tossed each dog a biscuit. Jesse put the box back in the cargo area and walked around and opened up one box. A red houndy-looking dog of about 40 pounds came out. She had flop ears and white legs with red freckles. Except for the thicker coat and the typical husky dots over the eyes, I would have thought she was a small Shorthair Pointer. "This is Cindy," he said. "Her brother, Junior, looks just like her."

"Scandinavian Hounds," I said. That's the nickname for German Shorthaired Pointer crossed with Alaskan Husky.

Jesse nodded. "They're fast—but trying to get them to slow down to twelve miles an hour is a chore. One I'm really not sure I'm up to."

"How much did you pay?"

"A thousand for the lot." I must have gasped because Jesse grinned. "I thought that was low too, but in retrospect, I should've spent the money on a Stage Stop dog."

I nodded. "It's a fair price. I'll take them." I paused. "There was another lead dog—a gray and white husky named Blue—that ran with Shep. Do you know what happened to him?"

Jesse shook his head. "I didn't see the dog, but Matt's wife said she had already sold some."

"You know to whom?"

Jesse shook his head. "No." He paused. "But I know someone who might know."

"Who?"

"Alan Freeman—he told me about Matt's dogs."

Chapter Seventeen

"Why would Alan care about Matt's dogs?" I started the truck and waved at Jesse before pulling the truck around and starting back towards Frazer. Jesse and I had come to an agreement on price. I put a $500 check down as earnest money on the Alaskan Huskies in exchange for a promissory note. Jesse lived near Nederland—a couple of hours drive away from Pine Junction. I would be able to pick up the dogs after the race and pay him then.

"I don't know," remarked Amy. "Maybe Alan is interested in helping Gina out."

I shook my head. "Gina isn't interested in mushing."

"Gina isn't interested in mushing, but maybe Gina is interested in mush*ers*," Amy said pointedly. "Maybe Gina thought it was time for a little payback."

"Hmmm, maybe she did. Gina *did* know Matt was fooling around on her."

"What's good for the goose…"

"Is good until the goose gets cooked," I remarked dryly. "You might have something there."

"But would Gina have given us Alan's name if he had bought dogs?"

"Alan didn't buy dogs," I said. "He's a Siberian musher, remember? Matt's dogs are Alaskans, like mine. They're mixed breeds."

"So, Gina wasn't technically omitting anything."

"Actually, if Gina's having an affair with Alan, she is," I said. "But, I just don't know. Gina doesn't seem interested in mushers."

"I swear, Steph, you've got your head in the sand. Alan is a hunk."

"Alan is a slimeball. Alan's got Vicki around his finger, he's probably boffing Gina, and he puts some moves on me. Ick." I stuck my tongue out for emphasis.

"I'd consider him."

"You have no standards."

"I do too."

"What? A pulse?" I snickered. "Or is that optional?"

"Whatever," Amy said, crossing her arms.

"Okay, Gina may or may not be having an affair with Alan," I continued. "If she is, then we know her connection with Alan and why Alan is helping her place dogs."

"Jesse is an Alaskan driver, right? What is Alan's connection with Jesse?" Amy asked.

"Seems about a year ago Alan was running distance with his Siberians," I said. "Jesse helped Alan get started with distance but Alan decided to go back into sprints. That's why the ISDRA points were meaningless to Alan—Alan let his ISDRA membership drop this year."

"Okay, so Alan mentioned Matt's dogs to Jesse and Jesse talked to Gina."

"Right."

"Then, how did Gina meet Alan?"

We drove over the railroad tracks and I turned back onto the highway towards Granby. "A very good question," I said. "Alan said that he barely knew Matt. I accepted it because Alan is a Siberian driver and Matt's an Alaskan driver."

"Alan could be lying."

"He could, but why? And what purpose would Alan have to deal with Matt?"

"Alaskans and Siberians are a bad mix," Amy said.

"Huh?" I glanced at her.

"Remember what you said to me about Alan when I met him the first time? You told me that Alaskans and Siberians don't mix."

"Yeah, it's bad blood."

"So, how did Gina meet Alan? How did Alan know that Matt's Alaskans were for sale?"

I didn't have an answer. We were approaching the motel where we were staying and I slowed the truck and pulled into the turn lane. "There's still one dog missing," I said. "I found Shep and two Scandinavian Hounds with Jesse. Jesse is selling them to me. But neither Sam nor Jesse have seen Blue."

"So, who has Blue? The murderer?" Amy asked.

"Maybe," I said. "Whoever it is, I'd bet money he's got Tasha too."

We arrived at the Silver Spruce motel. Sam Horton had parked his truck towards the back of the parking lot. Sam had dropped his dogs and, from the sound of the barking, was feeding them. I parked next to him, leaving enough room to provide a safety zone between my dogs and his, so I could drop mine.

"One person who might be able to shed some light on this might be Sam," I said while shutting down the engine. I got out. "Drop the dogs for me, could you?" I closed the door before Amy could reply. "Hey Sam!" I waved and shouted.

Sam looked up from ladling a meat and kibble mixture into a dog's bowl. "Hiya, Steph. What's up?"

"How did you find out Gina was selling the dogs?"

"Gina called me, why?"

"Did you tell anyone Gina was selling them?"

Sam scratched his head. Consternation creased his large features. "No, I don't think so. Why?"

"I spoke with a distance musher who bought a few Alaskans from Gina. He told me Alan Freeman told him about the dogs."

"That's odd," Sam mused. "I didn't think Matt and Alan were friends. How would Gina know to call Alan?" Sam put down the bucket and ladle. "Are you sure it was Alan?"

"That's what the distance musher said."

Sam chewed his lip thoughtfully. "Why would Alan even be interested in the Alaskans? Alan runs Siberians."

"What about Gina?" I pressed. "Why does Gina know Alan well enough to call him?"

Sam's expression grew dark. "So, that's who it was. Matt knew that bitch was screwing around on him. I ought to…"

I grasped his massive arm. "No, don't," I said. "This is all conjecture. I've got to find out more."

"We've got to tell the police."

"Yes we do, as soon as I have something more substantial. Right now, I can't go to them with hunches."

Sam nodded and relaxed. "You're right, Steph."

"Look Sam, whoever killed Matt has had it in for me. I nearly became the cop's number one suspect. Thank God there was a witness." I paused. "Sam, can you think of anything that might tie Alan to Matt besides Gina?

"Matt was thinking of divorcing her. He told me Gina hadn't been faithful."

"Interesting," I mused. "Gina wasn't the only one who was

fooling around."

"Well, Matt wasn't getting any," Sam smirked. "Gina decided to hold out until he got rid of the dogs."

"No way," I said. "You're kidding, aren't you?"

Sam shook his head. "Matt mentioned it on more than one occasion. I told Matt he ought to just divorce the bitch—I think Matt was going to before he got murdered."

I nodded. "So, Gina could be a real suspect, only…"

"Only what?"

"Only Gina isn't strong enough to kill him," I remarked, thinking about the snowhook. "That was pretty bloody— remember? Gina's so small and dainty; I don't think she'd able to do the extent of damage we saw."

"What about Alan, then?"

I shrugged. "I don't know."

~ * ~

Little Joe's is a pizzeria not far from the Silver Spruce. Although technically this was a "banquet," it was by far the most informal one I've seen. Little Joe's was a drafty place with two hot wood stoves, rough pine walls, and a variety of mounted animal heads. There was a beautiful bull elk with a five by six rack, a buffalo head, two mountain goat heads, one bighorn sheep ram, several bucks with assorted racks, and a number of pelts. I recognized coyote, fox, bobcat, lynx, mountain lion, and even a black bear. We didn't have a separate room from the patrons, so Amy and I took the red booth with a red and white checked tablecloth underneath the elk's head.

I looked around the pizza parlor, looking for Alan Freeman. I saw Lee and Sherri Johnson at one table talking to Shawn Bailey and Cindy and Joe Travis. Liz Smith was sitting in a booth with Vicki Thompson and Paul Jorgenson. Other mushers sat in booths, talking about the day's race, the standings, and the teams' performances. As I scanned the room, Shawn Bailey caught my eye and motioned for me to come over. Leaving my order with Amy, I walked to their table.

"Join us," Shawn said waving his hand at the empty chair next to him.

"I'd love to, but my handler is alone," I said as my gaze fell on Sherri and her expression. If it were up to her, I could see she'd rather be in another state.

"Nonsense!" said Lee. "We've got chairs. Please join us."

I waved at Amy and she came over. "We've been invited," I said. Amy took a seat beside me.

Shawn eyed me appraisingly. "I watched your team—they look really hot."

"Thank you," I said. I craned my neck to look for the scoreboard—it was nowhere in sight. "I bet I'm going to have quite a time catching up with Lee tomorrow."

Lee snorted and Shawn stared. "You're kidding me, right?" Shawn said.

"No, I'm not." My gaze went from one to the other. "Did I say something funny?"

"You're in first place," Cindy said quietly.

"No, you're kidding me, right?" I repeated, stupidly. The stares told me she wasn't. "Look, I had to leave after the run; I didn't catch my time…"

"Blow us all out of eight dog and then split," Shawn laughed. "Typical."

"Why isn't the scoreboard here?" I asked.

Cindy made a face. "The manager didn't want the sign up, seeing as this isn't a private party. But, I did manage to copy all the times down before the club took the board." She pulled out some paper and put her glasses on. "Whose times do you want?"

"Mine?"

"Twenty minutes and twenty one point zero five seconds."

"Wow, we were that fast? That's over twenty-three miles an hour," I said.

"I noticed," Shawn said dryly. "What did Lee come in at?"

"Twenty minutes and thirty five point fifty six seconds," Cindy said.

"What about Alan's team?"

Cindy shuffled through the papers. "That's odd. I don't see his name."

"I don't remember seeing his truck either," Lee offered. "Maybe he didn't come."

"To the Grand County Triple Crown?" Joe remarked. "The Rocky Mountain Sled Dog Club made an extra effort to put together Siberian awards and a Siberian purse. I would think Alan would want to come."

"Maybe something came up?" Lee offered.

"Gee, I hope Alan's all right," Sherri said. "I hope he didn't have an accident or something."

Or something, I thought darkly. The pizza arrived with a waiter and waitress carrying two extra large pizzas with all the toppings, except anchovies. As I bit into a slice with the cheese still bubbling, Lee tapped me on the shoulder. I looked up.

"Isn't that the cop who is investigating Matt's murder?" he asked in a conspiratorial tone.

I scanned the room until my eyes fell on Jack Tallon. He was standing at the entrance, looking around. I almost didn't recognize Jack without the uniform. He could have been just another ski bum, albeit, a little old. Jack's eyes met mine and he smiled.

I glanced back at the group. Lee and Shawn were snickering like schoolboys. Amy had grabbed my arm and gave me a push forward. I shrugged. "My own personal cop," I said lightly as I got up. "Save me some pizza, will you?"

I didn't look back, because I didn't want to see their behavior. "Hello, Stephanie," Jack said. "Nice race."

"You saw it?" I asked.

"Yeah, I was watching the races this afternoon—I wanted to talk to you then, but you left before I had a chance." He paused. "Let's sit down and talk—was I interrupting anything?"

"Just dinner," I said.

"Well, let me order…"

"No, no—they're saving me some."

"It'll be cold, let me buy you some pizza—I haven't eaten either."

I was about to object when he added, "Department's tab."

I acquiesced. "So this is not a social call?"

"I wish it were," Jack said, perhaps noting the disappointment in my voice. "We found the murder weapon."

I held my breath and my heart began to pound in my ears. Did he know? "You did?" I said, trying to keep my voice steady. "What was it?"

"I was hoping you'd be able to tell me." Jack pulled out some photographs and passed them over to me.

"It's a snowhook," I said. "Yeah, that would explain much." I looked up and noticed Jack was staring at me. Did he suspect something? "The blood when I got there—it was all over."

Jack paused and decided to continue instead. "What is a 'snowhook'?"

"Mushers use them to anchor the sled to the snow," I quickly explained. "See those talons? Those grip into the snow when you pound it in."

Jack nodded. "So anyone would have one."

"Matt bought one from Mary the night he was killed," I said. "I was waiting in line at Megan's and saw him purchase a new one."

Jack hesitated. "It did look new and it was sharp."

"You can ask Mary about it, but I think Mary said she had the edges sharpened for ice."

The waitress came and took our order. "Pepperoni fine?" he asked me. I nodded. "A large pepperoni with extra cheese and a coke."

"Ice tea for me," I said. The waitress scribbled down the order and left. A few moments later, the waitress returned with our drinks.

"Look, Steph, I don't think you're being quite honest with me," Jack said.

"I don't understand."

"We've cleared you, and yet I think you're holding back."

I sighed. "It's pretty transparent, isn't it?"

Jack shrugged. "I just know what to look for."

"Let's see," I said. "You found the snowhook in the third trash bin on the Frisco dock, right?"

His expression darkened. "How would you...?"

I took a deep breath. "I threw it there. After the run, Amy and I found a snowhook with dried blood in the back of my truck. Somebody put it there."

"Why didn't you call the police?"

"I was scared," I said. "With all the questions from the night before, I was sure I was a suspect and I was positive Detective Jenkins wouldn't believe me if I walked over to the Frisco Police Station to turn it in."

Jack sighed. "Tampering with evidence."

"I didn't 'tamper' anything. I knew if you guys were on the ball, you'd be searching the trash bins for the murder weapon. I just facilitated the process."

"What else do you know?"

Our pizza came. Between slices of pizza, I recited everything I knew: Matt's old girlfriends, the lack of money, but the nice house, the brokering of Alaskan Huskies, the missing lead dog, Blue, the names on the checks, everything. Jack listened with rapt attention, asking questions where appropriate and furiously scribbling down notes. When I had finished, he sat back and flipped through the notes.

"Wow, that's more than I thought."

"Are you going to arrest me?"

"For what?" Jack looked surprised.

"For throwing away the snowhook?"

Jack shook his head. "I ought to, but not this time." He flipped through the pad, ripped out a sheet, crumpled it up, and stuck it in his pocket. "What they don't know won't hurt them. Listen, what you've told me is that we need to focus more on the widow…"

"I don't think Gina did it," I said. "She isn't strong enough."

"Gina could have had someone else do it," Jack replied. "Maybe this 'Alan Freeman' whom you think she might be having an affair with. A favor for money, sex…that kind of thing."

I thought about it. "I still don't believe it," I said. "Sure, Matt and Gina had serious problems, but Gina just doesn't seem like the type."

"Then, who do you think did it?" Jack's blue eyes stared intently at me.

"Off the record?"

"I can't promise that."

"All right, then. There's something fishy going on with this dog brokering. These dogs are being bought and sold for hundreds of dollars."

"Look, Steph, I told you once and you didn't listen to me…"

"And look at all the good information I gave you."

"Don't go confusing me with the facts," he laughed. I grinned. "Look, I don't want you involved anymore. I'll handle it from here on out. We'll talk to Gina."

~ * ~

The next day, the dogs looked better than the day before. The sky was overcast and the clouds kept the temperature down ten degrees as Amy and I harnessed the dogs. On Sunday, the teams were run in reverse order. Ten-dog went first, followed by my class, eight-dog. My winning time put me in first position today—if I could maintain my lead, I could guarantee a run free from passing. Lee Johnson's team was second, but only by a small margin. My tenuous lead was only fourteen seconds—this had to be a clean run. I'd been in first place before, only to lose it because of a mishap or tangle.

Shawn Bailey, my competitor for the ISDRA 8-dog bronze medal, had placed an abysmal sixth. Everyone had forgotten to take into account the high altitude and its effect on both dogs and mushers. I live at 8500 feet—Granby's altitude felt like home.

I should have been focused on the race, and for the most part, I was. But, occasionally my mind drifted to Matt Rayburn, Tasha, and Blue. Where was Blue? Did the person who bought Blue steal Tasha? Someone had wanted Blue bad enough to pay cash outright. Earlier that morning, I tried visiting different mushers while they dropped dogs to see if they had either Alaskan. It was a long shot and I felt as though I was searching for the proverbial needle in a haystack.

Where did Alan fit into this? Who else had he told about the dogs? Why was Alan not racing today? I finished harnessing Lightning and turned to Amy, who was struggling with Jasmine's harness.

"Can I borrow your cell phone after the race?"

Amy frowned.

"I'm calling Alan," I quickly explained.

That drew a smile. "Had second thoughts?" Amy teased.

"Actually, I have—though not the kind of second thoughts you think."

"What then?"

"Hey, Steph!"

I turned around to see Mary Palmer walking towards me. "Want a little help?"

"I think we can handle it." I grinned. "Thanks anyway."

Mary looked at my sled and tsked. "You know, you're only fourteen seconds in front of Lee—you could use all the help you can get."

"Huh?"

"That boat anchor you call a sled—you going to run that?"

I paused. "What do you mean?"

"How about a state-of-the-art Risdon?" Mary smiled. "A real

deal at only three hundred bucks."

"I thought it was five hundred."

She shrugged. "It can be, if you insist."

"Three hundred is fine," I laughed. "But I said I'd buy it on payday. I just put cash down on three Alaskans."

"Pay me on payday. Hang on—let me get it."

I held my breath—I saw Lee coming in from ten-dog.

"I hope Mary hurries up, we have to hook up soon," I said. "It won't be long."

At that moment Mary appeared, carrying a lightweight sled with a half-basket. She pushed aside my old sled and put the Risdon beside it. "Here—let's get your lines, dog bag, and snowhooks transferred. You don't have much time."

I stood and watched stupidly as Amy and Mary transferred the lines and sled bag to my new sled. *My* new sled. I couldn't believe it. It was maybe seventeen pounds with composite runners and lightweight wood. I tentatively stepped on the runner and tried warping the sled by tugging on the driving bow. It warped perfectly under my hands—this was like driving a race car as opposed to the semi-truck I was used to.

"Well?" Mary asked.

"I don't know what to say," I said after a few moments. "It's perfect!"

"Tell me you'll win and send that Minnesotan packing," she snickered. "You win this, and you've got the Bronze sewn up."

"Maybe," I said. "Thank you—it's almost half the weight of my old sled."

Mary looked around. "Well get hooked up. It's almost time for you to go."

Amy and I hooked up my team and waited. The dogs were screaming loudly when one of the gate stewards waved at me. I pulled the snub line and we lurched forward. The brake screeched against the rough slush that had turned ice, giving me a bumpy ride. Amy nearly fell twice before leading us to the line.

"Thirty seconds," the timer said as we stopped at the line.

Where was Alan? Why hadn't he shown up at the race? Why was he interested in placing Matt's Alaskans? And why had Alan lied about his relationship with Gina? Assuming there *was* a relationship. Amy's suggestions seemed plausible: Matt fooled around on Gina;

Gina fools around on Matt. But how would Gina even know Alan, assuming she did?

"Ten, nine, eight, seven..."

I could feel my muscles tighten as the dogs pounded the line. The first few hundred yards would be a real white-knuckler. I didn't hear the "one" or "Go!" above the barking. Instead, the people holding my sled released it and we flew out of the chute.

We flew down the straight and towards the first turn. "Let's see how this baby handles," I whispered and warped the sled as we hit the first turn. The sled kicked around the turn, taking it effortlessly. "Woo Hoo!" I shouted. The old sled would have never done that.

Freed from the extra weight, the dogs flew. Eight miles felt like four and I never saw Lee Johnson once. We crossed the finish line, beating our time from the previous day.

"Wow!" Amy shouted as she led me to our truck. "The timers couldn't believe it—you shaved a full half minute off from yesterday!"

I grinned. I knew it. I had won the ISDRA bronze medal.

Chapter Eighteen

The exhilaration of winning lasted for maybe an hour. Everyone who knew me—and some who didn't know me—dropped by and congratulated me. I noted, with some disappointment, that Jack Tallon wasn't there. But then, I knew Jack was probably working.

I had hugged Sam and Mocha so many times Sam actually growled at me when I approached him again. I couldn't blame him. It was, after all, only a twenty-minute run. I didn't have steak to give them, but I did have meat and liver and gave them each a large chunk. Then, I gave them more water and a good rubdown before putting them up.

~ * ~

The awards ceremony was a bit anticlimactic. What few mushers were left—namely those who won something—were standing in a giant semi-circle in the middle of the parking lot as Kirk Shaffer, the Race Marshall, read off the winners. A girl stood next to Kirk, holding a clipboard with the final standings. She looked about thirteen years old and was probably Kirk's daughter. She was bundled up in a red down parka with the hood pulled tightly over her head. She hopped from one foot to the other, even though she was wearing a warm snowmobiler's suit and Sorrels. She also held the ribbons and the envelopes with the purse winnings.

Kirk looked at the clipboard and then extracted some envelopes and ribbons.

"Ten-dog, first place, Lee Johnson!" Kirk shouted.

Lee stood beside me and grinned. He walked up, shook Kirk's hand, and came back with a blue rosette ribbon and a check. I clapped and cheered along with the few other mushers. He peeked in the envelope and then showed me. I whistled. It was twelve hundred dollars.

"It's a lot less than last year," he confided. "Last year, before the club instituted a Siberian purse, the check was two thousand dollars."

I nodded.

"Ten-dog, second place, Sam Horton!"

"Yay, Sam!" I cheered as Sam picked up his ribbon and check.

"Ten-dog, third place, Shawn Bailey!"

A few people clapped and then became silent when they realized Shawn wasn't there. "Must have gone home to Minnesota with his tail tucked between his legs," Lee whispered to me.

The awards went to fifth place. I didn't have long before Kirk called my name.

"Eight-dog, first place, Stephanie Keyes!" Kirk said. I walked up with a silly grin on my face and took the check and the blue rosette ribbon. He gripped my hand for a moment and said "And our new eight-dog ISDRA bronze medal winner!"

Everyone started whistling and clapping. I could feel my face flush. I shook his hand and took my place beside Lee.

"Look at the purse," he whispered.

I flipped open the envelope and gasped. Inside was a check for one thousand dollars.

~ * ~

It was dark when Amy and I had finally arrived at my tiny cabin just outside of Pine Junction. The exhilaration had given way to exhaustion, but the dogs came first. We unloaded the Alaskan Huskies and then put them in their kennel runs. I had enough leftover dog food so we fed them and gave them extra baited water.

Amy and I were so tired she called Dominoes Pizza instead of cooking. Dominoes delivers even up here. Well, sort of. We have to go meet the driver about five miles away, but that's ok. It's easier than going into town. While Amy hopped in the little Dodge Colt to pick up the pizza, I made a fire in the woodstove to heat the house and save on propane. The energy costs have hit propane gas too. It's actually more cost effective to use wood now.

I fed Winnie and collapsed on the couch. I spied the blue ribbon and the check on the end where I had dropped them when I came inside. I picked them up. Winnie finished eating and came over for a pet. She pawed me as I examined the ribbon and the check. I would soon receive a bronze medal to go along with the ribbons I'd won this year. I'd probably get a plaque and a trophy too from club standings.

I rubbed Winnie's ear as I looked at my winnings. The check would pay for the dogs I had bought from Jesse Brown. I could use it easily. But, I began to think about Matt again. Matt would be enraged to see me with this placement. I found that sad and petty. Just as petty as when I held Matt up in the Free Zone at Frisco. Was that all I wanted to do—win?

Sam and Mocha were getting older now. Mocha was already four and Sam would be turning four soon. They might be fast enough next year to make the team, but what about the following year? I had Shep now, but he wouldn't be competitive forever. If I found Blue and Tasha—what would I do with them? Heck, I didn't even know how Tasha ran. I'd always found good homes for my older dogs. All of my retired sprint dogs ended up going to slower sprint teams or even a distance team or two.

Anything to stay on top.

Anything?

I knew the answer before I asked the question. Not *anything*. What got me in this sport were the dogs, not the racing. Somehow, I had let my competitive side take control. I stopped enjoying the races for the sake of the dogs. Instead, I had let myself get embroiled in the politics of winning. Matt had gotten caught up in it too. It was easy, if you had a competitive nature.

But, there were others who hadn't gotten caught up in it. Lee hadn't and he was consistently on top. He was always there to help people out and lend a hand, even to me, a competitor. There were others too—Liz, Ray, and Paul. They ran their teams for the enjoyment, even though they knew their purebred dogs could never match the speed of the Alaskan Huskies. Then, there were the distance mushers—these strange renegades who eschewed ISDRA points and high purses.

It gave me a lot to think about. I picked up the phone and dialed Alan Freeman's number. The phone ran four times and his answering machine picked up. I set the handset back in the cradle. No one had seen him at the race. Maybe he was busy with dogs or maybe he was avoiding me. I knew I was getting close.

I rubbed Winnie's ears and let the big Malamute paw me. "Maybe it's time for a change, Winnie," I said to her. I placed the check and the ribbon on the end table and rubbed her neck.

I heard a car drive up. It was Amy with the pizza. I promised myself I would relax tonight. I had Monday off and that meant time to talk to Gina. I knew Gina was holding back now and I knew she held the key to Matt's murder and to Tasha's and Blue disappearance.

~ * ~

"Why didn't you tell me about the affair?" I demanded.

I sat across from Gina's breakfast bar, ignoring the hot liquid she had place in front of me. I was almost out of my seat, leaning forward on the pristine ceramic tiles.

Gina withdrew, pale and shaking. The calico cat sitting in her lap, stood up, ruffled by her owner's sudden movements, and gingerly stepped onto the breakfast bar. She meowed plaintively.

Gina looked down at the cat adoringly. "Hang on, Honey. Momma will get you some nice warm milk." She stood up, walked to the fridge, and poured a bowl of 2% milk. The calico followed her meowing as she slipped the milk into the microwave. Gina smiled. "You know, Matt never let me get a cat."

"Did you tell the police about your affair with Alan?" I asked.

The microwave beeped and Gina took the milk out. The cat followed her expectantly to a placemat that said "Cats Rule, Dogs Drool." Gina put the bowl down on the mat. She petted the calico as the cat began to lap the milk up. "Here, Puss-ems, Mommy brought your some milk. Snook-ems, you ter-sty?"

The cat looked up and meowed again before turning her attention to the milk. Gina turned to me. "Her name is Crystal—isn't she the most wonderful cat?"

"Yes, she is," I said. "You know, it's not good to feed a cat milk."

"It's not?" Gina asked, not looking up.

"No, cats are lactose intolerant."

Gina frowned. "It hasn't hurt her yet."

"It causes diarrhea," I replied. I paused. "Look, Gina, are you going to answer my question or are you going to ignore it and continue croon to that cat?"

She sighed in exasperation. "No," she said finally. "The affair was none of their goddamn business."

"How can you say that?" I asked incredulously. "Matt is dead, the police are stumped, and you're holding out on them..."

"I'm not holding out..."

"I think that's called 'obstruction of justice' if I remember my cop shows right."

"I didn't obstruct anything!" Gina wailed. "I just told them I couldn't think of anything else."

"Lying under questioning? My, my, my—this does add up."

Gina bit her lip. "What should I do, Steph?"

"I think you should call Officer Tallon and tell him what you've told me. You have Tallon's number, don't you?" She nodded. "Good. Tell him you were afraid to mention this, but you've thought about it and you think it may have something to do with the murder."

"But won't it get Alan in trouble?"

"Why are you protecting a potential murderer?" I asked.

"Alan—a murderer—no!" Gina shook her head. "Steph, Alan could never have killed Matt. You just don't know him, he's wonderful."

"Funny, Vicki said something very similar."

Gina had been looking at Crystal. Now, she met my gaze with uncertainty. "Vicki?"

I grinned. I knew I had her. "Yeah, Vicki Thompson. You know Vicki—she's the woman who 'trained' with Matt, remember?"

Gina bit her lower lip and her brow drew together in consternation. "Vicki is seeing Alan?"

"Oh, Vicki's doing a lot more than 'seeing.' Oh yeah and while I was over at Alan's place, Alan was interested in showing me a lot more than just the trail…"

Gina slammed down the mug of hot espresso, sloshing its contents over the white ceramic. "That bastard!"

"I'd use a stronger word," I remarked dryly. "But don't take *my* word for it, call Vicki and ask how good Alan was in bed."

"That no good, son-of-a-bitch! That…" Crystal fled out of the kitchen at Gina's tirade. I calmly watched. Gina slowly cooled down and she turned to me. "Okay, Steph, you've got my attention. Alan's a loser. But why would he kill Matt?"

"I don't know. I was hoping you could shed some light on it."

Gina took a couple of sheets of paper towels and blotted the spilled espresso from the countertop. "I don't know what I could tell you."

"You could start by telling me how you met Alan and what his relationship with Matt was."

Gina shrugged. "Alan was always coming over here to look at

Alaskans. One day Alan came over when Matt wasn't here and we—you know."

I knew. "Look at Alaskans? Alaskan Huskies?" I asked. "Are you sure?"

Gina nodded. "Alan was always buying dogs."

"But Alan runs Siberian Huskies, not Alaskans…"

Gina looked at me blankly.

"Matt ran unregistered Alaskan Huskies. Alan ran AKC registered Siberian Huskies."

"Is there a difference?" she asked.

"Yeah, I…"

At that moment, my cell phone began ringing. I cursed and picked it up. "Yeah, what?"

"Uh, Steph, this is Liz. Where are you?" Her voice sounded tentative.

"Oh damn! I'm so sorry, Liz, I forgot! The puppies dews, right?"

"If this is a bad time…"

"No, no, no!" I said hurriedly. "I promised I'd be by to clip their dewclaws and I will. See you in a half an hour. Bye." I pressed the END button and turned to Gina. "Look, I've got to run. I want you to call the Frisco police and tell Sergeant Tallon everything you told me. Promise me you'll do that?"

Gina nodded.

"I'll call you tonight to make sure," I said. "I have to go now and show Liz how to clip dewclaws on a litter of pups."

"Okay," Gina said. "I'll see you later. Thank you for opening my eyes."

"Bye!" I said and left in a hurry.

~ * ~

Siberian Huskies and Alaskan Huskies. Two breeds intertwined throughout history and yet miles apart. One with a limited gene pool; the other completely boundless. Why would Alan buy Alaskan Huskies? He owned Siberians.

I knew I was getting close. I didn't know if Alan had the opportunity to kill Matt and I wasn't sure of a motive—all I had were a number of inconsistencies that were starting to add up. I needed an answer and perhaps this required a little trip to Alan's home after I stopped at Liz's place.

Liz Smith lives in Pine, just south of Pine Junction. Pine is a small town with old Victorian homes nestled in the floodplain of the North Fork of the South Platte. It's a narrow valley with a lush, green plain in summertime, surrounded by pine forests—hence the name. In the summer, you'd think you died and gone to heaven. It's that beautiful. Unfortunately, it was close to the terrible Buffalo Creek fire and the Hi Meadow fire. A few miles south, Buffalo Creek sits, wasted from fires and the subsequent floods. To the north and west, you can see the scars from the Hi Meadow Fire. The town of Pine, thankfully, was spared from the fire. Liz lives just within Pine's town limits in a small two-story. She raises working and show Samoyeds. During the Buffalo Creek fire, Liz called me up and gave me reports. The night when danger looked imminent, I had her load her Samoyeds and stay with me. Thankfully, she had only six—I had an extra pen and doghouses. The barkers, we kept indoors in crates. It was a cramped week. During the Hi Meadow fire, we both got evacuated.

If you aren't familiar with the breed name, "Samoyed" (or Sammies, as the enthusiasts call them) you'll recognize the dog immediately. They are beautiful, pure white dogs with standoff coats, pricked ears, and tails that curl over their backs. They're a favorite with crowds—there's nothing more beautiful than a team of Samoyeds in contrasting red harnesses pulling a sled. Many breeders and owners insist these smiling dogs hold Christmas in their faces all throughout the year. They're smart and capable too. Originally bred by the Samoyed peoples on the steppes to pull sleds, herd reindeer, help hunt, and to be a loyal protector and watchdog, these dogs have won the hearts of many.

Samoyeds aren't fast dogs, but that isn't where their charm lies. The Samoyed racers run their jovial dogs in teams because they love them and their history. They work well freighting, packing, herding, and sledding, but don't excel in any one in particular. The Alaskan Husky, for example, is faster in a team and the Alaskan Malamute is a better freight dog. But, the Samoyed does all things relatively well. They are the northern dog equivalent to the jack-of-all-trades.

Most of Liz's dogs are outside in large kennel runs outside. As I pulled up to her house, the Samoyeds in the exercise began barking loudly. Two larger Samoyeds, obviously males with their fuller coats, stood on their hind legs against the fence and barked.

"Quiet, you guys!" Liz shouted out the sliding glass door off the balcony. She looked over and saw me. "Hi, Steph!" she waved. "Come down to the lower level entrance."

I walked over and two white dogs, one much larger, whom I presumed was the male and a smaller, daintier Sammy that was certain to be a female, greeted me at the door. The male barked, while the female watched me intently.

"Easy, Kishka, easy Misha," Liz said. "Let Steph through." Kishka snuffed at me once and then hung back to let me enter. "They're always like this, especially with puppies in the house."

I stepped inside and looked around. I was in a brown den area. All around me and throughout the carpet were white clumps of Samoyed hair. I ignored it. If you're in a house with more than one northern breed, you expect it. "Where's Momma and puppies?"

"Sasha is in the laundry room," she said. "The pups are doing great—there are six of them in all."

"Great, could you take Mom and put her someplace else?" I asked. "She won't like the sound of this."

"Sure…" I could tell Liz was a little apprehensive. "Will it hurt?"

"Only for a moment," I said. "Most pups go right back to sleep once it's been done."

Liz chewed her lip. "I wish we didn't have to do it."

"It is better they come off now, than risk getting one ripped off when they're older," I replied. "That's far more painful when they finally attach to the bone, only to get ripped off while playing or working."

"Here," I pulled a leash off the hook that hung by the door. "Take Sasha for a walk."

While Liz obediently took Sasha outside, I walked into the laundry room and closed the door. The air smelled warm and of freshly licked puppies. The Samoyed pups, themselves, were fat white bundles of fur. I pulled up a stool from just beyond the puppy box and scooped up a fat pup. Using surgical clamps, I quickly removed each dewclaw and dabbed the spot with surgical glue. As normal, the pup squawked or squealed loudly once and then fell silent as the pain was past.

I was done with the dews by the time Liz returned. Sasha was quick to jump back into the puppy box and thoroughly inspect the sleeping pups. Sasha gave me a long, cold look and then settled down to nurse.

"That's all the thanks I'll get," I grumbled.

Liz laughed. "How about some tea and cookies upstairs?"

"Sure, twist my arm," I said.

"You know, that was some race!" Liz said. "I still can't believe how well you did on the second day."

"It was that Risdon," I said. "It handles like a dream and weighs almost nothing."

Liz nodded. "That was so kind of Mary to sell it to you."

I nodded. "I don't know if I could have pulled out another victory over Lee's team without it."

We walked upstairs. Winning photos of Samoyeds lined the walls. I paused and considered them. Liz stood proudly next to each dog next to the judge holding the ribbons. "Best of Winners," "Best in Show", "Best of Breed", "Winner's Bitch,"—the titles continued through the long line of photos. Liz paused by the "Winner's Bitch."

"Look, that's Sasha in full coat. She took Winner's Bitch at Terry-All last summer. It was a major. She's finished now."

I nodded. To decipher the dog show was at first daunting, but by now, I understood pretty well. Dogs and bitches compete for "points" at conformation dog shows. Dogs win points by taking the "Winners" class. A major is when a dog earns three, four, or five points. The number of points a dog can earn in a show depends on the number of dogs entered. A dog or bitch is "finished" when they earn enough points for their championship. "She's beautiful and they're nice looking pups. I assume the sire is a champion as well?"

Liz led me into the kitchen. The kitchen was small, but functional. The walls were beige with framed photos and needlepoint renditions of Samoyeds. Most were of cute puppies, but a few showed Sammies in harness.

"Oh yes, Takotna, the sire, is being campaigned on the West Coast."

"So, is this your next sled team?" I asked as I took a seat at the kitchen table.

Liz laughed as she poured water into a cobalt blue teapot and set it on the stove. "I wish! They're all going to homes except for the bitch puppy with the red collar. This is a repeat Sasha and Takotna breeding." Liz opened up the pantry and took out a Ziploc bag of cookies. "Chocolate chip? I made them yesterday."

"Absolutely!" I said.

"If I had known this breeding was going to be so nice, I would have kept more than one," Liz admitted, carefully arranging the cookies on the plate. "Misha is from an earlier breeding two years ago. She's their sister." Liz set down the plate of chocolate chip cookies.

"So, it's a money litter."

I heard the click-click-click of toenails up the steps and the tell-tale whine and scratch. "Can I let them in?"

"Sure," Liz said, as the teapot began to whistle. I opened the door and Kishka, led by Misha, pushed their way out. They headed straight for the table with the cookies.

"Watch them," Liz said. "They're thieves. They'll raid the cookies before you'll even get a bite."

"I'll keep that in mind," I said as she handed me tea, served in a blue cup with a smiling Samoyed's face looking cheerfully back at me. Misha eyed the cookies. "No cookies for you, dear. Chocolate is poisonous to dogs."

Misha sat directly in front of me and laid her ears back in annoyance. She pawed me pitifully. Kishka circled around the oak table like a white, furry shark.

"Oh, for Pete's sake!" Liz exclaimed, watching their antics. She opened a cupboard and pulled out two rawhide chews. They rushed over to her and accepted them. Kishka took his chew and lay down next to the patio door. Misha was happy to thread her way under the table and lay there. "There, that will give us a little peace and quiet for a few moments," Liz said as she sat down across from me with a cup of tea in her own hands. "I decided to do a repeat breeding because the pups turned out so nice. Problem is Misha is too straight in the back."

"How can you tell through all that fur?" I glanced down at Misha.

"You feel," Liz replied.

"Do all judges do that?"

"Thankfully, no, or she wouldn't have a point on her."

"What about Kishka? He's a beautiful dog."

"I can't—Kishka's a rescue dog. I don't have his registration."

I took a bite of the chocolate chip cookie. It was soft and I let the chips melt in my mouth. Pure ecstasy. I considered Kishka again. "I was watching him move—he's got good movement. He's of good quality, isn't he?"

"Oh, most definitely," she agreed. "He's probably a Nikita grandson."

I looked blank.

"Nikita or Champion Sno-hills Nikita's Laughing is my foundation dog," Liz said. "Nikita had won more Best of Breeds and Best in Shows than any Sammy in Colorado. He was number two in the nation for a time. Kishka looks just like him."

"But Kishka's a rescue dog?"

"Yeah—I work for Samoyed Rescue. Park County Animal Control called me—someone had left him tied to the door of the shelter. When I got there, I knew Kishka was out of my dogs. I tried going through my records and calling puppy buyers, but that was a dead end. Although I have contracts requesting right of first refusal and requiring pet owners to contact me if they move, several seldom do. The owners could be lying too, just to avoid my lecture. So, Kishka's parentage is a dead end."

On hearing his name, Kishka sat up, alert and ready. He chomped the chew a couple of times before swallowing it. Liz slipped a dog biscuit from a ceramic cookie jar and tossed the biscuit to Kishka. Snap! Kishka caught the biscuit in midair. I clapped. "I bet your non-dog guests are surprised when they reach in, expecting cookies and end up with a Milk-bone," I snickered.

"The last non dog-person to visit was two years ago. My aunt was utterly horrified when she saw me spinning Samoyed hair into yarn. She's convinced we're all nuts."

I laughed too. Kishka continued to sit; his dark, soulful eyes stared at Liz intently. "Too bad you can't register and breed him," I said.

Liz held up another biscuit. "Don't think I wasn't tempted. Kishka was unneutered when he arrived at the shelter. An unethical breeder would have."

"How? Kishka's an adult."

"Easy—Kishka was about two years old when he came to me. Let's say I had a litter anywhere from one to three years ago. Out of the litter of puppies, I might sell a dog and a bitch without papers or

I could have added another two puppies to the litter when I registered the litter with AKC. If I had those papers around, Kishka would now have a name, registered parents, and a registration number."

"So, you register a bogus dog or transfer papers from a registered dog to your rescue—isn't that fraud?"

"Big time—and AKC will prosecute you if they find out."

I nodded. "Yeah, but that would be if you are planning ahead. Suppose you weren't just willy-nilly registering bogus puppies."

"Well, if I were to show Kishka, I'd have to have him assume the identity of a show prospect that didn't turn out."

"What if you weren't showing, only breeding?"

"Then, I could put down any dog I owned—it wouldn't matter." Liz tossed the biscuit to Kishka. Liz paused and looked at me strangely. "But you know, AKC is starting to clamp down on breeding, especially breeding sires multiple times. They now require genetic testing of sires that produce seven or more litters." She took a sip of tea. "Why? What's the interest? You're not planning on going into some sort of canine black market?"

"No, but I believe someone else has," I said.

"Who?"

"This is strictly confidential, okay?"

"Yeah, yeah, of course."

"Suppose I knew a guy who bought and sold Alaskan Huskies like a broker…"

"Okay…" I could tell by Liz's expression, she was unsure of the whole conversation.

"Hang with me here," I said. "And suppose I found out this broker sold the Alaskan Huskies to a purebred Siberian Husky breeder. And the Siberian breeder wasn't telling anyone he had mixed breeds."

Liz whistled through her teeth. "You're asking me how tough it would be to breed and register Alaskan Husky and Siberian Husky crossbreds?"

"Yes."

"Piece of cake."

"Damn! Are you sure?"

Liz shook her head in anger. "AKC relies on the breeder's integrity."

"Then, the Siberian breeder could crossbreed an Alaskan Husky and a Siberian Husky and register the pups as purebred Siberian Huskies."

Liz nodded. "Faster Siberians. Only, they wouldn't be Siberians. They'd be crossbreeds."

"Let's say the crossbreeds looked Siberian and the Siberian breeder did register them as purebred. How much would they be worth?"

"Hundreds, if not thousands of dollars," Liz said. "It would be extremely dicey, though. If anyone found out, the breeder could be forever barred from AKC, all his dogs and their ancestors could have their registrations revoked, plus the breeder would be facing criminal fraud charges."

"Most likely a felony," I mused. "Now, I know."

"Know what?" Liz asked. "Look, what happens to the pups that look too Alaskan? Does Siberian breeder keep them for breeding stock, sell them back to the broker, or…" Her mouth twisted in rage. "Who's doing it, Steph? I'll kill the jerk!"

"No need, I think," I said. "The broker is already dead."

"Huh?"

"Matt Rayburn."

Liz opened her mouth, but no words came out. "Then, who is the breeder?"

"Matt Rayburn's murderer."

The room grew cold. "Who, Steph?" she whispered. "Who?"

"Alan Freeman."

Chapter Nineteen

As I drove towards Kenosha Pass, I kept thinking about Alan Freeman. It was all so clear now. Puppies. Not just your run-of-the-mill Alaskan Husky mutt puppies. Purebred Siberian puppies—only not. Alan Freeman was breeding Alaskan Huskies and Siberian Huskies and passing them off as pure Siberian Huskies. That was how Alan's team was so fast and could compete with the Alaskan teams. The only thing AKC had was the honesty and reputation of the breeder. How could someone prove these dogs weren't Siberians? There was such variation in the breed that color, body shape, coat length, and size could all be accounted for—after all, weren't race Siberians not typey?

Flop ears and a hound body might be a dead giveaway. A short coat with weird splashes of color might not. A flop-eared mutt would most likely been given back to Matt Rayburn or worse—put down for not conforming to the minimal standard. The only way to know the dogs weren't purebred was to be there. And Matt was there.

I shook my head. It must have given Matt great pleasure to see the Siberian Husky line sullied like that. It was so like Matt to take perverse pleasure ruining one of the top Siberian lines for the sake of money. Matt had to have known that, like the proverbial house of cards, the whole plan would sometime come crashing down on Alan. Perhaps Matt was the one who might have even pushed on the cards. In which case, Matt's plan backfired and he was now dead. Matt had pushed Alan a little too far.

Alan had everything to gain from Matt's death too. Alan had Gina, if he wanted her. Alan got first pick of the dogs when Gina sold out. Alan's little dirty crossbreeding secret would be safe because Gina didn't know an Alaskan Husky from a Siberian Husky.

I shook my head at my own stupidity for not seeing it all sooner. Alan had me help put Matt's dogs up at the murder scene—no doubt checking to be certain he hadn't left some sort of trace at the crime scene. Alan had helped me with my dogs that Sunday morning, perhaps using the opportunity to slip Matt's bloodied snowhook into my truck bed. Tasha must have somehow gotten loose from

Alan's truck that day—Tasha still had Matt's collar on her and Alan wouldn't have dared claim Tasha when I found her. Wednesday, Alan had come in from his run and saw Tasha on my stakeouts. Alan must have come back and pried the box open to retrieve Tasha. He then took a bolt cutter to my lines to cover the real reason. That afternoon, he boldly made a play for me. Perhaps, Alan felt invincible knowing he had gotten away with vandalizing my equipment. He had even offered stakeouts for my dogs—if I had been quick enough, I would have realized Alan meant truck stakeouts instead of dog yard stakeouts. Alan had inadvertently given himself away, but I was too flustered to have noticed it. Alan's disappearance from the Granby races concerned me—perhaps Alan knew I was getting close. Rather than face me in a crowd, Alan decided to skip the races.

The truck sputtered as I began the uphill climb towards Kenosha Pass at Hall Valley. You can see where the old railroad bed cuts into the hill. Highway engineers built Highway 285 along the old railroad bed. Long ago, the only way to travel southwest towards Fairplay was either by rail, foot, horse, or stagecoach. The tracks are long gone, except at the very top of Kenosha Pass, but most of the roadhouses enroute are still standing. Hall Valley is the site of the ghost town of Webster. If you follow Hall Valley Road, you can cross Webster Pass on a jeep trail to the near ghost town of Montezuma and further to either Breckenridge Ski area or Idaho Springs, depending on the route you choose. It is not for the mere passenger car or the faint of heart.

Puttering up Kenosha Pass, I ran into snow. Typical, since Kenosha is 10,001 feet above sea level. The downward trek brings you out of the Kenosha Mountains and into Southpark. Southpark is a vast glacier field cut through the mountain thousands of years ago. A visitor will see a vast high altitude plain surrounded by a ring of mountains. I love Southpark because it reminds me of Montana with its wide grasslands and mountains surrounding it. Now the grass and scrub was brown with patches of snows dotting the fields. The Tarry-All Mountains surround Southpark to the east while the Ten-Mile and Mosquito Ranges guard the west.

The truck shuddered as the wind hit it. The wind thunders down the western passes of Boreas, Mosquito, Georgia, and Hoosier, scrubbing the plains. It's a cold, forbidding wind. This along with Southpark's distance from Denver is perhaps the reason why few people inhabit this region. Still, I find the ruggedness very beautiful.

The first town you will reach is Jefferson. Its claim to fame is it is the home of Ginger Greene, Colorado's 1991 Rodeo Queen. The sign still stands proudly announcing her accomplishment. Drive further south and you will pass the near ghost town of Como where the old train roundhouse still stands and the railroad museum. Follow the road northwest out of Como and you will follow the Boreas Pass road where the train crossed the continental divide to Breckenridge. It's barely passable by a passenger car in the summer and dangerous in the winter with avalanche chutes spilling onto the road.

As I continued to drive southward towards Fairplay, I caught movement in my peripheral vision. Antelope bounded along the hill line a half-mile away. Antelope and rabbits were perhaps the only creatures out in that unrelenting wind. The road wound its way towards Red Hill Pass, a mere 9993 feet above sea level, that loomed over the town of Fairplay.

After driving through Fairplay, I took the turn off to Alan's house and followed the Beaver Creek. I glanced at my watch as I pulled into Alan's driveway. Alan's dog truck was not there. No doubt, he had gone to run some errand. The red Yamaha snowmobile still sat just under the deck.

I slid out of the truck and tugged on my parka. Although sheltered somewhat from the biting Southpark wind, it was still pretty breezy. The sky was clear though and when you stood in the sun, the temperature could feel almost balmy. I hesitated for a moment before I closed the truck's door. My .44 Magnum sat invitingly in my pack. I closed the pack and tossed it in the back seat. I could be all wrong about Alan, I rationalized. I tried my cell phone. The phone said "scanning" but was unable to lock on a cell. I was too far out of range. I shut off the cell phone and tossed it on the seat.

I walked up to Alan's front door and knocked. I really didn't expect a reply. Now, I hesitated. Did I dare check out Alan's dog yard and confirm my suspicions? I walked past the snowmobile. It was a late model Yamaha four-stroke with the key still in the ignition. Out here, thefts were rare, so that wasn't unusual to find. Many people still leave their homes unlocked. I held my hand near the exhaust pipe. It still radiated heat. Alan must have just left for some errand. He would probably be gone for an hour. I strode over to the dog yard gate and found it locked—no surprise there. The dogs started barking when they heard me fuss with the gate. I knew better than to try to quiet them. Instead, I walked around the fence, looking for a means of getting into the dog yard.

Luckily, the privacy fencing only ran the length of the road. The rest of the dog yard fencing was six-foot chain link. Alan kept a number of dogs on stakeouts. Like most mushers, Alan had the two sexes separated and a puppy and heat pen in the back near the kennel office outbuilding. I could see the puppies bouncing up and down against the chain link. I guessed by their size and overall demeanor, they were five weeks old.

One dog caught my eye. She was a red husky staked out towards the back of the dog yard. "Tasha?" I called. The dog seemed to respond, but at this distance with all the dogs spinning on chains, it was hard to tell if indeed this was Tasha. I considered the chain link. I hadn't switched to my Sorrel's—instead I had on my hiking boots. Still, they wouldn't be the best for climbing chain link. I leapt up and grasped a handful of chain in my gloved hands. I scrambled with my feet to grasp even a tiny toehold. My right foot caught and I pulled myself over the fence, allowing myself to drop the six feet to the ground and tumble. It wasn't pretty.

This roused a new chorus of barking and howling. I fished some biscuits out of my parka pocket and tossed them to the noisiest dogs. The barking subsided enough and I walked through the yard towards the dog who had caught my eye. I stopped about ten feet away and stared. Before me danced the beautiful Alaskan Husky. There could be little doubt. "Tasha?" I asked.

The Alaskan Husky stopped in mid-motion and leapt up on her hind legs to greet me. I ran up gave her an ear scratch as she carefully washed my face. From a distance, I could have easily mistaken the Alaskan for a Siberian, if I had not recognized the dog.

Another Alaskan Husky caught my eye. "Blue?" I turned to the dog next to Tasha. Blue danced on the end of his stakeout and I petted him. "I've been looking for you," I grinned as he washed his face. Like Tasha, I might have mistaken Blue for a purebred Siberian from a distance. Blue's legs were a little too long and his body a little too houndy to be a Siberian. His head was narrow and ax-like—unlike a Siberian's head. Blue's tail too was longer than any dog's ought to be—it nearly touched the ground. Somewhere in his background, Blue had Saluki or some other sighthound blood. He clung to me in adoration, as sighthounds are wont to do. I stroked his narrow head. "What'cha doing here, Boy?" I crooned.

Blue nuzzled me and then looked up at me with a quizzical expression, his ax-like head cocked sideways. I chuckled and slowly peeled the husky off. As I walked away, Blue threw himself against the end of the chain, whirling on his hind legs, trying to reach me.

Two Alaskan Huskies. I made a mental note. Still, having a couple of Alaskans in a dog yard filled with Siberians does not make a crime, I reminded myself. I scanned the yard and could maybe pick out a half dozen Alaskans. Maybe. I couldn't be certain. I had put the pieces together, but now I needed proof.

I approached the puppy pen. This must have been the litter of six pups Vicki mentioned she had bred her top Siberian to. I knelt down and clapped my hands. The puppies came readily to my invitation and licked my fingers through the fence. The momma dog peered out of the doghouse. She shook herself and stretched slowly out of the doghouse. She was a completely white dog with a short coat and a long greyhound-like tail. Her ears were floppy, not pricked as a Siberian should be. If she was a Siberian, then it just snowed in hell.

I counted and recounted the pups. There were eight, not six, as Vicki said. I stood there for a long time, wondering why. Then, I noticed two of the pups had floppy ears, brindle markings, and longer bodies than their siblings. The others looked like Siberians but these two didn't. I scratched one of the brindle pups' chins. He rubbed against my finger in delight.

I didn't see any other puppies, but I was willing to consider that maybe Vicki was talking about another litter. Still, Alan didn't let anyone in his dog yard—not even Vicki who owned the sire. It made sense—Alan wasn't breeding Siberian Huskies. Alan was breeding Alaskan Husky and Siberian Husky crossbreeds and registering them as Siberian Huskies with the AKC. He offered his "purebred" Siberian Huskies which were faster than anyone else's at $800 to $1000. His "purebred" dogs gave him fame and recognition throughout the mushing community. Only they weren't purebred.

I slid past the puppy pen towards the small barn I guessed was the kennel office. I hoped Alan kept his records where he did his veterinary work. I tried the door and found it unlocked. Musty air greeted me. I walked inside.

Alan's office furnishing consisted of a large metal desk, chair, and filing cabinets from a used office furniture store. Alan had set up a tack box and grooming table in the corner and a small trophy case, filled with various ribbons and trophies sat behind the desk. Multitudes of framed photographs, some of show wins, others of various teams Alan ran, lined the walls.

AKC requires all owners to register their purebred litters. I remembered receiving a blue AKC puppy registration form that breeders refer to as "blue slips" when I bought Winnie from her breeder. I then registered Winnie with her AKC name and received an adult AKC registration. If Alan indeed intended to register the crossbreed puppies, he would have blue slips with the name of the sire and the supposed dam. The sire would be Vicki's male while the dam listed would be a purebred Siberian Alan owned. It might not even be a purebred, I thought as I scanned the desk. God only knew how long Alan had been fraudulently submitting papers. Certainly, the past three years. Maybe longer.

I was warm beneath my parka, so I pulled it off and left it on the chair. Although musty, Alan must have had the electric heat on. I removed my gloves and hat and laid them in a neat pile on top of my parka.

I found a folder underneath a receipt for 500 pounds of dog food, various purebred race forms, and a week-old newspaper. I opened the folder and found six AKC blue slips. I pulled out one and squinted in the dim window light. The sire was listed as Icy Paw's Shadow Stalker—Vicki's dog. Vicki's kennel name was Icy Paw. The dam was listed as Silverheel's Grey Morning: Alan's kennel. I looked at the puppies' birth date: January 24th. Five weeks old. I had my proof.

The light came on. "What are you doing?"

I turned. Alan's face was grim. He knew what I was looking at. I decided to play dumb. I knew it wouldn't work. "Hi Alan, I was looking for you."

"Nice try," Alan said as he closed the door. He carried a rifle.

I drew a quick inward breath. I regretted my decision to not carry my gun. The rifle looked like a .22 caliber—a rather light load, but it could be lethal with a well-placed shot. "Nice pups," I tried again. "I didn't know drop ears and brindle coats were part of the Siberian standard. I counted eight pups—what are you going to do with the other two?"

Alan shrugged. "What nobody knows won't matter. They will disappear—as you will." He pointed the rifle's muzzle towards me. I'd kill you here but you'd make an ugly mess on the floor..."

"Like Matt did on your Carhartts?" I asked. Alan winced—a direct score. "Did Matt get a little jealous over your success?"

"Matt was an idiot with a big mouth," Alan replied curtly. "Matt didn't know when to keep his trap shut."

"Matt made a lot of money selling you those dogs, didn't he?"

"Yeah, he did. Matt didn't know when he had a good thing."

"And you killed Matt because he threatened to tell someone about your little dealings? My what a big man—you screw his wife and then you screw him. Nice job."

Alan frowned. "You don't understand. Matt was the one who got me into this in the first place. He was so damn sure of himself. 'Hell,' Matt used to say, 'all the top Siberian teams have Alaskan in them, Alan. Just *look* at them. Those aren't purebred. How could you call those dogs anything but Alaskans?' Matt had a point, you know."

I nodded. Alan expressed a frustration I've heard and seen among Alaskan drivers before. "So you bought some of Matt's Alaskan Huskies and bred them to your Siberians."

"No, it started as an experiment—we just intended to breed one litter to try out some new genes. Only they looked like Siberians. Fast Siberians. I had to register them. They were incredibly fast."

The road to mushing hell is paved with minor indiscretions. Once Alan started, he couldn't turn back. "So, Matt was your broker—he bought the Alaskan Huskies you were interested in and you bred the fastest Siberians in Colorado."

Alan nodded. "You know, Steph, if you hadn't been so damn curious, we could have had something."

"What? Me in jail for you? I don't think so."

Alan chuckled. "Yeah, well I didn't expect you to find the hook before the police did. You were convenient, that's all."

"Like Matt was convenient? Like Vicki is convenient? Like Gina is convenient?"

Alan didn't reply, instead, he produced a roll of duct tape. "Come here and turn around."

I eyed the rifle, wondering how good of a shot Alan actually was. I walked over.

I knew I had maybe one chance. I turned around and waited until I heard Alan put the rifle down so he could fumble with the tape. At that moment, I kicked backwards like a mule. It wasn't good karate form—just a hard backward kick—but it did the job. Heel impacted knee and Alan screamed. I whirled around with a solid right cross. My fist hit him squarely in the nose. Blood poured from Alan's nostrils and he screamed again from pain. He crumpled to the floor. For a moment, I hesitated, looking around for the rifle. Alan had knocked it over when he fell but was already scrambling for it. I ran.

Once outside, I sprinted across the dog yard. The dogs yapped and whirled with excitement. I arrived at the gate to find it unlocked. I threw it open and at that moment, I heard a loud pop, followed by successive pops. My right leg cramped up and I almost collapsed. Instead, I tumbled. I shuddered and pulled myself up. My hand went instinctively to my thigh and felt the hole in the Gore-Tex and felt something warm and sticky. In shock, I pulled my hand away—it was slick with blood. More pops. I kept moving along the side of the house.

"God damn it!" I screamed in rage. My throat tightened up. Alan shot me! He just out-and-out shot me. *Two could play that game*, a voice in my head said. I had the .44 magnum in the truck. If I could just get to it. I stumbled towards the truck and fumbled for my keys. They weren't there. I must have lost them—maybe when I fell? I didn't feel like going back.

Another successive volley of rounds. Alan was limping across the dog yard towards me. It would take no time for Alan to get to me if I didn't act soon. I pulled myself back towards the carport, hoping the wooden slats would afford some protection. Alan fired repeatedly towards the carport. Bits of wood flaked off and slats split where the bullets hit. I jumped on the snowmobile and started it.

"You bitch!" Alan screamed and began running towards me as fast as his injured legs would carry him. Alan threw down the rifle—he was most likely out of bullets—and came charging around to the carport's entrance, but I had already shifted the snowmobile and nearly ran him over as I took off.

Fairplay would have been the most sensible place to go. But Alan still had his truck and he could have possibly caught up with me. Snowmobiles are fast, but in truth, I hadn't much experience riding one, so all that speed would be completely useless if I crashed the damn thing. I took the trails that led to Mount Silverheels. The snow there was too deep for a truck, even with four-wheel drive. Alan would be unable to follow me except by foot, snowmobile, or sled team. By the time, he harnessed and hooked up some dogs, I could maybe double back to the Fairplay Nordic Center and call for help there. Maybe I could get to Fairplay, itself, and find the police station.

That was the plan, until the damn snowmobile died. I was maybe a mile into National Forest when the snowmobile coughed and sputtered. I tried giving it more throttle, but to no avail. It coughed twice before expiring. I hit the electric start, but the machine stayed defiantly dead. For some reason, the image of Prunes the Burro popped into my mind. I wondered if this was how the old gold prospectors felt when their mules wouldn't budge. Only, they could shoot the mule to end it. I didn't even have a gun.

I stood up and looked around. I had stopped at the crossroads between the main forest service road and a narrow jeep/snowmobile road that went across Beaver Creek. The creek was more or less frozen now to a slushy consistency. Aspen, fire willows and other scrub grew in the creek's bed making a ten foot tall maze throughout the gulch. Giant ruts, a foot or two deep and several feet long crisscrossed the area as though somebody had snowshoed through, only there weren't any snowshoe prints. I didn't know what the tracks were.

I swore and tried to start the snowmobile again. Nothing. I sat there for a moment or two to consider my options. I couldn't wait here for Alan to come and find me and I couldn't walk to Fairplay.

I stood up and my thigh cramped again. Gripping my leg, I dragged myself towards the dense thicket that grew around the creek. I walked with a weird jerky motion, almost as though my leg had fallen asleep. I stumbled to the creek and put a foot on the ice. It crackled and I pulled my leg back. The cold water rushed deeply here. I couldn't walk across.

I turned left and walked onto the frozen marshy grass between the fire willows. The uneven ground made it tricky to move and I stumbled a few times. Once or twice sharp pains shot through my leg and I nearly screamed. Instead, I collapsed into a whimpering ball of jelly until the pain subsided enough for me to go on.

That's when I found the moose. I was so focused on the pain, that I wasn't looking where I was going that I nearly stumbled into the cow. By Alaskan standards, she wasn't a very big moose—maybe about the size of a horse—but she was plenty big enough. She was dark brown with the goofy Bullwinkle head and huge knobby knees. She looked up from browsing and eyed me suspiciously. I froze. Now I realized the giant ruts were moose tracks. They were made when the moose's legs cut through the snow.

Moose have three modes: charge, stand, or flight. I was probably too close for flight, so I hoped the moose would settle for stand. Never mind Alan, the moose would finish me off. Since she hadn't attacked yet, I prayed for stand. I said nothing and slowly backed off, hoping my jerky movements wouldn't upset the cow further. The cow moose lowered her head and took another bite of roots, still watching me. I retraced my steps and got out of sight. I took another direction through the brush.

I didn't realize how much I'd been shaking until I stopped when I thought I was safe. The cold wind chilled my sweat-drenched skin and I shivered violently. My fingers were numb. I searched my Gore-Tex pants and found a couple of unopened packages of Hot Hands chemical heat. I tore open the packs with my teeth and shook the chemical packs. Gripping the little packs, I prayed for warmth. It took a little while, but once the chemicals activated, they were good for six or seven hours.

The heat felt good to my cold, stiff fingers and I clenched and unclenched my hands to get the blood recirculating through them. I then searched my other pockets for something to eat. I found a half eaten chocolate bar. It wasn't much, but it's amazing how quickly your spirits can rise when you eat chocolate. I eased myself to the ground with a groan.

The bullet wound throbbed unmercifully. I was cold and tired, but alive. Now, that I knew Alan was the murderer, Alan wouldn't let me live. I had to figure out how to get back to Fairplay and notify the police. My mind wandered to Jack Tallon—the posse was still the next mountain range over Hoosier Pass. In retrospect, Jack was absolutely right about me not getting involved. Murders were not for amateurs.

I sat there for a while considering my options. I remembered there were private homes further up the valley. Certainly one would have someone home who could call the police—they all had to have phones. Even if they didn't, I could probably beg a ride back down to Fairplay. If no one was home, I'd have to break in. I hated that prospect, but I knew a judge would be hard pressed to convict me given the circumstances. Walking back out the way I came was deadly. Alan would be taking that route.

I stood up slowly, trying to keep from screaming as the sharp pain shot through my leg. Hell, this was worse than when it hit. The nerves were finally reacting to the shock, no doubt. I walked slowly towards the road, pushing aside the fire willows.

I felt more than heard the loud crack. Instinctively, I dropped to the ground, heedless of my leg's protestations. The willow branches rained down on me. That was close. By the resonance, I guessed it was a heavy caliber rifle—maybe a 30-06 or a 300 win-mag. I clearly heard the round eject as someone used the bolt action. A dog began yapping. "Shut up, you idiot!" I heard Alan snap. I also heard a loud thud and the dog whimpered.

I didn't dare look. Alan was maybe ten to fifteen yards away and my only protection was a bunch of skinny willows and dense brush. I heard snow crunch under foot. First, towards me and then away. I was afraid to move. He'd shoot if he saw movement, but he'd shoot if he found me. Gritting my teeth, I slowly rose to a crouched position and waited. Nothing. I hazarded a peek.

Alan stood where I had entered the marsh. Alan was off the runners and had pounded in a snowhook. Beside him stood Blue, Tasha, and two other huskies, leaning into their harnesses. Blue was looking right at the spot where the moose was, his ears pricked in attentiveness. Alan was so focused on finding me that he was oblivious to his dogs' reactions. Most mushers would have noticed.

Alan was holding a Winchester model 70. Evidently, he traded the .22 for something with more power. I did the math. If Alan had a round in the chamber, he had three bullets left. While .22 caliber rounds are used to kill more people than any other round, they're pretty wimpy. The bullet in my leg was testimony enough. The .300 win-mag, however, didn't need to be entirely accurate to blow a big hole in me. It's big enough to take down elk and elk are usually 1000 lbs. or more. You do the math. I sure did.

Once again, I longed for my .44 magnum. What in the hell was I thinking when I left it in the truck? I quickly assessed the situation. Perhaps if I could lure Alan towards the moose, which might slow him down enough for me to grab the sled and make an escape. I almost irritated the moose by nearly trouncing on it, I wondered what Alan and his dogs were doing to it now.

It wasn't much of a plan. I scooped some snow in my still frozen fingers and quietly packed it into a snowball. Then, I hurled it towards the moose.

Alan spun towards the sound and shot. I pulled a chunk of ice and my digging nearly gave me away. Alan shot again. This time, much closer. The snow sprayed up into my face where the bullet hit the ground, a few feet away. I hurled the ice chunk towards the moose and again Alan fired.

The next thing that happened was surrealistic, almost like a dream. The moose bellowed and crashed through the willows. Alan stumbled back in shock, trying to fire at the enraged, charging animal. Alan worked the bolt action, but to no avail. The rifle was empty. The dogs pulled the snowhook and went right for the moose. The moose bowled Alan over and brought her huge hooves down on his chest and head. I heard a sickening crack as bone shattered under the moose's weight. The dogs were barking and snapping and the moose turned on them. She pounded the lead dogs with frightful ferocity and turned to the wheelers who cowered in fear. They too were smashed down in an instant. They screamed in agony and terror.

"Oh God!" I yelled and without thinking, I ran out of the thicket. I didn't even feel the pain in my leg.

The moose turned to me as she walked out of the screaming mass of fur and blood. I stopped dead. The moose lowered her ears as she considered me. Then, she paused. Her ears pricked towards the trail.

I hesitated too. Then, I heard it. Snowmobiles. I backed up and the moose's ears lowered slightly. She turned her head and trotted away with frightening agility for an animal so large and ungainly.

Then, everything turned fuzzy. The adrenaline that held me together faltered and I began to shake from cold and fear. My stomach turned inside out and I retched uncontrollably. My leg ached. I thought I was going to pass out. Perhaps the snowmobiles were a figment of my addled senses. I closed my eyes, no longer wanting to fight the pain or the cold.

Chapter Twenty

The horrible sound of a dogfight brought me back to my senses. The dogs were still thrashing and screaming. I pulled myself off the ground and stumbled over to them. The blood was incredible. I could see bones protruding through skin where they splintered and cracked under the moose's hooves. Blue lay unconscious with a nasty slash across his ribs where the moose stomped. The ribs looked broken. Tasha was the other lead—she was semi-conscious. The wheelers—the dogs closest to the sled—were in a terrible fight. I yelled and grasped one of the wheel dog's collar, pulling him off the other dog. It was a big black Siberian Husky who had not been injured severely enough to lie quietly. He backed off.

The snowmobiles drove up. I glanced at the riders and took a double take. "Jack?" I said, hardly believing what I saw. Jack Tallon rode up. He was wearing a thick, black military issue parka and Sorel Glacier pac boots over his police blues. Jack's face was red from windburn and he must have still been really cold. The second rider was a police officer from Fairplay. He too wore a thick parka but had sewn the Fairplay police emblem on the parka's outside sleeve. They both wore white snowmobile helmets and goggles.

"Jesus, Steph, what happened?" Jack was off his snowmobile. "Amy called me and said you were going to confront Alan Freeman."

The Fairplay officer had already gone over to Alan. "It looks like a moose did this."

Jack stared at Alan's body. "Is he even alive?"

"I don't know and I don't really care," I croaked. My voice had gone hoarse. "Alan tried to kill me. Do you have a knife? I've got to muzzle these dogs."

"Well, Freeman's in no position to kill anybody at the moment," the officer said. "He's been banged up really good." The officer turned and spoke into his police radio.

"Alan chased me into the thicket and irked a moose," I said lamely. "I didn't help, I'm afraid."

Jack handled me the knife. I started cutting strips off Blue's harness, but my hands shook with cold. Jack took the knife from me, cut the dogs' harnesses and lines, and fastened them tightly around each of the dogs' muzzles.

"I've radioed the EMTs and they're calling in a chopper," the Fairplay officer said. "We'll have a Flight-for-Life in about forty minutes."

"We got to get these dogs to Rachel's," I said. "They'll die otherwise."

Jack looked strangely at me. "Freeman just tried to kill you and you're worried about the dogs?"

I rubbed a grubby and bloodied hand against my face. "Yeah, anything wrong with that?"

Instead of answering, Jack glanced down. He started. "Jesus, Stephanie, you're bleeding!"

"Yeah, Alan shot me," I said, so matter-of-factly, I think Jack almost panicked.

"You've been shot?"

"Yeah, a twenty-two. Alan picked up the first rifle he found when he saw I was in his office snooping around. He later chased me with that Winchester when I escaped."

"You better lie down."

"I don't want to lie down. These dogs are in worse shape."

"Look, I'll take care of the dogs. You need to rest."

"I don't need rest. I need warm hands."

Jack took my hands in his own. He pulled off his parka and gloves. "Here," he said, wrapping the warm parka around me.

I slid my hands into the warm, oversized gloves. I flexed my numb fingers, enjoying the warmth.

~ * ~

The EMTs arrived on snowmobiles and began treating Alan. They looked grim as they worked. I heard words such as "chest wound" and "head trauma." One EMT checked me over and started to bandage my wound, but I wouldn't sit down. The EMT gave me something hot to drink, but I was more concerned about the dogs than my own safety. To quiet me down, Jack Tallon called Rachel. She left the clinic with a fill-in veterinarian and drove to Fairplay. Although it was only forty-five minutes, it seemed like an eternity when the Flight-for-Life Helicopter finally arrived. They took Alan Freeman and that was the last I saw of him. They wanted to take me, but I refused and instead opted to meet with Rachel.

One of the EMTs let me ride down with him on the snowmobile as he carried two of the injured dogs in the stretcher. When we arrived at the bottom of the trail, I saw the outside of Alan's house was swarming with Fairplay and Park County police.

"Oh Steph! Are you okay? I heard you'd been shot!" Rachel exclaimed as she jumped out of her blue Ford Expedition.

I pointed to the struggling dogs. "I'm okay—we've got to take care of the dogs."

I was helping Rachel administer triage to the dogs when I started feeling fuzzy again. Rachel stared at me. "You don't look well," she said.

"She shouldn't," Jack Tallon walked up behind me. "She HAS been shot. Stephanie—I'm taking you to an emergency clinic for treatment."

~ * ~

I don't remember much after that. Rachel says I passed out. When I woke, I was in a hospital bed with IV tubes sticking in my arms. My leg hurt worse than it had when I got shot. My hand slipped down to the leg to feel bandages. No doubt, the pain was due to all the pulling and prodding the surgeon did when he took the bullet out.

I looked over and saw the nurse call button on the cart by the bed. My mouth was dry and I pressed the button. A few minutes later, the nurse walked in. She was a large woman with dark hair and eyes and wore a cheery smock with rainbows across it.

"I see you're finally awake," she said. "Are you thirsty?"

"Yeah," I said. "Where am I?"

"Swedish Medical in Denver." She handed me a large plastic cup of water, complete with lid and a sport sipping straw that said Swedish Medical Center on its side.

I took the water and drank gratefully. "I think Tallon overreacted."

"The officer?" the nurse asked. "Actually, the officer did the right thing. The bullet was up against the femoral artery—it wouldn't have taken much more movement and you would've died."

"Great," I sighed, wondering if my piddly little health insurance policy would cover this.

"Well, since you're awake, I might as well ask if you're up to see-ing some visitors?"

"I have visitors?" I asked. I must have sounded surprised. "Sure, I guess."

"I'll bring in the whole group," the nurse remarked. "They've been waiting for you."

Group? I didn't like the sound of that.

"Hey, Steph! You're awake!" Amy led the way, followed by Lee Johnson and Liz Smith. "We were hanging around waiting—the rest of the gang got tired of waiting and will probably be back this even-ing. Sherri went and got sandwiches for those of us who decided to hang around a little longer."

"The rest of the gang?"

"Oh yeah," Liz remarked. "Everybody's heard how you took on Alan Freeman. Wow! I couldn't have done it."

"What happened to Alan? Last time I saw him he was getting choppered out."

"You don't know?" Lee asked.

I looked from one face to another. "Hey, I just woke up—cut me some slack," I snapped.

"Alan died enroute to Denver. I hear that moose did a real number on him," Amy said. "We've been trying to pry more infor-mation out of Tallon, but he's been pretty tight-lipped about the whole thing."

"I bet," I said.

"So, fill us in!" Amy said, sitting down in the chair.

I quickly went over the whole story. When I finished, I looked at them. "One thing I can't figure out is how the posse showed up. It's not supposed to happen like that."

"After you left Liz's house, Liz called me and told me the mur-derer was Alan Freeman and you were going to confront him," Amy said. "I remembered the card with Officer Tallon's number on it and called him. Amazingly enough, the dispatcher put me through when I told her what it was about. Tallon called the Fairplay and Park County police and headed over Hoosier Pass to meet them."

I nodded. "I guess I owe you both."

"You stupid idiot!" Amy said finally. "You could have gotten yourself killed."

"I nearly did," I said. "The nurse just told me the bullet was against an artery. Honestly, it didn't feel like much."

Lee snorted in disbelief. "You get shot, pass out, and all you can say is that it didn't feel like much? Honestly, Steph!"

"I guess I'm out for the rest of the season, though," I sighed. "I don't think the doctors will let me run this weekend."

"I don't think you're going to have too much to worry about." Lee said. "Shawn Bailey packed up and went back to Minnesota. Even if he took first place at Grand Lake, he wouldn't have enough points to beat you. The Bronze is as good as yours. Sherri calculated it out." Seeing my expression, Lee added, "Sherri told me about the 'Inquisition.'"

"How can you possibly talk to me?"

"Water under the bridge, Steph. You dredged up a very painful memory for Sherri. We almost got divorced over Matt and she has never reconciled herself with the affair. After Sherri heard what happened in Fairplay, she knew you were on the right track. She'll be back soon—with sandwiches. I assume they'll let you eat sandwiches?"

"There's nothing wrong with my stomach—it's my leg," I replied. "Unless the nurses are feeling particularly sadistic, I can't see why not." I paused and turned to Amy. "What about the dogs? I left them with Rachel."

"I checked on them today," came a familiar voice from the doorway. Jack Tallon stood there with flowers in his hands. Amy grinned and I nearly hit her. "The nurses told me you'd probably be coming around today, so I thought I'd drop by. Here." He brought the flowers, complete with a vase to the table by the bed.

I was almost blushing. "Thank you" I stammered. "You didn't have to."

"Well, I figured your musher friends would sneak a dog in, so I thought perhaps I would try something more conventional." Jack paused. "Your vet..."

"Rachel?"

"Rachel told me the dogs were pretty banged up, but should be okay. She doesn't know if they will run again, though. Rachel said they needed physical therapy, but she said once you were out of the hospital, you'd be up to it."

"You bet!" I said.

"If they're as badly injured as I've heard, they'll never be competitive," Lee said. "I hear Blue was really banged up. He'll never have that top speed."

"It doesn't matter," I said. "I don't think I'll need top speed in what I'll be doing next."

At that moment, Sherri showed up with a large brown paper bag. She briefly met my gaze and smiled. "I've got club sandwiches for everyone."

"Terrific!" I said. I turned to Tallon. "I don't know what happened after I blacked out. Could you fill me in?"

"We searched Freeman's residence and found a set of bloody Carhartt overalls in his truck. We've sent them to the lab for analysis, but it's likely that's Rayburn's blood."

"What about Gina?"

"Gina Rayburn has been charged with obstruction of justice."

"Gina didn't know Alan killed Matt."

"I don't think she would have cared," Sherri said dryly. "With all the playing around on her Matt did, it's little wonder Gina didn't kill him herself."

I shook my head. "Gina was in total denial over it. I really didn't think she suspected Alan." I looked at Tallon, who shrugged.

"This is Gina's first offense and if she didn't know about Freeman's involvement, then the courts are likely to be lenient."

"What about Alan's dogs?"

Lee smiled. "You wouldn't believe it. You know how adversarial mushers can be? When the Siberian Husky drivers heard about the dogs, they were shocked at first. You should have seen Vicki—she was livid…"

"Half Vicki's stock is from Alan's kennel. She either has to rebuild her breeding stock or accept she's driving Alaskans," Liz added.

"Slow Alaskans," Sherri corrected.

"The dogs were going to be impounded," Lee continued. "But Cindy Travis held an emergency club meeting. Everyone there decided to foster one or two dogs until they can be placed."

"No!?"

"Yes!" said Sherri. "Mushers don't agree on much, but in this case it was unanimous. Anyone with an extra kennel or stakeout took a dog or two. Vicki is fostering the bitch with pups."

"Wow! I didn't realize…"

"None of us did," Lee said. "I guess when it's the welfare of the dogs at stake, people can shine through."

"Now, Lee, not all of it was altruistic," Sherri said. Sherri turned to me and cupped one hand to her mouth as though telling a great secret. "Sam Horton and John Wasik were looking for the faster dogs."

"Can't say as I blame them," Lee remarked. "A fast dog eats as much as a slow one. And Alan had some pretty fast dogs. You better watch out, Stephanie, there's going to be some fast up-and-coming drivers with those dogs."

"I'm not worried," I said. "I'm thinking I'll take a break from sprint racing for a while."

"Really? What would you do?" Liz asked.

"I don't know. I kind of like distance races," I admitted. "Being on the sled for more than twenty minutes sounds like fun."

"The ones around here have limited purses," Lee remarked. "If you run any longer races, you'll have to go to Montana, Idaho, or Wyoming."

"So, I travel," I shrugged. "The races are nice, but I realized something. I'm not in it for the competition. I'm in it for the dogs."

"That's how it should be," Lee said.

"Too bad Alan couldn't see that." I remarked. "But then, neither did Matt. Matt put his own desires ahead of the dogs. So did Alan. They lost sight of what attracted them to mushing in the first place: the dogs. Sure, they took good care of the dogs, but they were no longer in it for the dogs. They were in it for the money. That's where they failed."

About the Author

M. H. Bonham or Maggie Bonham or Margaret H. Bonham (she does this regularly to confuse her publishers, but her fans figure it out) is a multiple award winning author and editor with more than 35 books published. A semi-retired sled dog racer of Alaskan Huskies and Alaskan Malamutes, she has raced sprints and mid-distance with her sled teams. She is a world-renown pet expert having published more than 20 books and hundreds of articles on dog and cat care. She is the publisher of Sky Warrior Book Publishing, LLC. www.skywarriorbooks.com.

Other Books by M.H. Bonham
from WolfSinger Publications

The King's Champion

For over fifty years, fireworms have ravaged the city of Citadel Heights. Warriors and wizards have sought to find the answer to the attacks, but to little avail. Each raid has decimated the Chi'lan warriors, the elite guard of King Romarin, the son of Rhyn'athel, the warrior god.

Kalena, a young squire to Cahal, the King's Champion, knows all too well the peril that the fireworms bring. As she watches her friends and fellow warriors die in the attacks, she knows something must be done. A tragic loss sends her on a quest with Romarin, himself, to find the source of the attacks and to perform daring rescue. But an ancient evil lurks in the fireworms lair that even the magic of Romarin may not be able to fight, and forces Kalena to face an enemy even more dangerous than the fireworms…

WolfSongs 2 – edited by M.H Bonham

The wolf has long been a source of folklore and mystery, since the dawn of humankind.

Sometimes reviled and feared.

Sometimes revered and loved.

The wolf's fate has intertwined with our own.

Follow the latest myths and legends of the wolf as written by Science Fiction, Fantasy and Horror authors.

In this Award Winning anthology, you'll discover that as the dusk fades in the night, you'll hear the wolfsong calling you into stories of the imagination.

More Mysteries and Thrillers to intrigue you from WolfSinger Publications

da sticks – *A Harry Mickey Shorts Mystery* – by Rich Kisielewski

Not long ago, Harry had moved back to the town where his ex-wife and kids reside and was trying to rebuild his life. The "work hard and play hard" attitude that carries Harry through life is balanced by the softness evidenced in his dealings with his children. Once again, he was going to have to be away from them and the new life he had been trying so hard to establish.

Going undercover at MechInsCo, Harry gets exposure to executives within the company including his lifer accounting boss, the psycho senior finance executive and a frantic company president. They all paint the same picture-a company losing money with no idea how, or why. His stint at MechInsCo supplies Harry with some raucous times: large amounts of information, booze and ladies provide him with much more than he signed on for.

da bug *A Harry Mickey Shorts Mystery* – by Rich Kisielewski

Harry Mickey Shorts gets a call from M. Randle Trundle, a New York business tycoon, who is in need of Harry's help. Without a thought, Harry drops what he is doing and races off to help his benefactor, and his friend.

Trundle is a part owner in Board Room Farms — a horse racing stable—which is run by his brother, Danny Trundle. He informs Harry the stable's stud breeding stallion was found dead in his stall and Trundle feels something is wrong. Harry agrees to help Trundle with the case and does what he does best by going undercover and begins digging into the world of thoroughbred horse racing. Having bet on more than a few nags before in his lifetime, Harry is comfortable around the track and blends in very smoothly.

During his investigation, Harry forms an alliance with the ranch's female vet—in more ways than one. She agrees to provide needed intelligence on the current and prior goings-on at Board Room farms. Along the way, she becomes a serious love interest in Harry's life. Unfortunately, that conflicts with Harry's renewed part-time interest in his ex-wife that may prove to be a "pick one" dilemma, sooner, rather than later. His love for, and continued attempt to become part of his two children's lives, remains paramount in Harry's thinking.

In Adam's Fall – by Pheobe Wray

Old New England towns are infamous for their odd murder stories, but that had never happened before in Halton, Massachusetts.

When history teacher Nikki Sheridan trips over the dead body of a young Muslim girl in her backyard she finds herself at the center of a murder mystery. A mystery that will take her on a perilous journey with the police, the FBI, a nervous town ready to point fingers at neighbors who seem different, and a man calling himself 'the Patriot': a dangerous zealot whose hateful agenda could destroy the small town or bring them even closer together as they face a homegrown terrorist in their midst.

www.ingramcontent.com/pod-product-compliance
Lightning Source LLC
Chambersburg PA
CBHW070702280626
47159CB00022B/1764